# Somewhere Between Water & Sky

## Elora Ramirez

Elora Ramirez

Copyright © 2014 Elora Ramirez

Kick-ass Cover Design Sarah Hansen from Okay Creations

Editing by Lindsay Tweedle from Lindsay Edits

All rights reserved.

ISBN: 1500834327
ISBN-13: 978-1500834326

Somewhere Between Water and Sky

Elora Ramirez

Sarah and Ritz,

without your friendship this book wouldn't exist.

Somewhere Between Water and Sky

Elora Ramirez

# CONTENTS

| | |
|---|---|
| Chapter 1 | 1 |
| Chapter 2 | 11 |
| Chapter 3 | 23 |
| Chapter 4 | 43 |
| Chapter 5 | 66 |
| Chapter 6 | 82 |
| Chapter 7 | 103 |
| Chapter 8 | 118 |
| Chapter 9 | 132 |
| Chapter 10 | 143 |
| Chapter 11 | 153 |
| Chapter 12 | 169 |
| Chapter 13 | 183 |
| Chapter 14 | 197 |
| Chapter 15 | 211 |
| Chapter 16 | 229 |
| Chapter 17 | 242 |
| Chapter 18 | 252 |
| Chapter 19 | 259 |
| Chapter 20 | 268 |
| Chapter 21 | 277 |
| Chapter 22 | 289 |
| Chapter 23 | 297 |

| | |
|---|---|
| Chapter 24 | 309 |
| Chapter 25 | 322 |
| Chapter 26 | 332 |
| Acknowledgments | 336 |
| About the Author | 339 |

## CHAPTER ONE

I heard it said once that every human is a story with skin.

If this is true, paragraphs would be etched in the scars on my wrists.

Whole chapters could be written about the way my heart pounds when I startle awake.

And every single one of my tears could fill a book.

I watch the people sitting around me on the bus. The single mother with two rowdy toddlers, the older couple on vacation with cameras strapped to their necks, the boy rapping beats under his breath and writing in a journal—all of them breathe into this poetry of life.

Normally, I'd want to know their stories. I'd wait for hints of who they were inside, the poetic shifts that make us human. Now I just watch.

The boy rapping pauses with his hand in mid air and thinks for a minute. Breaking into a smile, he nods vigorously and lowers his hand to his paper. I frown. I used to have a piece of that poetry inside. It's just all a little broken now. I don't know how to fix the one thing that used to put me back together. The poems still come; I just don't know what to do with them anymore. If I'm feeling particularly brave, I'll attempt to scratch them into a journal.

Usually, I just write them with my finger on my jeans. No one needs to read them anyway. Besides, I can't hold on to them for very long. The silence is on fire and the sentences and scenes that used to extinguish those flames do nothing but fan it hotter and brighter.

I'm a new person here—no one knows anything about me. All of my journals are in various trash cans around the city. I fill one up and then throw it away, shedding the skin and finding someone new underneath every single time.

This is how I dare to move forward and believe in a new beginning. I let go of the old. I just grab the new and run. I don't wait around anymore. I can't.

*Like clockwork*
*the words disappear at dusk*
*empty cans filled up*
*like dust.*

Rapper boy looks back up and catches me watching him and then offers a shy smile. My fingers pause their lines and curl in to the protection of my hand. I flip my lips upward into a quick grin and then look away before he can strike up a conversation.

I don't want to know his story.

Stories, with all of their promise, only leave room for disappointment. I don't have room for that anymore. I left it all—the hope, the love, the promise—back in my old life with the ghosts I'd rather forget: Jude. Emma. Pacey.

Kevin.

Something like grief catches in my throat and a small burst of air escapes through my parted lips.

I miss him. I miss him and I *can't* miss him. If I give into these feelings…this emptiness…I shake my head and wipe the stray tear on my cheek.

*This is ridiculous.*

Reaching into my bag, I pull out my phone. *One missed call* shows itself on the screen and I frown. No one has my number. I swipe the screen open and scroll through until I notice UNKNOWN NUMBER in red font.

*Red like blood.*

I shudder.

After the life I've lived, I'm nothing if not over-dramatic. It's whatever. I feel I've earned it.

With a few more quick swipes, I delete the notification and sigh the misgiving away. There's no voicemail, and so there's nothing to worry about yet.

*No harm, no foul. No one knows your number. No one knows your number.*

I've learned different but I'm choosing another way of living. I repeat these phrases in my head, tapping the rhythm of the words on my knee.

"This seat taken miss?"

A gravelly voice cuts into my silence and I fight a groan. A downside to public transportation: everyone thinks they're a friend and worthy of your personal space. I glance sideways and see a hairy hand resting next to me on the seat, the flesh bulging over a gold ring with a sapphire placed securely in the middle. I squint as the sun grabs a piece of the jewel and paints pictures with it on the side of the bus.

I lift my eyes to the voice in question and curl my lips into what I hope looks like a smile.

"Sorry. I don't think you want to sit next to me. I have a cold."

I sniff and rub my nose for good measure, building a cough from as deep in my lungs as I can muster. The guy laughs and taps me on the shoulder before pushing my bag over to where I'm sitting.

"Nonsense. I'm the healthiest I've ever been."

He wheezes and squeezes the seat in front of us to help guide him down to the leather.

I just raise an eyebrow and try to count to three.

My anger is a little volatile these days. When counting doesn't work and I'm working on fighting the need to punch the guy's meaty arm for not listening to me, I transfer the anger the only way I know how: words. A few lines come to me and I pull up the notebook app on my phone. These lines are keepers. I can feel it in my bones.

*You will know the taste of me
by the scars I leave in your sleep.*

Out of habit, I open up my photo gallery. I have one picture left of Kevin—the only one I allowed myself to keep. I scroll through until I find him and for a moment, imagine what it would feel like for him to look me in the eyes like that again.

I let my mind wander to when I took the picture.

We were at Emma and Jude's. I smile thinking about those dinners and Jude's inquisition of Kevin. It took forever for Jude to accept him as a viable possibility for me. I flinch. At least that's how it seemed. Looking back I wonder what those questions were really about, and if they were a symbol for something entirely different.

This particular dinner, I talked to Emma about some poetry I was writing. I had pulled out my phone to show her the lines I wrote earlier that day and before I was able to hand it over to her, I caught him staring at me. I hadn't even hesitated. I put the phone in front of my face, pulled up my camera, and snapped the picture.

"Caught ya." I said. "Now you're forever in my memory."

He leaned forward and kissed me square on the mouth, his hand firmly placed behind my neck—something rare in the presence of Jude and Emma. He eventually moved away and leveled me with those eyes of his.

"Oh you already did that a long time ago, Steph."

I rolled my eyes.

"Oh please. Go take your charming self somewhere else."

He'd just winked and I'd just smiled and we'd just carried on like we normally did for the rest of the evening—giggling, finding ways to touch, catching the other's eyes.

It wasn't so much about me catching him, and he knew it. He caught me the second he walked up to that coffee shop table and said hello.

I look at it now and feel my chest tighten. Those eyes I memorized—I find my finger tracing the outlines of his skin before I set my jaw and click *delete*. The picture vanishes and my heart squeezes in on itself.

I wish memories were that easy to erase.

Names and faces roll through my head and heart like broken records. I glance down at my phone again and before I can second guess myself, delete one of the last pictures I saved of Emma and Jude's baby Benjamin.

Slowly, I'm erasing the Stephanie Tiller I left behind.

I'm realizing what it means to be free.

From obligation.

From worry.

From the terror of my father and the brokenness of my mother.

I'm learning what it is I'm made of in this flesh and bone. Maybe it's words. Maybe it's not. I'm not sure anymore.

Staring out the window of the bus, I watch as LA comes into view and I feel my heart grow lighter by the second. I'm quickly falling in love with this new city. The life—the movement—it's like poetry in motion. I may not be able to drop words on paper right now, but I can take it in through my eyes. It's a form of freedom to recognize beauty. I'd seen pictures of the ocean—watched videos and movies with people who lived near it and often imagined what it would be like, sitting on the sand and watching the waves crash over each other.

I think of where I'm staying, a hotel with a kitchenette right outside the city limits and in full view of those waves. Smiling, I wrap my finger around a strand of my hair. The crimson pieces are a sharp contrast to my ivory skin. I raise an eyebrow slightly.

Even though changing my hair color was one of the first things I did when I got here, it still startles me sometimes when I see it attached to me in mirrors or falling into view. I glance at my phone to check the time and position myself to look around the heads in front of me toward the traffic. I twist my lips. I may be late for work today. We pass the culprit for traffic—a movie set taking up two lanes of the road—and I crane my neck to see who may be working. Despite the magazines with all of the "they're one of us!" photo montages, I've yet to see anyone noteworthy.

We turn the corner and I gather my bag to make a quick exit at the next stop. I'll be running to make it on time, but I'll make it. I glance at the man sitting next to me and sink back against the seat when I realize I'm going to have to talk to him again.

"Um. Sir. I'm going to need off at this stop."

The bus slows down and the brakes squeal and the man just turns and smiles and shifts his feet *just so.*

"Sure thing…" He trails off as if waiting for me to share my name.

When I stare and refuse to move, he offers a broader smile and a low chuckle. "Don't worry, pretty lady. It's been a while since such a tight ass brushed up against an older man like me. I promise to behave." He waves his eyebrows suggestively and I tilt my head and smile.

"Gosh. Thanks." I move to slip past him and at the last minute, swivel around and bring my knee into his groin. He puffs his cheeks out in pain and breathes out slowly and I pull my bags past him, making sure they all hit him on the way out. I catch his eye one more time.

"I didn't give you my name on purpose. You might want to learn how to pick up on some social cues if you want to remember what a *tight ass* feels like…"

And then I turn around and rush off the bus and out on to the street only pausing long enough to hear *"whore!"* thrown out the window as the bus passes me. A voice echoes in my head and I breathe in quick.

*You're nothing but a whore. Whore. Whore. You're nothing but a whore.*

Only when the bus is out of view do I feel my insides shaking. It's been weeks since I've heard his voice take over internally and I try and shake my head to erase the words.

It doesn't work. It never does.

I take a few steadying breaths and continue down the street to the coffee shop where I've been working as a barista. These tremors will not help in making drinks tonight. I clench and unclench my fists and keep walking—keep moving—keep doing *something* because I know when I stop it won't be pretty.

The thoughts can wait. I have a shift to cover and I need this job.

I'm close to saving up enough of my own money for a car. College will wait. I couldn't risk following through with the USC acceptance and so I let the offer hang—I haven't even contacted the university because if I know Kevin and Jude like I think I do they'll probably call and ask around for information surrounding a Stephanie Tiller who just enrolled. I'm not worried about turning down the acceptance—my mom's money sits comfortably in a bank waiting for the right moment for me to pursue a degree. It'll happen, just not right now.

My scars won't dictate the story I live. They can't. The second they do, all of my new beginnings will be lost.

## CHAPTER TWO

I get to work right as my shift starts and clock in before making a mad-dash for the espresso machine. I flip the switch on the grinder and close my eyes as I inhale the smell of delicious addiction. Grabbing the portafilter, I flick the doser and watch the grinds fill the cup.

Benefits of working at a coffee shop: free coffee while on the clock.

"Hey Steph."

My hands jerk in surprise and I glance up and nod toward one of the coworkers resting on the wall outside the kitchen. Standing at least a foot above me, he absolutely towers over everything in the room. Judging by his gait and overall style I would assume he doesn't play any sports—definitely the artsy type. Longish hair, skinny jeans, *accessories*.

"You still don't remember my name, do you?"

I tie my apron around my waist and shake my head, blushing a little at the realization that he just caught me staring. "I don't—sorry."

"It's Ren."

"…Ren."

"Short for Renfro, which was my grandfather's middle name." He bows at the waist, his hand extended toward me. "My family has a penchant for the dramatic."

I widen my eyes in recognition. *Ah. That's right. Ren. The actor.*

"How was the audition? You were looking at a…pilot for a tv show? Right?"

"It was alright. I don't think I'll make the cut. But, chalk it up to experience—some shit like that."

I laugh despite myself and mutter under my breath."Yeah. Some shit like that."

He rubs his fingers under his lips and crinkles his eyes.

I twist my cheek inward and look away, focusing on tamping the grounds evenly before they're polished enough for the Astoria, our espresso machine. I call her Asti for short. She's basically my best friend.

*Why is he staring? This is awkward. Really awkward.*

"So are you in school?"

I shake my head and reach for the button that signals a double shot. The machine whirs to life and I let it go quiet before I answer, trying to figure out how much to say. He doesn't need to know everything. Hell. He doesn't need to know *anything.* But the old Stephanie would hide. I don't want to hide here. I look his way and twist the portafilter loose on the machine to empty the used grounds.

"I got into USC but decided to take a break for a little while before taking classes."

He studies me and walks over to make his own drink. I maneuver away from him so he can have his space. He stares at me underneath the mop of hair that looks stylishly uncombed. He reaches out for the portafilter and I hand it to him with a towel to dry off the residual water.

"A break to travel? Like a gap year?"

I turn toward the low-boy and pull out a Topo Chico, popping the cap. Twisting back toward my cup, I drop two pumps of simple syrup and shake it around the ice before grabbing the bottle and filling it to the first line on the plastic cup. The water fizzes and tickles my nose. I take a slight step back and then pause, making sure not to bump into him as I finish prepping.

Downside to working at a coffee shop: everything is a finely tuned dance of moving, shifting, leaning and reaching with other humans in close proximity. Slight problem since I don't dance. I turn around and lean against the counter, resting my hands behind me.

"Gap year? Um. Sure. I guess." I shoot him a glance. "I don't really know what that is, but if it involves taking a break, then yes."

He laughs.

"You're intriguing, you know that, Stephanie?"

I need to finish my coffee. I reach around him for my two shot glasses of freshly dropped espresso. I wrap my fingers around the shot glasses and then turn around to face my cup and pause before pouring it into my cup. I wrinkle my nose. Kevin used to tell me I was a mystery he loved solving.

"…I'm intriguing? You just met me."

"I just can't figure you out. I have this sense, you know? I can normally spot people who aren't genuine." He taps my shoulder with his finger and I step away, gun shy by the sudden touch. He continues and I try to breathe through the quickening of my pulse. This isn't the rushed pulse of excitement or terror—this is being found out. Known.

These are the moments his voice is loudest.

*Whore.* The guy yelled out of the bus window.

*Whore.* My dad would call me on days I didn't bring in enough money.

*Whore* was the look in Kevin's eyes when he found me in the shed.

*This is why I don't do relationships.*

I force myself to stand still and not run. I look him in the eyes and say nothing.

"I can't read you. Ever. I ask questions and you answer them, but there's not any emotion behind the words. Like who turns down an acceptance from USC?"

"Are you saying I'm not genuine?"

He looks me over and answers with another question. "What are you, like 18? Did you graduate early?"

"Do you always ask this many questions?"

He's not deterred. He steps toward me. "And your hair." He glances at my roots.

*Rude.*

"This isn't your natural color."

He grabs a strand and I jerk my neck away from his touch. He smiles.

"Do you mind?" I'm getting a little angry and a lot antsy at him pushing for answers.

"You don't like people touching you."

"No shit, Sherlock." I have no clue whether or not his questions are considered within social norms but I'm not used to it and they make me uncomfortable. I'm not used to this level of friendly intimacy between strangers. I feel my armor lock into place and my gaze steels.

"I thought I already had my interview."

He raises an eyebrow and chuckles and then pauses to glance over my shoulder, our conversation momentarily forgotten. I notice the distraction and turn to follow his gaze as I stick a straw in my cup and take a sip.

There's a girl walking up to us—someone I haven't met before. Her hips sashay with the music playing overhead and she's waving at the cooks in the back as they holler their welcome.

Everything about her is color. Her hair, although a dark brown, is streaked with blues, purples and reds. Her lips are magenta. On her forearm is a dream catcher tattoo with feathers. Her shoes are khaki wedges with rainbow stripes wrapped around her ankles. And when she grabs an apron out of a locker and looks at both of us, her bright green eyes pop out of the highlighted eyeshadow.

Standing next to her technicolor, I feel monotone.

She smiles at me and bumps my arm with hers as she ties her apron.

"Damn, Ren. What are you doing to this girl? She looks like she's seen a ghost." She reaches for a rubber band on her wrist and doubles over to throw her rainbow hair into a high bun. I notice Ren looking away and hiding a smile. Straightening up and sighing, she reaches for my hand.

"Hi. I'm Jessa. You must be the new girl. I've seen you on the schedule but just got back from vacation with the family. Your name's Stephanie, right?"

I nod and she glances back at Ren, still staring out the window toward the bikes and people on roller skates passing us. I catch a smile fly across her face and she leans sideways to whisper in my ear.

"Don't pay attention to him. Seriously. He thinks he can figure anyone out in less than thirty minutes."

He jerks back to attention, crossing his arms.

"If I remember correctly, it took less than that for me to figure you out."

She looks him up and down and shakes her head.

"No, love. You remember wrong. There's far more nuance in these bones than you'd care to admit." She slaps her hip and winks. Ren swallows.

She looks back at me. "Nice meeting you, Steph. We need some more girls around here." Squeezing my forearm she smiles and juts her chin toward Ren. "Remember: all bark no bite."

I furrow my brow and watch her walk over to our chalkboard to write the evening special — along with the daily quote minus the attribution. Anyone who can tell us who said it gets a coupon for a free drink. She throws the chalk on the floor and bends over to write, ass to the sky, legs stretching out for eternity.

"Give me a quote, guys!"

Her hands fly over the chalkboard and I see an intricate border forming underneath the stick of chalk. Ren looks at me and shrugs.

I search my mind for a lesser known quote and land on a memory.

My voice comes out breathy.

"You ripple, like a river, when I touch you."

Jessa pauses mid-stroke and turns, straightening her back. Tilting her head she smiles.

"Nice. Poetry?"

"…Neruda."

She turns back around and writes the quote down, adding swirls and what looks like a river in between the words. Ren is staring at me again.

"I didn't take you for a poetry girl."

I avoid his gaze and shrug.

"I'm into it, I guess."

*If into it equals twenty or so journals filled with stories and poems scattered around town in dumpsters.*

Ren snorts and shakes his head, realizing he won't get much from me other than those simple words. He doesn't get this story of Kevin leaving those lines in my locker one day after a particularly heinous fight. I smile at the memory of what happened *after* — how he showed me all of the ways his touch sent ripples down my skin.

*Shit.*

I watch both of them out of the corner of my eye—Jessa doing a great job giving Ren a show of what I imagine she *won't* be offering him and Ren doing a horrible job of trying to ignore it.

"Whatever, man." He reaches into his apron and grabs his booklet and cash and after untying it, shoots it into a nearby laundry basket. "Lunch was slow today. Too slow. Hopefully you'll have better luck with the dinner rush. I think there's a concert or something down the street so you should get some business from them. If not, you can always get

Steve to let you out early. There's a party tonight at Seth's place. Jessa will be there."

*Too close.*

I sniff and avoid eye contact.

"Thanks but I need to head home after my shift and get some stuff done."

He stares at me for a few beats and turns to walk away.

"You can't avoid us forever, Stephanie." He looks over his shoulder and turns to walk backward, smiling at me and motioning to the sign hanging above the employee area that reads *here, you're family.* "You wouldn't avoid your family, would you?"

He doesn't see my reaction because he turns around before I can even answer.

But I'm not answering—I'm not even breathing. My vision begins to blur. I know he knows nothing of my history but those words—they do something internally. My breath returns in gasps and I cup my head in my hands.

My arms feel like cement. There's fire in my bones.

*Shit. Shit. Not here. Not here.*

I close my eyes and reach for a nearby stool and fight to breathe deep—to remind my body that I'm safe. It doesn't help. I can't stop hyperventilating with Ren's words on a loop in my mind.

*Avoiding your family. Avoiding your family. Your family. Family.*

*Dad chasing me with a baseball bat. Mom reaching for Nyquil. Pacey.*

*Oh god.*

Images of the past break through and I'm done for—running for the restroom and barely making it before throwing up everything I ate in the toilet, the tears falling as if they had their own say. When I'm finished I collapse on the floor and lean against the wall, my hands underneath my legs to keep them from shaking.

*I'm fucking certifiable.*

The door to the bathroom swings open and I see Jessa's wedges walk in and point toward my stall.

"Shit, Stephanie. You okay? Are you sick?"

"No."

One of her feet pivot slightly.

*Please leave. Please leave.* I think to myself.

I sniff and wipe the tears off my cheeks with the palm of my hands. Straightening myself up, I breathe in a few times and open the door and almost run into her.

"I'm fine."

She watches me.

"You look horrible."

"…thanks?"

She crosses her arms and won't let me pass. My eyes flicker up to meet hers and then back down.

"Would you…can I get by please? I need to wash my face."

"Oh. Sorry."

She squints and nods, stepping aside and pulling her purse away from her and onto the counter next to me. She catches my glance in the mirror.

"I hope you don't mind. I saw you running toward the bathroom and figured you may need some help freshening up…" she pauses and I watch her consider her words. "Listen…is this…I saw you collapse against the stool back there…."

I reach for a paper towel. Turning off the water I motion toward her bag and wipe my face.

*Holy hell what is it with these people and their questions?*

"Thanks, but I think I'm good. I wasn't wearing make up today anyway." I look down to my loosely fitted black shirt that falls to mid-thigh, black leggings, and black boots. I make an attempt to smile. "Not sure all of your…color…would go well with this ensemble of doom I have going on here."

I pat my cheeks and drag my hands down toward my neck. She's too silent. As if she is just waiting for me to spill my secrets. I don't do well with silence. I can feel the flames inching closer and closer and the words forming. I have to get out—get away—there's something about her that begs for explanation.

"Well, I mean, technically yes. The color would look fan-damn-tastic with that black. Contrasts and all." She winks.

I roll my eyes.

*Who is this girl?* I think of the last person who drew me in with curiosity and possible friendship and I stiffen with suspicion. Another level of armor locks in place.

"I'll be okay. I promise. I just am getting over some weird food poisoning and it hits when I least expect it."

Her eyes squint and she sets her jaw.

*Stop. Looking. At. Me.*

"Okay well, if you need anything let me know? I've worked sick before. It blows." She grabs her purse and walks out the door.

I place my hands on the sink and look at myself in the mirror again, the red tendrils falling around my face. I know Jessa didn't buy my excuse of food poisoning. But what do I say? *Sorry. I puke when I think about my family?* How's *that* for an explanation? I moan and let my head fall.

Maybe these new beginnings are harder than I thought.

## CHAPTER THREE

I get to my room that night and notice a journal propped up against my door. I frown, looking around. It's a Moleskine, my favorite. I haven't bought one since moving here though because I just throw them in the trash once I'm done anyway.

Leaning over to pick it up I crack open the spine, the blank pages calling to me as they always do. I snap it shut and let it fall out of my hands and onto the floor, unwilling to think about how or why it appeared here. It's not like anyone knows me.

*Maybe someone dropped it in the hallway and then someone else thought it belonged to this room.*

Satisfied, and leaving the journal behind me, I swipe my card over the door handle and walk into my room, kicking off my shoes and rolling my head to stretch my neck. I curl my lip at the thermostat, noticing that room service adjusted the temperature again.

Benefits of living in a hotel: you don't have to pay for electricity or cable.

Bumping it down to a comfortable setting, I shuffle to the bathroom, turning the faucet to run the water for a long soak in the tub.

I walk back toward the bed and turn on the TV. Flipping through the channels, I grimace.

*Gameshow. Gameshow. Crime show. Dumb sitcom. Infomercial.*

I settle for a show about Amish teenagers losing their minds in New York City and turn back toward the bathroom, goosebumps lining my skin as the air kicks on above and around me. I sink deep into the scalding water, rolling forward to light the candles I hide in a drawer while I'm gone. The candles were one of my first purchases when I realized I had a tub. I remembered Emma talking about her nights with a bottle of wine and candle-lit bubble baths and decided to splurge. Once the flames are dancing on the tile, I lean back and let the water hold me.

Finally I can breathe.

Water has always been healing to me. When I was little, mom would tell me stories about how when I would get in a rage and start crying, all they would need to do is run the water for a bath and I'd begin to breathe again—it's always been my reset button. I lift my left leg and watch the steam swirl off my skin and frown at the scars left behind from the last night in the shed. They aren't as red as they used to be, but they're still obvious. Long streaks snake across my shins from where I was tied. I close my eyes and put my leg back underneath the water.

Now's not the time to be thinking about the past.

Work tonight was weird. As promised, we were slammed with business from the concert down the street. I took the orders and Jessa made the drinks. My feet still throb from standing for so long. But it wasn't the business that took me by surprise—that just made the shift go by faster. It was the conversations. I stretch my neck, rolling it around by shifting my shoulders and feeling the tension of the day fall away.

Relationships are such a fickle thing.

Ren, despite his incessant questions, doesn't set off my douche-o-meter. And Jessa is way too intuitive for her own good. I both crave and fear their ability to waver my defenses and I don't know what to do with that—how to be strong Stephanie starting over when wounded Stephanie cowers from touch.

I think I want to be friends with them, but what does that even mean? I'm not sure I know. Jessa invited me to the party tonight, and I don't think I'm quite at the spot of tailgating at some stranger's house. She'd looked at me and smiled, twirling her rainbow hair, and bounced her eyebrows up and down.

"Come on, Steph. I just met you and I can tell you need some adventure. Just come see? There may be someone there worth your while."

I had snorted—I'm nothing if not graceful in those moments of assumption—and stood my ground.

"Yeah that's just not my scene. And I've had plenty of adventure to last me a lifetime, thanks."

Her turn to snort.

"Suit yourself. But how will you know if it's your scene if you don't show? And don't think I'm letting you off on not spilling the secrets behind those adventures. Your day of story-telling reckoning will come, my dear."

I focus on the noise coming from the television set and close my eyes. Slowly, I lower myself until I'm completely submerged, the echoes of the world outside coming through as a garbled mess. Opening my eyes, I see the separation of here and there—it looks like a sheet of glass and ripples with the laughter of kids running down the hallway. I lift my head just enough to breathe in and then lower myself again, letting the heat and water wrap around my body like a womb. I stay here until there's no more oxygen, and lift myself slowly until I'm resting against the towels behind me.

This is when the fire of silence beckons. When the flames stay far enough away to hypnotize me by their beauty but won't overwhelm me with the heat. I let my limbs float freely and imagine myself held.

I startle awake by the sound of knocking. The water sloshes up and out of the tub with my movement and I squirm for one of the towels, just in case.

I roll myself up and out of the liquid cocoon so I can hear better, not allowing myself the time to think about how my heart rate has increased with the possibility of it being *my* door. I hear the banging again and the yelling from the couple across the hall from me and I relax, the adrenaline dying in my throat. I bend at the waist to dry my legs and notice that I'm shaking.

*No one's found me yet. It's okay. I'm okay. No one's here.*

I swap one cocoon for another, throwing on some clothes and gathering the comforter around me on the bed. My heart is still racing despite the deep breaths I'm working through my lungs. This is when I'd reach for my journal, letting the poison out in between the lined pages. I haven't purchased a new one yet, and the last one was burned, the ashes let loose over the Pacific.

*What do you do when your coping mechanisms aren't letting you cope anymore?*

I let my body sink into the mattress and go through my mental checklist.

Dad's in jail.

No one knows my local number.

I deactivated Facebook.

I am alone.

I fall asleep before I'm able to think about just how much I miss the feeling of arms around me.

.:⋮:.

Jessa calls me in the morning.

My phone, hidden underneath my hip, buzzes me awake.

"…hello?" I scratch out a greeting, confused and squinting against the sun peeking through the hotel blinds.

*Note to self: shut the curtains tonight before going to bed.*

"Stephanie. Don't freak out, but Ren and I are down in the lobby. We're taking a day trip to San Diego. Come with us to Sunset Cliffs?"

My heart slams in my chest. I pull the phone away from my ear and stare at the screen and see *The Best Friend You Never Knew You Had* as the contact name.

"What in the actual fuck?"

"…she's freaking out." Jessa whispers away from the receiver.

"I can still hear you. How'd you get my number?"

"Listen. We're not crazy, just curious, and I may have followed you home last night after work. Oh and um…never leave your phone unattended at work. Just trust me. I saved you from many a picture last night. You're welcome."

I wrinkle my nose.

"I'm so confused right now."

"Understandable. But you should also be excited. Two strange people are waiting for you in the lobby to take you on a road trip! It's like Ren's dream movie role."

I hear him snort in the background.

"Seriously?"

Ren's voice cuts through the line, low and rumbly.

"What will it be, Stephanie? The red pill? Or the blue pill?"

I hear shuffling and Jessa pushing him away.

"Don't. Be. Weird, Ren. I told you. Harness the Nerd."

He just laughs and mentions something about grabbing a muffin from the continental breakfast area.

*What the hell?*

"Jessa…I don't know you."

"Fact."

"You could kill me."

"Not possible. But I can see how that scenario would play through your mind right now."

"Do you normally try and kidnap strays who live in hotel rooms?"

"This isn't kidnapping, sweetheart. And you're not a stray. This is a rescue mission. You need fun! You mope and grow all self-reflective at the coffee shop. It's starting to freak customers out."

"Wait. Really?"

She laughs. "No. But. You do dart around like you're ready to run at a moment's notice. And, chalk it up to my dad being a professional counselor, but I can spot the ones who need some extra attention."

"You're calling me broken."

"I'm calling you needing a friend."

"I can't believe I'm actually considering this."

"I'm very convincing *butplusalsotoo* I think you just really want to get out of that stuffy hotel room. Come onnnnnn. It'll be fun. See you when you get down here."

She doesn't even let me respond. She hangs up and I sit there, staring at the ceiling, the phone still stuck to my ear. I didn't even talk to her for five minutes and I'm already exhausted. What would a whole day be like? I smile and jump out of bed, grabbing the nearest and cleanest clothing I can find. Throwing my hair into a pony tail, I brush my teeth, slide on some lip gloss and walk out the door. It's only after I get to the elevator that I realize exactly what I'm doing and I laugh under my breath.

*Yep. Certifiable.*

But for once in a very long time, the silence of the morning brings nothing of distant flames and memories. I lean my head against the wall and feel the equilibrium balance itself internally as I shoot down the floors. When I reach the lobby and the doors slide open, I hesitate for just a moment before I hear a squeal and feel fleshy arms wrap around me. The slight smell of jasmine and a rumble of male laughter to my right clue me in that the arms belong to Jessa. She pushes away and holds my upper arms in her hands.

"Oh that's right. I forgot. Ren told me you don't like people in your personal space."

She winks and lets go of me before I can even respond. I look at Ren.

"How does she have this much energy? And where can I get her supply?"

She lifts her arms above her head and walks in front of me, lifting her chin to the chandeliers in the lobby.

"This is all natural, Stephanie." She drops her arms and reaches for Ren's belt buckle, pulling him closer so she can lean on his shoulder. Her lips part in an unbelievably wide smile. "I can't believe you actually came down! Ren owes me twenty bucks." She blinks her eyes at him, holding out her hand. "Now or later, loverboy?"

He blushes and grabs her hand. "I will choose to evade that question in favor of hearing Stephanie's favorite breakfast food."

Jessa's eyes pop even wider than they were and she turns to me.

"Breakfast! You haven't eaten and this continental shit is *no* match to local cuisine." She snarls and points toward the small enclave where scents of stale waffles and contrived sausages take over. "What'll it be, Steph?"

I think for a moment.

"I want real eggs. And bacon. And maybe french toast."

Jessa and Ren look at each other and smile.

"Americana!"

Jessa grabs my hand and pulls me toward the door. "You'll love this place—it's about halfway between here and San Diego, so it'll be a bit of a wait, but I promise—it's so worth it."

"How far is San Diego from here?"

"About two and a half hours, if we leave now."

*Two and a half hours?*

I'm beginning to second guess things. That's two and a half hours in the car with people I don't know. Two and a half hours away from this nice safe place I've found for myself here. My mind shifts back to Marisol and I know I look panicked. I can't help it.

"Wait." I pull my hand away and begin to back away slowly. "I'm beginning to realize just how crazy this is…sorry. Go without me."

"Oh no you don't." Jessa leans forward and grabs my hand again. "*Relax.* One of my favorite places in all the world is in San Diego. Have you heard of Sunset Cliffs?"

I pause.

"Sunset Cliffs? Is that what you said?"

"Yeah. It's this incredible place where you can watch the sun set over the Pacific. If we're lucky you can see the surfers who risk getting slammed up against the rock." She winks. Ren rolls his eyes.

"I know about Sunset Cliffs. I've always wanted to go…" I can't help but offer a small smile. "Okay. Just one question. Do you know Sam Tiller?"

Confused eyes stare back at me.

"Who?"

I ignore the question, satisfied.

"What about a Joey? Do you know a Joey?"

Ren leans in around Jessa. "Tribiani?"

I blink. "Um. No."

Jessa swats at his arm.

"Ow! Jesus." He scowls and rubs his arm, shaking his head. "I don't know a Joey, Stephanie."

I breathe easier. I'm not sure what's happening, but for the first time in months, flesh and bone conversation has me almost giddy with anticipation.

"Okay then. I'm in."

We walk outside and Jessa shivers.

"It's chilly today."

"…it's 50 degrees."

She turns and nods, her eyes serious.

"Right. Chilly. Where are you from, Canada?"

I shake my head, offering no other specifics.

She grunts and turns to Ren, her voice taking on a British lilt. "You're right. She's an enigma, this one!"

We get to the car in the garage and I walk right past Ren's car before realizing it. Turning around, I stare at the car and then back at him.

"This is yours?"

His lips curve up a little.

"Yeah? Why?"

"It's a Jeep! With like…no cover!" My face breaks into a huge grin.

Jessa hops in the front seat and stands to face me. "Stop gawking and just get in, girl! The green eggs and ham are calling my name!"

I blink. For the millionth time in less than an hour I'm speechless.

*What…in the hell?*

I make my way to the side behind Ren and Jessa shakes her head, motioning me behind her.

"You'll want this side. Promise."

"…Why?"

"Just *trust* me. It's not like Fabio has gas or anything but…" she widens her eyes and looks knowingly at me.

"What the fuck, Jess? No." He catches my gaze. "It's for the ocean view. You'll want to be on that side to see it." He turns back to Jessa and shakes his head muttering under his breath. "I swear."

Jessa just giggles.

"You know you love me, Renfro."

Given how Ren burns rubber squealing to get out of the garage, he doesn't necessarily agree. I fight back the laughter building in my throat.

When he gains control and we find ourselves on the road, Ren clears his throat and glances to his right. "Jessa, you will be the end of me."

She answers by throwing up her arms above her head and screaming at the top of her lungs.

.::.

When we get to Americana, I almost don't want to get out of the Jeep. For the past thirty miles, I've been staring at the waves crash against each other on the shore. I want to be out there—feeling my toes dip into the sand and watching the way the waves rush to meet me, trying to pull me out into the depths with them. If I were standing there on the sand, I have no doubt I would feel the temptation deeper than my bones to walk as far as I could go.

The waves are alluring. Hypnotic, even. Watching them crash against the seawall, I remember a poem from my literature class with

Mrs. Peabody. It referenced the constancy of waves. The going, the pulling, the bringing back. Like memories and time, it all comes back. Everything changes and moves and disappears or ages, but not waves. Waves are constant. A moving piece of time.

Waves are like the sunrise.

Jessa steps down and stretches her back.

"Oh my gosh I am so hungry."

My stomach roars and gives away my own need for food and I realize I haven't eaten since lunch the day before. I think of french toast drizzled with syrup and runny eggs and bacon and it's all I can do to keep from running ahead of Jessa to find a spot inside.

Ren meets us and asks for a booth, and we are seated within minutes—just beating the rush of travelers stopping for brunch. By the time we grab drinks and are looking through the menu, the line stretches out the door.

Jessa looks up at me from behind the menu. "Are you 21? The mimosas here are *amazing*."

I raise an eyebrow. "I'm…18."

She squints and I look away.

*Why does she always do that? It's like she's trying to see into my soul.*

I cross my arms in front of me. Just in case.

"You hesitated."

"I did."

"Did you forget your age?"

"Do you have something in your eye?"

She blinks and Ren spits out his water.

Jessa turns her head and looks at Ren then back at me. "What?"

"You were squinting. Looked like your eyes were dry or something. I don't know. Made me uncomfortable. And to answer your question, yes. I did forget. I just had a birthday and it slipped my mind."

She beams and claps her hands, completely dismissing my comment about her habitual squinting.

"A birthday! And an important one! Did you have a massive party? What did your parents do? Tell me everything."

Her face is earnest and Ren glances from me to her before leaning forward. "Or, rather than telling us your life story," he makes a face at Jessa and she shrugs, taking a sip of her water. "How about you just decide what you want to eat and we can talk once we have food in our stomachs."

He jerks his thumb toward Jessa as she studies her eyeliner in a compact. "This one gets feisty when hangry."

I take a sip of my water to hide my own laughter and nod. "Noted."

Jessa snaps the compact shut and looks from Ren to me. She twists her lips.

"Seriously?"

I focus on the people outside on the patio. Ren's smile twitches. Realizing she's not going to get anything from him, she shakes her head.

"Oh Renfro," she whispers. "Don't you know not to poke the bear?"

Renfro and I exchange a smile while she pouts behind the menu.

.:.

Jessa and Ren have taken to a game they call Figure Out the Stephanie. All I have to do to participate is say yes or no. I placate them—for now. What I really want is to dig in to this massive plate of cinnamon dusted french toast.

"You were part of a circus."

"No."

"You're a foreign exchange student from Canada who's running from the Mounties."

"Um. No."

"You're part of Olivia Pope's team of gladiators."

I blink at Jessa.

"I have no idea what the fuck you are talking about…."

Jessa makes a face and looks at Ren. "So obviously she doesn't know television. Noted." Her eyes widen. "Oh! You're totally running from your Amish community."

I sigh. "No."

Ren snaps his fingers and points. "I got it. You're the love child of some has-been actress and you're trying to find your roots."

I shake my head. "You guys are reaching. Like…far out reaching. These don't even make sense."

"But you are running."

I pause and Jessa pounces.

"She paused! She paused. She's running." Her eyes grow in diameter.

"I'm not running. I'm very comfortable in my moderately priced hotel room. I don't plan on going anywhere." I hold out my hand. "I have a job. I wouldn't have a job if I were running."

I swallow, forcing myself to stop explaining. Simple answers are always best. The table goes quiet for a few moments and I finally chance a look up from my french toast to find them both staring at me.

"Do I have something on my face?"

Jessa smiles and shakes her head.

"You're new to California, right?"

I swallow.

*Where is this going?* I think.

"Um, yeah. I guess you can say that."

She laughs, picking up her fork again and waving it around before stabbing her eggs. "You're either new to the state or not, Steph. It's not a difficult question."

"I moved here in December."

I grimace slightly—remembering those weeks of hiding. I spent Christmas holed up in my hotel room, binging on Swiss Miss rolls and watching a marathon of America's Next Top Model. A week later, on New Years' Eve, I found two bottles of champagne waiting outside of a room down the hall. I didn't even second guess my impulse of grabbing them and running back to my room.

I drank both of the bottles that night while reading through my journal. In a rage, I shredded every single page and set them on fire in the wastebasket. I decided two things that day: I can set fire to the silence before it sets fire to me, and I'd never keep another journal again. My words are too volatile. Too meaningless. The stories once deeply embedded in my bones have been replaced by hollow pieces, ashes of words I thought would stay forever.

Words like *you can trust me.*

And *I love you.*

And all of the million ways they crashed into hopes and dreams and promises of future.

A future I had to take in my own hands when it collapsed right in front of me.

I blink and realize Ren's hand is waving in front of my face. Blushing, I look back at him and Jessa. Her eyebrows are raised and she has a slight smile.

"You okay? You went somewhere for a while."

"I'm fine."

She waves off the waitress, stopping by to see if we need anything else, and looks me in the eye.

"So, if you just turned 18, and you moved here in December, did you graduate early?"

"Um…" I can feel my heart rate increasing. The overhead lights suddenly feel really warm on my skin. I shift in my seat, trying to figure out how to answer this question.

Ren coughs and nudges her arm.

"What?" She shrugs and scratches a spot underneath her shoulder. "I'm just trying to get to know her. She intrigues me."

"I tested out of high school once I moved here."

She nods and studies me.

"Listen. I'm trying not to be nosy. But it's kind of ingrained—you can thank the sociology lessons my father started giving me when I was five—so I apologize for the third degree. But like I said earlier—I can tell when someone needs a friend, and you have this neon arrow above your head that's blinking like mad." She lifts her hands to her eyes and flashes her fingers open and closed, signaling the blinking effect. I clench my fists underneath the table. She reaches for her water and takes another sip.

"Whenever you're ready, I'll be here to listen."

I clear my throat. "Thanks," I whisper.

"It's just…" Ren rubs the palms of his hands over his face and peeks at me from between his fingers. "You aren't in trouble are you, Stephanie? Like…this isn't some matter of you running away from something that will find you here?"

I keep my face neutral and shake my head slightly.

*God I hope not.*

My voice grows quiet and I look him in the eye. "I don't know what you mean, Ren."

They exchange a glance and I rub my fingers over the middle of my forehead.

My father's voice breaks through and echoes through my mind.

*They don't believe you.*

I close my eyes and act like I'm stretching a kink out of my neck. I fight to push the voice away and breathe through the fear.

*This can't happen here. Not now. Just look them in the eye. Be confident. Smile.*

I rest my hands palms up on the table. Ren's attention shoots down toward my fingers and then back up to me. I wait for Jessa to look and then smile.

"Listen. It's really simple. My parents are kind of deadbeat. I don't know where my mom is—my dad's in prison. I skipped town after my brother found a place through foster care because I just couldn't take it anymore."

*Just give them enough of the truth that they don't question. A dad in prison isn't a big deal. Plenty of people deal with that—plenty of people come from fucked up families.*

That's when I notice the slight tremor to my hands.

*Shit.*

I lower them before they notice and place them under my thighs. I need to figure out a way to keep them from shaking so much.

For the moment, they seem satisfied with my explanation. My dad's voice returns, softer than before. *They wouldn't believe you anyway.*

I shake my head slightly, enough to catch the questioned gaze of Jessa.

I wave my hand in front of me. "I just don't like talking about it." I rummage through my purse and find enough cash to cover my breakfast and tip. Placing it on the table I move to stand, turning my head back toward the table as I check to make sure I have everything.

"I'll be outside. I need some air."

I can hear Jessa whispering to Ren as I walk toward the door. Before I can reach the hostess stand, I feel Jessa's hand on my arm, gently pulling me off to the side. I maneuver my arm out of her grasp and shake my head. Her eyes widen.

"Oh right. Sorry. Personal space." Her hand grabs a strand of her hair and she begins twirling it around her finger. "Listen, Steph. I'm sorry. My father says I have this problem with not knowing social graces—" she rolls her eyes. "I get caught up in the curiosity and become invasive pretty quickly."

"You're pretty invasive."

She chuckles. "I know."

I straighten my shoulders and take a look at my phone. Feeling someone's eyes on me, I look up and see a man at a booth with a woman. She's vacant. Like she's a robot—here but not here—turning and humoring him with laughs that don't even reach her eyes. He smiles at me, toying with his mimosa glass by twirling it around and resting it on his fingers. The light catches his ruby ring and my heart jumps. He turns back toward the woman, but I keep staring. There's something vaguely familiar about him—about that ring. I shake off my unease.

*There's no way I would know anyone here. Be realistic, Stephanie.*

But I know him. I know I do. I stare at him for a few more seconds and nothing comes.

And then I remember. The bus. This was the douche sitting next to me. My breath quickens and my knees go weak. I grab a nearby booth to gain control.

*Surely it's just a coincidence. Surely. Same bus. Same place for brunch. It can happen…right?*

"I think Ren is done paying. Are you ready to go?" Jessa's voice cracks through the silence and I blink.

"Oh. Yeah. Sure. Let's go."

She studies me for a moment and then follows my gaze to the man eating.

"Do you know him?"

"What? Oh. No. Not really." I wave my hand and start making my way to the door. "He just sat next to me on the bus yesterday. Was kind of a douche. It's weird seeing him here."

Jessa just nods and follows me out the door, turning around to catch a glance at the booth one more time.

I can't shake this feeling of uneasiness or dread snaking its way through my bones.

## CHAPTER FOUR

We arrive in San Diego early afternoon, Ren intent on heading immediately to Coronado Island.

"Let's just stick to the La Jolla area, Ren. Avoid all these tourists."

"It's San Diego, Jess. Tourists will be everywhere."

She tilts her head half a degree. "I guess you're right. I really don't care where we go between now and sunset. But why Coronado? Any reason?"

"The beach. Beaches equal bikinis."

"…in April?"

He looks at her and raises his eyebrows. "Spring break."

"Well then. If I knew you wanted to go to the beach I would have come prepared."

He laughs under his breath. "Oh Jess. You're being innocent for our guest. We both know you've stripped down to those lacy underthings and deemed those appropriate."

Jessa's eyes jump to mine and then back to Ren.

*Ohmigosh she's actually blushing.*

"If I remember correctly you liked what you saw. Mentioned something about me being so colorful you wanted to lick me like a Jolly Rancher."

*Welp. My turn to blush.*

Ren clears his throat. "Proof that some things are better left in the memory tank."

Jessa smiles slightly and glances out the window. Suddenly she jumps up and down and waves her hands around, hitting Ren's arm in the process.

He jumps. "Jesus! What the fuck, Jess?"

She looks at him and smiles and my eyes go wide. I know that smile. I've known this girl less than twenty-four hours and I am beginning to read her. That smile? It's the one she gets when an idea pops into her head.

"I know what we can do."

He looks at her.

"Go to Coronado?"

"Get a tattoo."

"Get a…" Ren's face blanches. "You want another tattoo?"

Jessa laughs. "No. I want a septum piercing." She pokes him in the arm. "But *you* want a tattoo. Remember?"

He glances at her out of the corner of his eye. "I do. But I can't just *get a tattoo*. Not when I have scripts and stuff I'm supposed to be reading."

"Lame." Jessa rolls her eyes and then turns her attention to me. "How about you, Steph? You want a tattoo?"

"Actually yes. I do."

"NO. WAY."

Jessa is so excited and moving around so much I'm not sure she's going to be able to stay in her seat. I lift my hand to calm her.

"Yes way. I've wanted one since seeing a piece on this hairstylist back home." I brush my finger against my forearm and look back at her. "It'll be on my forearm. A girl holding a quill and dancing in a field of flowers."

"You write?" Ren looks in the rearview mirror at me.

"I did."

"No time now or what?"

"…some shit like that."

Recognition flares in his eyes and he looks back at the road.

"A poetry-loving, tattoo-wishing, crimson-haired writer-runaway" Ren turns on the blinker and catches my gaze again in the rear-view mirror. "If you're not careful, Steph you're going to tell us all your secrets."

I shrug. "Go ahead and believe that, Renfro. I got some deep ones though. Those are vaulted. I threw away that key a long time ago."

They stare at me for a few seconds in their respective mirrors before breaking contact. Things grow quiet for a few moments as Ren waits for a green light.

Jessa places her hand on Ren's arm. "So what do you say, Renfro? Adventure at the tattoo parlor?"

He sighs and then nods his head. "You know what? Screw it. Yes. Adventure at the tattoo parlor."

.:::.

Thirty minutes later, we're waiting in the front of a tattoo shop. This place is nothing like your typical tattoo parlor. There are multiple stations built up like a hair salon. The floor is a deep ebony wood. And the ceiling? The entrance has a gold tile ceiling — each tile imprinted with a roaring lion. Ren looks up, his hair falling like a false mohawk behind him.

"Whoa." He whispers. "That's intense."

He pulls out his phone and snaps a picture and I just shake my head.

The girl at the front desk finally walks around the corner and gives us a smile.

"Hey y'all!"

We glance at each other and Jessa leans closer to me. "Is that accent real?"

I study her bright purple hair and multiple tattoos and shrug. "Who knows," I whisper back.

"I'm Stacy. Paco and Tim are working today. What were you guys looking for?"

Jessa walks forward. "I wanted a septum piercing." She jerks her thumb back toward me and Ren. "Those two want tattoos."

Stacy nods. "Groovy. You guys got lucky. Paco was supposed to be out of town for a convention but he canceled it because his son got sick. His whole afternoon is free." She turns and stretches to look around the pillar next to her desk. "And it looks like Tim is almost done with his morning appointment so you'd only have to wait like…thirty minutes?"

A guy walks around the booth and leans his elbow on the wood.

"What's up guys?"

Stacy presses her hands on the desk in front of her and leans over to point at us.

"Paco, one of them is here for a tattoo with you."

"Alright alright. Which one? Who's doing what?"

I speak without even thinking, telling him my idea. His eyes brighten. "Oh yeah. Let's do that. Come back here. We're gonna make this fucking perfect."

I smile and follow him, my gaze resting on a poster on the wall.

*Baby Cheesus wants you to buy a t-chirt.*

I frown and Paco catches me. "Oh. You like that? I swear people here are always fucking wit me about my accent. Whatever man. I'm Aztec. I win."

I smile and he motions for me to sit in the leather chair.

He sits down next to me and focuses solely on my eyes.

"What are we gonna do to you today, sweetheart?"

It takes less than an hour for him to sketch up something amazing. I'm leaning back against his leather chair and watching as Paco balances the paper against my skin. He talks to himself softly as he positions it just right. He looks up at me.

"This is your first tattoo? You're getting a big piece. You ready?"

I nod.

He rubs the paper smooth and lifts it gently.

"What do you think about the placement?"

My breath catches at the outline covering my entire forearm—from elbow to wrist not a piece of skin is clear of his sketch.

*No one will be able to see the scars anymore.*

I blink furiously to keep the tears at bay. There's nothing more hopeful than for me to douse the flames of self-harm and abuse with vibrant color.

He taps on the ink with his finger.

"This may take a few hours. Do you have time? We could just do the outline today if you want…."

Jessa's voice bounces off the walls throughout the shop.

"Fuck, Ren! Squeeze my hand a little harder why don't you?"

Ren wheezes. "Why didn't anyone tell me it would hurt this bad? Holy hell I want my mom."

Paco shakes his head and whispers under his breath. "What kind of fucker thinks a tattoo is going to tickle? I'm almost 40 and I still cry when I get these things."

I laugh.

He swivels the chair around to his station and preps the colors and gun. He gives me a quick look. "One time I had this girl come in and get a whole side tattoo. It was banging. Although, it *sounded* like she was *being* banged while my guy was working on her." He shakes his head and does a little hip thrust. "Talk about awkward."

My eyes grow wide.

"...Uh. Yeah. Awkward."

He laughs and throws his long black hair up into a ponytail. He shifts his head toward me while he wraps the rubber band around a few times. "This means it's business time."

"...Okay?"

He sits back down and rests his arms on the back of his chair while putting on some rubber gloves. He nods toward Ren, still moaning about the pain.

"Do you know those guys?"

I nod. "Kind of? We met yesterday."

"Did they talk you into this?" His eyes grow serious. "This is my art. Everyone who asks where you got this—you're gonna tell them good things?" Shifting in his seat he calls for the receptionist up front.

"Um. Yeah?"

*This guy's intense.*

"Hey Stacy—these kids aren't drinking are they? They signed the waiver?"

Stacy answers with a middle finger pointed in Paco's direction.

I straighten my shoulders and nudge his arm. "I'm fine. I've wanted this tattoo for a long time. You can start."

He studies me for half a beat before turning back toward his station. When he scoots closer with the gun in hand, black ink glistening on the tip, I lean my head back and close my eyes. I gasp on first contact, but slowly, the sharp sting of the needles makes me smile. My breath evens and I find myself in another place entirely. If I listen close enough, the sound of crashing waves drown out the buzz of the tattoo gun.

"What's the story behind this ink?"

I open an eye and look at Paco. His face is inches from my arm, focused on the detail. I didn't even realize how long I'd been lying there. He's already finished with the outline, shading and moving toward the color. I quickly look away, not wanting to see the tattoo until the end. I move my other arm behind my head and study the laminate above me.

"I guess you can say it's a reminder."

"Oh yeah? Of you?"

I nod.

"The girl represents innocence and hope. The flowers are beauty. And the quill signifies the stories we're made of—where we come from and what we make of ourselves."

He glances up at me and then back down to my arm. "You've been through some shit?"

I frown. "Why?"

"You haven't even moved. You practically fell asleep as I outlined your entire forearm. And now, as I'm shading in the color, you're making conversation without the slightest waver in your voice." He shakes his head. "Trust me. Nine out of ten people are asking me to wait, to give them a smoke break, to get a drink of water—stupid shit."

I look at him.

"You though, you just go somewhere else." He pauses and waves his arm around. "People who can separate themselves from this kind of pain know how to from experience."

When I don't respond he grunts and returns to silence.

I'm beginning to think Jessa's right. There has to be some kind of sign or target or something that makes people believe I want to go all kumbayah and shit. I focus again on the cracks in the laminate above me until I hear Paco clear his throat. When I look down I realize he's done.

"What do you think?"

I move my arm for a better view and suck in a quick breath.

*Ohmigod.*

My arm looks like color-exploded. Surrounded by a gold frame, the girl twirls through a field of peonies, her dress blowing in the wind. Her arm is out toward the sky, her hand holding the quill. But what makes me lose every single word I ever thought I had—is the little girl's hair.

It's crimson. Just like mine. And with the strands flowing behind her in the wind, it looks like wisps of flames trailing in her wake.

"I love it. I do. It's amazing." I look up and try to blink the tears away so I can see him but they just keep falling. They just keep falling and I don't even care, don't even move to wipe them off my cheeks.

He claps his hands. "Good. I'll be right back with some instructions on how to care for it." He walks away and hollers for Stacy. "Grab my phone! I need to instagram that arm." He fist pumps and then points to Tim. "Go look at that arm, fucker. It's amazing."

I can't stop staring. For as long as I can remember, my body has been something to hide. I hated myself. Hated looking at myself in the mirror and seeing hints and reminders of what it was like to feel razors sliced into flesh. Now? Now it's just *color.* Color and art and beauty and I can't stop staring. I'm so transfixed I don't even hear Jessa and Ren walk over to where I'm seated.

"Damn, Stephanie. That's amazing." Jessa's voice is slightly nasal, and I glance up at her new piercing, not surprised to see that it looks as if she's always had it, outside of the slight swelling in her nose.

"Thanks. I love it. The metal suits you, Jess."

She smiles and curtsies. "Doesn't it? Hurts like a bitch, though." She wrinkles her nose and whimpers at the pulling of newly-pierced skin.

Paco comes over with a paper towel soaked in water. "Okay. This is gonna sting like hell for a few seconds but it'll draw out the excess blood and plasma. Do this once when you get home today as well. Put some regular soap—none of that fancy shit—and then get the water as hot as you can take it. Speeds up the healing process." He gently places the towel on my arm and I breathe in quick and sharp.

I exhale between my teeth, closing my eyes and breathing through the pain.

"Dude, Stephanie. You're such a badass. I need you to teach me your buddhist ways." Ren moves to scratch his forehead and then winces, realizing he's using his newly tatted arm. He points to me. "My guy did that and I cried. *Cried.*" He shakes his head and looks away.

"Fucking embarrassing."

I laugh and motion my chin toward his arm. "Let me see!"

He takes his finger and gently moves back the binding around his arm. I sigh in appreciation.

"Ren that's incredible."

I lean forward so I can get a better look. His tattoo stretches from the back of his shoulder to his elbow. There are trees—huge Redwood looking ones with incredibly detailed trunks and branches and leaves—lining the top of his shoulder and snaking their branches around his back. Beneath the trees is the profile of a man playing the trumpet. Coming out of his trumpet are the words *we're all stories in the end.*

"What does this even mean? And how can you fit all these things together and it look so…*natural?"*

Paco laughs at me and glances up at the tattoo. He turns his head and hollers toward Tim in the back, still cleaning his station.

"His arm looks baller, dude."

He looks up and smiles. "Thanks, man. It would have been easier had he not been squirmy."

Ren looks offended for half a second before turning toward me to explain. "I grew up in Northern California—spent my time playing in the Redwood forests. This guy? He's my great-grandfather and spent time as a famous trumpet player in a jazz band during the 20s. And this quote comes from one of my favorite episodes of Dr. Who—because it's true. We really are all stories in the end." He shrugs and I keep staring.

Paco dries my arm before bringing out a small tube of Aquaphor. He motions toward Ren's arm. "Deep shit, man."

Ren nods in agreement. I keep staring.

"Wait. Wait. I love it, I do—especially the quote—but Dr. What?"

His eyes bug out of his face.

"You don't know the doctor?! That quote is basically from the best monologue in the history of talking. You're hurting my heart, Steph." He clutches his chest.

"…um. No? Should I?" I look between Paco, who's chuckling under his breath and Jessa who's muttering something about harnessing the nerd under her breath.

Ren shakes his head slightly and then looks away. "How can you not know the Doctor? It's like this whole relationship is a lie."

I look at Jessa. "This is one of his nerd things?"

"Correct."

"Is it like a book series? TV show?" Paco pats my arm, letting me know the wrapping and doctoring is completed, and I hand him the rest of the cash I have in my pocket.

"It's a TV show. And don't worry about him. Seriously. He gets borderline batshit when we start talking about these things so the offense isn't real. He'll get over it."

Ren widens his arms and juts out his chin. "Hello? Ladies? I'm right here." Dropping his stance he gives us a defeated look. "Fuck's sake."

I hide a smile and gather my things, gingerly wrapping my purse around my chest without bumping the tender skin. Jessa does a good job not laughing at Ren's expense until I catch her eye. We burst into giggles and walk out the door, laughing at the hilarity of nameless doctors and colored pills. Ren follows us, grumbling the entire time.

.:..

Before heading to Sunset Cliffs, we eat at Luigi's. We walk in and see people at tables covered with a single pizza. Like, the pizza coves the *entire* table. Ren claps his hands.

"Good. I'm so hungry."

It's a small local restaurant—beach front and run down in all the best ways. The owner, a burly 60-something year old surfer, takes our order and strikes up a conversation with Ren and Jessa while I find us a seat.

It doesn't take long for our food to arrive. Garlic bread that steams with the aroma of salty goodness, pizza that has cheese on top of cheese on top of every meat imaginable, and ice-cold cokes. My stomach growls and I place a hand over it. I had no idea how hungry I was until I see the food and that surprises me. I think today is the first time in months that I've actually eaten two full meals.

We eat in silence for a few minutes, each enjoying the sound of the waves and listening to the small conversations around us. A couple a few tables down begins to argue and we share gleeful moments of eavesdropping on their disagreement.

"Babe. You *told* me I could go with the guys tomorrow to see the game. I have the text to prove it." He rummages in his pocket for his phone and his girlfriend sighs heavily.

"Just *whatever.* I can't even deal with you right now. Take me home?"

Ren whispers under his breath. "Just run, brother. Just run."

Jessa rolls her eyes. "Whatever. She's the reason all guys assume girls are needy attention whores." She licks her fingers and scoots out of her booth, grabbing Ren's arm with her other hand.

"Come on. Let's go check the jukebox. It's too quiet in here." They push and shove and slap the whole way to the machine, trying to beat the other for first dibs in song selection. I glance down at my pizza and catch more of the argument from the couple, now gathering their things to leave.

I curl my lip and chance turning around to catch a good look at them as they pass by our table. My breath catches. For a split second I think it's Kevin. Same hair—same build—same gait. He turns around and catches me staring and smiles.

*No. Not Kevin. Get a grip, Stephanie.*

I offer him a friendly smile and look down at my plate again, slightly embarrassed he caught me.

"Jessa. I'm not spending a dollar to listen to Beyonce."

I stifle a laugh and turn toward Jessa and Ren.

She points at the machine. "You won't spend a dollar for Drunk in Love but you'll waste *two* dollars on Taylor Swift?!"

"Don't judge my musical taste, Jess. Besides. It's not just any Taylor Swift." He grins. "It's our song."

"Damn straight it's our song. I knew you were trouble first."

He rolls his eyes. She flips her hair and reaches to lean her elbow on his non-tattooed shoulder, pressing into him while they flip through the offered songs. "Whatever you want, Renfro. I chose last time."

I tilt my head and try to figure them out. Ever since last night they've been glued together in a way I've never seen before. I watch as Ren presses a bunch of buttons and they high five each other as London Grammar fills the speakers around us. They turn to walk back toward the table and I smile in approval.

"London Grammar. Nice. I was concerned for a second."

Ren shakes his head.

"One of these days the world will understand the poetry of Taylor Swift."

I balk. "Nope. Never. Ren, *never* will the world understand her lyrics."

Jessa laughs and begins moving her hips in a sultry twist. I have no idea how she's moving her hips *and* walking *and* not falling on her ass. She sits down next to me and bumps my elbow.

I turn toward her, leaning against the back of the booth. I motion between her and Ren.

"Are you guys dating or what?"

Jessa's stops mid-bite. "Huh. Totally not expecting that question."

"Why?"

"Because," she flips her hand toward me and crinkles her nose. "You're the one with issues about every body knowing your business and shit. Didn't think you'd turn the tables so quickly."

I smile.

"I aim to surprise."

Ren swallows his piece of pizza in three bites and juts his chin toward me.

"Why do you want to know? You forming a crush, new girl?" He winks.

I roll my eyes.

"Hardly."

Jessa fights from spitting out her coke.

"I ask because the tension between you two is making *me* all hot and bothered and I just needed to clear the air before we go any further."

Jessa turns and focuses on Ren and raises her eyebrow. "Well, Renfro? Are we a thing?"

His eyes grow wide.

"Uh...."

Jessa throws her head back and laughs. She leans in and faces me. "Ren and I have a mutual-attraction agreement. He likes me. I like him. We both know it. But, we don't want a relationship." She shrugs.

"That sounds healthy."

She smirks. "Well, we've been down that road before—it didn't really work." She glances at Ren and his eyes have gone glassy, a sure sign he's wanting to evade the conversation. Realizing he's not going to chime in, she turns and looks at me again.

"What about you, Dr. Phil? You have any boy-toys back home?"

I clear my throat. "It's complicated. And no I don't want to talk about it." I take a sip of my coke.

Ren chuckles, now fully engaged. "Stop trying to be so mysterious. It's exhausting."

"Stop trying to pretend you don't want to be with Jessa." I jerk my thumb toward her chest and she blushes. "Everyone can see your hard-on from a mile away."

They stare at me gape-mouthed for a few seconds until I finally roll my eyes. "It's not like I just said something earth shattering. Like I said: *a mile away.* For both of you. Jesus. I don't understand the whole we-like-each-other-but-are-giving-the-other-one-space shit. Seems asking for trouble." Wiping my mouth with a napkin, I bring it down and start picking it to pieces.

*Reminds me of that time in the diner with Kevin....*

*Shit.*

Memories are dangerous. With memories come voices. I sniff and throw the shredded napkin on the leftover crusts on my plate and check to see if their plates are empty.

*I gotta get out of here.*

"So uh….can we do Sunset Cliffs now?" I point toward the sky through the window in the front of the store. "Looks like we only have a little over an hour of daylight left."

"Oh! Right. Sunset." Ren pats his jeans for his keys and begins to look worried before I push them forward on the table. Jessa combs through her hair and hazards a glance toward Ren before glancing at me and offering a small smile.

She leans forward as I maneuver myself out of the booth and tweaks my elbow with her fingers. Turning around to face her, her small smile stretches across her face into the grin of one who has a master plan.

"I like when you get feisty, Stephanie. You know, I feel like this is the beginning of what could be a beautiful and adventurous friendship." She licks her lips and jerks her head toward Ren. "I haven't seen him that flustered since I showed up to work licking a multi-colored lollipop.

I snort.

"You're evil, you know that, Jessa? Poor guy doesn't even have a chance."

She cackles.

"I know. It's glorious."

## CHAPTER FIVE

We pull up to Sunset Cliffs and there's not a soul in sight. Jessa takes the rubber band around her wrist and lifts and twists her hair into a high bun to fight the wind.

"I can't believe there's no one here."

I can't either. I breathe in deep—smelling the ocean and feeling the wind blow my hair loose of its braid. I don't even care. I walk to the edge of the cliff and hold my hands to my chest as if to keep the ache inside.

Sometimes beauty hurts you with her power.

The waves are rushing up to the cliff and crashing against the rock, spraying salt water up above. My flesh erupts in goosebumps and I shiver. I don't know if I believe in holy spaces. But here? I gaze out to the almost imperceptible line where water meets sky.

Here, everything seems sacred.

A wave crashes beneath me and the foam sprays up and over the ledge, baptizing my feet. I breathe in quick and blink away the tears. It's almost too much. I hesitate, wondering if I should just walk away. Maybe I'm making too much of things.

But the waves seem to take on a different chorus, beckoning me closer and closer to the edge.

I find a spot that's dry and sit down, curling my legs into my chest and resting my chin on my knees.

The sky is screaming too, but this time I'm not sure I want to hear.

She's begging me to remember mornings spent watching her grab hold of the blackness and edging it out for another day.

Begging me to hold on—to believe—to rest in second chances.

Because there's always another day coming, right?

But there's also the ending—the way the colors give in to the darkness and disappear for a moment.

Which one of those is truth?

I sit and listen to the chorus above and below me, wondering if just maybe, that's where my hope is: somewhere in the middle between water and sky.

Speaking of hope.

I bite my lip and close my eyes against Jessa and Ren's giggles behind me. Their happiness reminds me of piggybacks under the night sky and falling stars and running from trains and kissing to beat the storm. A tear trickles down my face and I bury my head in between my legs before raising it again to watch the sun dip below the horizon, the waves gaining intensity and rush as the tide moves inland.

*Never leave me,* he said. I roll my eyes and feel the anger brimming beneath the surface. If only I knew that "never leave me" meant more for job security than true love. The fissure within cracks a little more and I let my shoulders slump inward to mind the pain.

Sometimes, a broken heart needs to see the darkness take over to know she's not alone.

I hear steps behind me and bristle involuntarily.

*Please don't come sit next to me.*

The steps continue toward me and I groan.

Ren laughs quietly.

"Easy, killer. It's just us. Wouldn't want you jumping off the edge or anything."

Jessa skips next to me and pops down on the rock.

"Oh. It's damp over here. Have you been sprayed?"

"A few times."

"Wow. The view is incredible."

She points toward a small enclave in front of us.

"See that fire?"

The flames light up the darkness blanketing the atmosphere. I nod even though she can't really see me anymore.

"If you listen closely, you can hear voices of surfers camping out tonight. Technically, that beach is off limits but they come down and hide in some of the caves so they can catch the morning waves."

"They stay over night?" I watch the flicker of campfire in the distance and feel a pang of jealousy.

"Yeah. Can you imagine? I'm sure they have grains of sand in their shorts for months."

Ren snorts.

It grows quiet and sure enough, the distant sound of laughter reaches us. I wonder what it would be like to feel that sense of adventure again: the rush of adrenaline moving in your veins.

Jessa falls on her back and lifts her arms toward the sky.

"Ren, will you be my Moondoggie?"

He's quiet for half a second before bending at his knees next to her head. She drops her arms and tilts her head in his direction. He stares at her and brushes a strand of hair off her forehead.

"Only if you'll be my Gidget."

And then they *kiss.*

"Are you guys serious right now?"

They don't answer me, too lost in each other's tonsils.

"Seriously? This is happening?"

Jessa raises her arm and gives me the finger.

I don't even admit I have no idea what the hell they mean by the Moondoggie and Gidget references. But it's annoying as fuck and I kind of want to push them over the edge. I sigh audibly and scramble to my feet.

"I'll be waiting in the Jeep."

Walking back to the street, I hear Jessa calling after me. "Don't act like you didn't want this, Stephanie!"

"Glad you came up for oxygen, asshole!" I holler back over my shoulder. And then without even thinking, I smile. A pure, genuine and unadulterated smile. I don't even care that I'm going home to an empty hotel room.

.:::.

We take a different route home, winding down side roads and back streets. I spend a majority of the trip with my head against the backseat, looking up at the stars. They're like shards of broken glass against a black sheet out here—vivid and crystal to the touch. I blink and let my eyes grow heavy with the rhythm of the wheels on the road and the wind at my face and the beauty around me.

I'm jostled awake by the Jeep going off road.

Opening my eyes I fight to to make out what's going on.

"What are we doing?"

"Jess needs to use the restroom."

I nod and close my eyes again, barely noticing a building in the distance behind some of the shrubbery. After a few moments we hear Jessa's voice calling out to us.

"You guys! Come here. Check this out."

Ren groans and rubs his face with his hands before answering with a muffled voice pressed in by his fingers.

"Jessa. Come on. It's late."

She reappears behind a bush. "Seriously? You don't even work tomorrow." She points at me. "Neither do you." And then motions us with her hand to come join.

Ren and I look at each other. I shrug.

"Your call, Moondoggie."

Leaning his head against the steering wheel he groans again. "You don't know the trouble she finds herself in or you wouldn't be saying that, Steph."

I laugh.

"Oh Ren. That's where you're mistaken. Trouble's my middle name."

He raises an eyebrow and catches my eye in the rearview mirror before shaking his head.

"Fuck it. Let's go."

And he opens his door and holds it open for me as I hop out and walk toward Jessa.

She's standing in the middle of a small field that used to be a parking lot. Turning to look at us with a glint in her eye, she tilts her head toward the building and smiles.

"Took you guys long enough."

I squint to get a better look at the structure and grimace. It's run down—missing doors and shingles. Noting the graffiti and debris around and inside, it's not totally abandoned. I imagine at any moment there are a variation of social misfits and dregs of society claiming this property as their own.

"Wanna go explore?" Jessa's voice is hopeful and full of excitement.

*No. No I do not want to go explore.*

"Um…."

"Oh come on. It's begging to be explored."

I squeeze my hands into fists. "It's begging for someone to step on any number of forgotten and rusty drug needles."

Ren holds up his hands and then points to the building.

"Jessa, that's a nightmare waiting to happen."

She laughs and then turns around, walking toward the building.

I shake my head, crossing my arms.

"Fuck *that*. I'm not going in there."

Ren groans and lifts his face to the sky, beginning to follow her and leaving me behind, dodging broken beer bottles and trash. I hesitate for a few moments, watching the distance between me and them get larger, and then feel a growing sense of being watched.

I turn around quickly, my pulse pounding in my ears; my arms growing heavy.

*No one's there.*

I bring my hands up to my face and massage my temples. *Breathe, Stephanie. Breathe.* I laugh under my breath and call out to Ren.

"Hey! Wait up."

He stops and Jessa throws her fist in the air in celebration. "I *knew* you guys would do this."

Ren mutters under his breath and steps in front of Jessa, his phone serving as a flashlight.

"Just let me go in first?"

She glowers at him.

"Whatever."

We walk through the door and I look around.

"Was this a hotel of some kind?"

Ren points his phone toward an area that looks like a lobby. In the corner on the other side of the room is the stump of what used to be one of those massive office plants. His voice isn't more than a whisper.

"It looks like it."

Something crashes against the floor upstairs and Ren jumps. Jessa screams and flings herself into his arms.

I just stand there, every piece of me tingling. If I thought I could hear my pulse in my ears outside, now it's roaring to life—I'm pretty sure I feel it in my fingernails.

"What the *fuck*." My breath comes out raspy—I'm barely moving my lips, as if in moving anything I'm giving credence to the noise above us.

Ren sniffs and moves his eyes upward.

"Hello?" A voice from above us wanders across the lobby.

*That's a kid's voice,* I think, swallowing my dread.

Our eyes go wide simultaneously. Ren puts his finger over his mouth, signaling for us to be quiet. Jessa's mouthing expletives.

"I swear to God if it's a fucking clown I'm fucking gone."

Ren rolls his eyes. "You watch too many horror movies. It sounds like a kid. I'm going to go up and check it out. You guys stay here."

Jessa and I look at each other as he walks away and immediately begin to follow him.

"Who's here?" Ren leads us slowly, his question bouncing off the walls in the hallway we're now walking in—rooms on either side of us. There are no doors and nothing inside the rooms until we get to the room by the window—the one at the very end of the hallway. We hear scratching inside and then a cough.

"Shit," Jessa whispers and I can see the vein in her neck bulging. Instinctively, I reach for her hand and give it a quick squeeze before letting go.

Ren taps on the door quietly.

"Is uh…is someone in here?"

We breathe in collectively.

Pause.

Nothing. Not even the sound of our breathing. We stand there and hold our breath, waiting. All of us staring at the door, hoping for nothing—hoping it's all just our imagination.

*That's possible right? That we all hear the same nothingness? A rat scratching against the wall in the framework or something?*

"Yes. I'm in here. Who is it?"

We breathe out the air we were holding and I don't know what's pushing me to grab the handle of the door but I'm remembering being caught and captured and locked away and there's nothing I can do except turn the handle and push open the door and collapse against an empty room.

An empty room minus a worn mattress thrown in the corner, a single wooden chair, a pile of clothes in the bathroom, and a young boy with a sling around his arm and a look of terror on his face.

"Please don't hurt me," he whispers.

I can't see anymore. My vision is tunneling toward him and my memories are mixing with reality and I'm falling toward the ground—I'm falling and I can't stop myself until I hit my knees on the cement and stumble backward until my back is pressed up against the wall and my dad's voice echoes in the spaces where I thought I would be able to breathe.

*You're nothing you're nothing no one will ever want you you're such a stupid bitch.* I whimper and put my hands over my ears.

Jessa bursts through the door, her eyes bulging and her hands shaking by her sides.

"Shit. Shit fucking shit holy fucking shit…."

Her eyes are wild and she's pointing at the boy and I can't hear anything she's saying even though I see her mouth moving. I blink once-twice-three times trying to get my vision clear.

*Too much noise. Too many voices.*

Slowly the room comes back into focus and I can hear her talking.

"Why aren't you answering me?"

I see Ren at the door, peeking in—his eyes wide.

I'm still in the corner, both walls closing in around me.

*I need to breathe. I need to just breathe.*

I somehow find my voice and barely crack open an eye to look at Jessa.

"He just startled me. I need a moment so I can breathe."

I'm lying, but that's not really important.

*Please don't hurt me,* the kid said. He didn't startle me. That's not what caused me to drop. It was the look on his face. The one of terror and defeat and resignation. I recognized it.

I walked into this room and found myself staring into my own eyes.

.:::.

Jessa turns and looks at the boy.

"What happened to your arm?"

He licks his lips and I can see his breathing grow erratic.

*Fear.*

"He told me he'd be back in about an hour."

"Who? Your dad?"

His eyes flicker between Ren and Jessa and then me.

"No. Not my dad. The guy who hurt my arm."

My breath is beginning to normalize and I wipe my hands on my jeans, pushing up to my feet. I walk over to the boy and kneel beside him.

"What's your name?"

"Oliver?"

"How old are you, Oliver?"

It's just us talking—Ren and Jessa might as well not even be in the room. I'm struck with the frailty of his voice and wonder how long he's been tied up alone. I search his face for clues but come up with nothing.

I should know by now you can't make sense of madness.

He swallows and looks me in the eye. "I'm 14."

Jessa clears her throat.

"Don't you think we need to call the cops or something?"

I can't stop myself. I blanch and jerk as if she just hit me. Oliver notices and tilts his head, studying me. Jessa reaches out toward me with concern. "Are you sure you're okay?"

I nod, holding up my hand to keep her from coming closer.

"I'm okay. I just had a foot cramp." I wiggle my foot for show and out of the corner of my eye, see Oliver's lip twitch.

*He knows I'm lying.*

Ren steps into the room and pulls out his phone.

"I'll call."

I look at him and nod, my throat threatening to close in on itself. Forcing my attention back to Oliver, I attempt a smile.

"We're gonna get you help, okay?"

I ignore the look of alarm in his eyes.

"How'd you get here? And what's with the arm?"

"I was walking my dog and a guy hit me with his car."

"His car?"

He nods. "And then he got out of his car, and forced me in his backseat, telling me he'd take me to the hospital." He's getting used to the audience now, warming up to us listening.

"When he turned down this road and it was this backwoods shit, I kicked open the door and ran. I almost got away. He ran after me and tackled me, and then started hitting me." He pointed to bruises on his forehead and eyes.

"And your arm?" Jessa's standing next to me now.

"He twisted it when he was leading me back to the car. Told me that was only the beginning of what he would do to me if I tried to run away again."

Something shifts inside and I push away the coils of familiarity growing taut within me.

*You run away again and I'll find you, bitch. And that's just the beginning. I'll make your life a living hell for leaving me.*

I suck in a breath and close my eyes for half a beat before opening them again.

*Focus on Oliver, focus on Oliver.*

But I can't. My dad said those words to me. Something skirts the edges of my mind and I lean back on my heels. I can't freak out. Not here.

*Something doesn't add up.*

I stand up and walk toward the window, looking for Ren outside. I see him right below us, talking on the phone.

Turning around, I find Oliver's gaze on me.

"You mentioned he was coming back. The guy who did this. Why did he leave you? And where was he going?"

Oliver shrugs.

"He just said he needed to go get something he forgot, and then he blindfolded me and threatened me again about leaving."

*Something he forgot.*

Lights flash in the distance and I blink them away, the tendrils of alarm threatening to grip tighter. I count them as they screech to a halt by the Jeep.

Three cop cars.

Two firetrucks.

One ambulance.

And down the street, hiding behind another area of shrubbery, is an unmarked car. The lights blink on and off twice and I stumble back, falling on my wrists. A sharp pain jolts up my arms.

"Whoa, Stephanie. What's wrong?!" Jessa runs up to me and helps me up to my feet. I bring my wrists up to my chest and look at her, my eyes wild.

"I have…I have to go. I have to leave. I can't be here. I can't…"

I don't even make it to the hallway before stumbling against the wall and falling on my knees for the second time. I'm crawling toward the stairs and begging myself to just move forward—just reach the stairs so I can reach the ground so I can get outside and run away.

Because the car. The car made me remember.

This is my dad. My dad is here. My dad is here and he hurt this boy and he's trying to let me know he hasn't forgotten.

## CHAPTER SIX

I don't even feel my legs as I run down the stairs. Grabbing the knob on the banister on the bottom step, I swerve and almost run into a police officer. He sidesteps me and then reaches for my arm to catch me from falling.

*Do not faint. Do not faint. Do not scream.*

"Whoa, there. Where's the fire?" His eyes move over my face and he frowns. "Are you okay? Wait. Weren't you one of the kids who found the boy?"

I bristle.

*I am not a kid.*

I can hear Jessa running down the stairs and calling my name but I can't focus. I can't process anything. I look down. The police officer is still holding on to my elbow.

I wriggle free and startle back a few steps, into Jessa who is running up behind us.

"Jesus, Steph you just bolted. What gives?" She looks up and catches the police officer and offers her brightest smile. I move to wrap my jacket closer around my chest and squirm.

I have no jacket.

Nothing to hide in.

I blink and focus again on Jessa, her hand landing gently on my shoulder.

"She's just a little shocked, officer. I think she just needs some air."

He nods, still eyeing me. "I understand. This is something serious you guys stumbled into—" His gaze lowers and he props his hands on his belt, fingering his gun. "You ladies realize you could have been seriously injured?"

I look away. I'm not interested in this conversation. At this point, safety isn't really my priority. It's almost impossible. The only thing I hear is my father—

*I'll always find you. I'll always find you. I'll always find you.*

Members of a SWAT team rush past us and run upstairs. I hear their footsteps above us as they look in the rooms. Jessa nods her head.

"Of course, sir. We just wanted to see an abandoned building." She juts her finger toward the second floor. "Who would have expected *that* to happen?"

"You'd be surprised," the officer mutters and Jessa just shakes her head.

"Come on, Steph. Let's get you outside."

We walk around the corner of the hotel to a back area. Our feet crunch who-knows-what and I keep darting my eyes back and forth, back and forth, half expecting my father to walk out of the woods at any moment.

"Okay, what's going on?" She points to my hands and I bury them in my back pockets. "You're shaking. And your eyes are all crazy. If I didn't know any better I'd say you were high on something." Her head jerks back. "Wait. You aren't high, are you?"

I shake my head. "No. I just need to get out of here."

I'm past the point of fear, the adrenaline burst leaving me numb and in shock.

*There's no way he could have known I was here. No way. Right?*

Jessa reaches for my arm and I jerk it away. I turn and stalk toward the Jeep, wiping my cheeks with the side of my thumb. I pass Ren and he turns and gives Jessa a quizzical look. She shrugs and whispers loud enough for me to hear.

"She just started walking away. I have no idea what's going on…"

Her footsteps falter just for a moment behind me and I hear Ren break in and call for her.

"Hey. Just let her go. She's fine."

I keep walking, urging myself not to run—not to break into a sprint and go until I can't go anymore. Let Ren and Jessa talk to the cops. I've done enough of that in my lifetime. When I finally sit down and rest my head against the back of the seat, I fight for control—for some type of reason. I close my eyes against the memories but they keep coming.

Back home, dad had a system with his men. They found the weak ones to use—to drag into their plot of determining how and when they'd find more girls. Whenever they were on a call or scouting, there was always someone in the background watching. They had a code. They would use the lights of the car to talk to each other.

One flash and the coast was clear.

Two flashes and there was nothing left to do but turn and run.

I think back to the car I saw in the distance and feel a sharp pang of adrenaline deep in my bones. Surely it was just coincidence—I'm just making something out of nothing.

*Right?*

I rub the chill from the back of my neck, willing Jessa and Ren back to the Jeep. I hear shouting and a snap—crack behind me. Turning around, I see the abandoned building engulfed in fire, Jessa and Ren running toward me.

"What-in-the-fucking-hell?" Ren screams as he jumps into his side and turns on the engine. "Seriously." He shakes his head maniacally. "That thing just burst into flames. No warning."

He jumps up and down and motions wildly for Jessa to hurry. Time moves slow-but-quick and I feel my vision clouding again. Something isn't right.

"What's happening?"

Ren turns to look at me as he shifts gears, ready to peel away as soon as Jessa's ready.

"No ones knows. It just happened. They say if they can't contain it'll blow. They told us to run."

"Who?"

Ren takes a big breath. Jessa's in her seat now and he's speeding through the dirt trying to get on the street as soon as possible. Her eyes are feral—nothing but fear and confusion. I watch her hands shake as she tries to button her safety belt.

"The SWAT team running out of the building. Apparently they went up to the room and the boy was gone—just completely vanished. His sling was the only thing left behind."

*Two flashes mean run.* I swallow back the despair and force myself not to show any emotion—mirroring the stoic look Ren gives me in the rearview mirror.

"So the fire?"

"That's the weird thing. It started downstairs. After you and Jessa left with the officer, and after the SWAT team ran upstairs, something in the lobby caught fire. They still have no idea what happened." He shakes his head and lets go of the steering wheel to run his fingers through his hair.

Glancing at Jessa, he reaches over and touches her knee with the tip of his finger and she grabs it.

"Let's just get out of here."

She doesn't respond, just stays silent—forehead pressed against the railing next to her, fingers gripped tight around his hand.

I can't keep my eyes off the flames, dancing around and under and in between every frame of the building. The firetruck immediately taps into motion, raising ladders and pulling out their hose.

It doesn't matter though. The flames have spoken. This building will be nothing but ash. I feel the hope of earlier rise with the smoke above us. I grimace and brush away a lone tear falling down my cheek.

*I should have known the silence would burn me.*

.::.

The ride home is a silent one. We get to the hotel and Ren pulls up to the front door to drop me off. He glances at me in his mirror again and offers a slight smile.

"Thanks for coming with us Stephanie. Sorry things got so….weird."

I don't respond except for a brief moment of eye contact. I step down from the Jeep and walk toward the front door when I hear Jessa calling my name.

"Stephanie! Wait. You left something." She reaches down by her feet and sits up again, holding something out of the window. I gasp when I see the familiar black ribbing with the yellow string hanging down from the pages.

*Another journal.*

"W-where did you get that? It's not mine."

Jessa shrugs and looks confused.

"It just showed up—I kicked it by accident on the way home and figured it fell out of your bag when we were leaving the building." She moves to bring it back inside the window and I lunge for the journal, grabbing it out of her hands. This one I'm keeping. I hug it to my chest and force smile.

"You're right. Sorry. It's late and I'm not thinking." I peek in my purse and glance back up at both of them. "Not here." Lifting the journal by head I laugh. "Thanks for finding it—and for giving it back."

And then I turn around before they can see me shaking from the inside out. I smile as I walk into the lobby and I keep smiling as I make eye contact with the guy behind the desk.

"Good evening." He nods.

I nod back and turn toward the elevator. The double doors. The steel. That's what I want—what I need before I can look down at this leather between my hands.

A couple turns the corner and almost run into me. She laughs and her fingers wrap around my arm.

"Oh darling. I'm so sorry."

My eyes catch on her jewels and I blink and look at her.

*Smile, Stephanie.*

"No problem. I probably wasn't paying attention."

I'm ten steps away.

Now five.

Three.

I close my eyes when I press the button, hoping to find an empty elevator. I open them again and watch the numbers fall to my floor. When the doors open and I am alone, I breathe a sigh of relief. The journal feels heavy in my hands.

I wait until it's just me and the dinging of the floors.

I open the journal.

*Thought you might like a fresh one. Try not to throw this one away? I love you. - Kevin*

The silence roars above and below me and I stare at the words for what seems like hours. I knew it was him. I knew it and I don't know how but as soon as I turned and saw Jessa holding the journal I knew he'd be the one responsible.

I can't explain the feeling inside me—elation, relief, anger, fear, joy, confusion—all of it. It's all coming and pushing up and out and I'm crying and screaming and ripping at the pages before I can even think twice. When I finally blink and realize what's happened, the journal is in pieces of ripped paper and torn binding around me and there's a lady bending over and looking at me curiously.

"Young lady, are you okay? Can you hear me?"

I jerk away and sniff, pushing myself up and looking around me. I don't even know when she appeared.

*How long have I been here?*

I blink and my eyes land on a piece of paper by the door.

I see his handwriting peering up at me and I'm falling again—I'm falling but this time falling feels like standing up and banging on the door and begging for it to open so I can just get into my room and lock the door and hide under the covers.

"Please just let me out! I need out. Just let me out…"

The lady steps away from me, shaking her head and reaching for her cell phone.

I turn to look at her, my eyes wild.

"I'm fine! I'm fine." I point to her phone. "Please don't call anyone. Please. I'm fine. I just need out." I turn to bang on the doors again as I hear the ding of a floor. I don't even wait for the doors to slide open all the way. I'm out and running to my room before they've even closed, the lady peeking her head out of the elevator to watch me swerve down the hall.

I struggle to lift my hands and end up holding one hand still so I can keep stop the shaking long enough to wait for the green light letting me know I can turn the handle and disappear. Once inside, I don't even reach my bed. I fall against the door frame, sobbing, clutching at my shirt and pulling until it rips. The sound awakens me. I'm clutching and pulling and ripping everything I can get my hands on—it's the only way I'll survive, to hear the ripping of my heart right out of my chest.

These past few months meant nothing. The ache of my new tattoo lifts me out of the fog only to suck me right back down again.

There's no field of peonies to dance in right now. It's all ashes and weeds and torn fragments of my past coming back to lay claim.

.:::.

In my dreams, my father isn't always a monster.

I'm little again—swinging in his arms as he walks around the house, whispering about the latest book he read. He talks to me of *East of Eden* and the secret of a good sentence.

"Did you know there's a one sentence chapter in *As I Lay Dying*? It's true. Flip the page and you see it: my mother is a fish." And then he laughs as if let in on some secret.

I reach my hand up and feel the stubble on his cheek, and he chomps down on my fingers playfully with his lips. He twists and carries me around his torso, plopping me down on the counter and looking me in the eyes. "Don't ever forget this, Stephanie," he says. His eyes are serious. My eyes flick toward the window where the light comes in and dances in shadow on the linoleum floor of our kitchen. My fingers play with the collar of his shirt.

"Sometimes, the best stories are the ones where the characters seem realistically disappointing." Stepping back he reaches for the stubble on his cheek just like I did seconds before. Instead of scratching or rubbing, he pulls the skin until taut like rubber.

My breath grows shallow.

*Why is daddy pulling off his skin? Why does he look different now?*

"In the end, sweetheart, we're all the villain." He says with a glint in his eye and a bottle of whiskey suddenly in his hands. Kevin stands behind him, holding a journal and laughing. I look down and my legs are not the ones of a little girl but my own—and I'm wearing the thigh highs he always had me wear on my nights in the shed.

Just like that, my daddy is replaced with the monster I know. And Kevin? Kevin is *laughing*. I move my eyes slowly up toward where they stand and Kevin makes his way to me, his eyes dark and brooding.

This is not the adventure-seeking boyfriend I grew to love—he's all together sinister. Menacing. His hands reach out to me and grab my hips with ferocity, pulling me off the counter.

I jolt awake, my hands clutching the sheets around me. When my hands only reach carpet and pieces of clothing, I realize I never made it to the bed. I bring my hands up to my throat, feeling the pulse race underneath my fingers. I breathe deep.

*It was just a dream Stephanie.*

I push the heel of my palms against my eyes, forcing the nightmare away.

*It's just a dream. Just a dream.*

My heart pounds as the city comes to life outside my window. When my pulse slows down and the images from my dream fade away, reality sticks to my bones and I shudder.

In my dreams, my father isn't always a monster, but he sure wears his dragon skin with ease—poisoning everything I've ever loved.

.:::.

I'm not sure how many days I spend locked up in my hotel room.

Monday.

Tuesday.

Wednesday.

Who knows what day it is anymore.

Thanks to the kitchenette, I have a small stash of food in the cabinets and fridge. But I'm not hungry. I can't remember the last time I ate. I've called in to work twice—both times claiming the flu. I'm aimless—not even turning on the television. I just walk around my room, lose myself to my thoughts, and then fall asleep to escape them.

I know I need to leave at some point, but right now, what's outside makes me cringe.

All of my thoughts are captured by the journal left in the Jeep.

Kevin is here.

I frown at the way my heart skips in tandem with my thoughts when it comes to him. There's a knock on my door and I jump, pulling at my robe. With a quick look at the clock on my nightstand, I know it's seven in the morning. I raise an eyebrow. I've lost all track of time. I had no idea it was that early.

I make no movement toward the door, knowing that housekeeping doesn't come until closer to noon and if I am quiet, maybe the visitor will go away.

Another knock.

"Stephanie. I know you're in there. I heard you startle."

Jessa.

I drop my head back toward my shoulder and sigh. She won't be leaving. I pinch my cheeks to make them look fevered, and open the door, sliding behind it to let her in the room.

She wrinkles her nose.

"It smells in here."

"You smell." I walk past her and collapse on the bed, pulling the sheets over my head and hiding from her gaze.

"Maturity becomes you." She mutters under her breath.

I feel the mattress shift underneath me.

"Go away, Jessa. I'm sick."

"You're not sick."

"Bitch. Yes I am." I cough and make a point to sniff from the base of my nose.

She places her hand on my foot and squeezes it.

"No. You're not."

My voice raises.

"Why won't you leave me alone?! Christ. You have to be the most inv…"

She interrupted me. "Kevin stopped by the coffee shop. He's the one who told me you probably weren't sick."

I pause and collect myself.

*Ohmigosh I'm going to kill him.*

"I don't know what you're talking about."

She sighs. "He didn't tell me much—but he did say that he fucked up pretty badly and was trying to figure out how to talk to you."

I snort.

"Did he say that he used me? Or that he lied? Or that I was a *job* for him like some horrible 90's teen movie? Or that he followed me here like a deranged stalker and tailed us when we went to San Diego so he could drop that journal in the Jeep and be a complete freak about it? Did he say any of that?"

Jessa's quiet for a few minutes. She clears her throat and moves to stand.

"He didn't say any of that—but he did tell me he was concerned about you. Said you had every reason to run, but wouldn't tell me why, and that he was worried you may try something."

I poke my arm out from underneath the covers.

"Fresh and clean for 18 months."

I know I'm being a bitch—but I can't help the poison oozing from my every pore. I wait for her to give up, to turn and walk away. I feel the mattress shift again and know she's sat down.

"Listen. Stephanie. I don't know your story." Her voice quickens. "And that's okay. I don't want you to feel pressured in any way to tell me your secrets when it's obvious you have a shit-ton of skeletons in that closet of yours. But I told you before: I can spot the ones who need friends."

I pull the duvet down to look at her with one eye. She smiles.

"And spoiler: I kind of need a friend right now too."

"Oh my god. Are you giving me a check yes or no speech?" Jessa blushes. "What are we, in kindergarten? Do you have a friendship bracelet that you made for me in case I say yes?"

"Smart ass."

I move my hand in a mock salute.

"I'm pretty fucked up, Jessa. And I don't trust people. I'll probably piss you off or overwhelm you at some point. I promise you. You don't want to be my friend."

She looks me in the eyes. "I spent three months in an out patient facility when I was 18. Overdosed on ecstasy." She stands up again and lifts the cuff of her shorts so I can see the markings on her thigh. "These are from high school. I was a straight-A student but overwhelmed with my father's expectations. I had to be the best—had to get into the best school—had to show myself as presentable to everyone."

"Wait-wait-wait." I throw the covers down and under my arms, pointing at her legs. "You cut because your dad wanted you to get straight A's?"

She grimaces. "Not really. That's not the only reason. My mom died when I was 14. It was sudden—a car accident. My dad tried really hard to take over for her, you know? And so he wanted me to be the best—to follow in his footsteps." She shrugs. "It was the only thing he knew how to do, really—point me in the direction of following his life path."

I nod.

Jessa sighs. "The pressure got too much. I know it sounds stupid and trite—but it's true. In school I was this wunderkind expected to go places and then…I just kind of snapped. I didn't want anyone to know. My dad wanted me to be a leading psychologist, my teachers wanted me to be this famous artist—so I did nothing. I hid the parties and the cutting and the drugs until one day, it all came crashing down."

I push my hands against the mattress and scoot to rest my back on the headboard.

"What happened?" I finger the rubber band on my wrist and scoop it off to twist my hair into a bun.

Jessa looks out the window.

"Ren."

I pause with hands still in my hair. "Ren?"

She laughs and falls on her back at my feet, facing the ceiling. "We were a hot mess back then." She turns her head and looks at me. "I met Ren when I was fifteen. We both went to the same fine-arts school."

"Oh."

"Yeah. We started dating at seventeen, and everyone thought we were perfect for each other—he put me back together in a way. I didn't have to worry about being good enough for my dad because I was good enough for Ren. And then he broke up with me out of the blue. Said I was toxic and couldn't handle the parties." Her face clouds over. "I didn't take it very well."

"What happened?"

"We can do some pretty shitty things to people we love." She moves her arm over her head and covers her eyes with the crook of her elbow. "I went to a party one night knowing he would be there. I made a big show of how happy I was, how I didn't need him, how I was fine without him. Got drunk and did a strip tease on the table." She peeks her eyes out from under her arm and a small smile plays on her lips.

"And then I left, slashing his tires and keying the side of his Jeep."

I chuckle. "Hell hath no fury."

She sits up. "Oh it just got worse. He sent me pictures with his new girlfriends at places that had been special to us. I texted him random escapades with strangers. He filed a restraining order against me. I got deeper into parties, becoming one of those cage-dancers for the really big parties here in town. Then he left for New York for a few months to film a mini-series and I just fell apart. I didn't know how to live without him near me."

"That's fucked up."

"That's *normal*. I had this amazing therapist for a father who lifted all of these people out of their darkness but no one was there to help me out of mine. So I kept falling." She shrugs. "When I took that Ecstasy, I knew what would happen. The dealer was notorious for potent batches. I just needed an escape from this..." she points to her forehead.

I nod. I know that feeling. I think back to the pill bottle on my nightstand back home. Jessa clears her throat and continues.

"Anyway. Ren flipped. He thought I did it as one last chance to grab his attention. Said I was twisted and manipulative. I think in a way he was right—that I was desperate for attention. But I don't think he was the sole target."

I blink. "So how did you get here? What happened next?"

She studies me. "Many hours of therapy. Lots of gym time." She looks away, her eyes unfocused and in a completely different world than where we are now.

"And eventually, cutting off all contact with Ren. I realized in the midst of all this drama that he was right—our relationship was just toxic. We *both* were—we were like moths to the flame with each other. Every time we got close we left the other burned."

She looks down and fingers the hem of her shirt. "We didn't talk for two years. It was the longest two years of my life but also the most healing. I found out who I was, you know? I didn't need my dad or some boy to tell me." She moves her shoulders and wags her eyebrows up and down. "Is this where I break into a Beyonce song? Cause I totally can."

I laugh.

"I'm being serious."

"I can tell."

"I woke up like this."

*Holy hell.*

I roll my eyes and divert her with a question.

"So how did you two get back to where you are now, though?"

"He groveled."

I slap at her leg and she giggles. "I'm only slightly joking. My dad and I came to an understanding during those years of therapy. He knows I don't have any desire to go into psychology or sociology or anything related to what he does. We're actually pretty close now. And Ren? Well. He realized how much of an ass he was and how he broke my heart for no good reason other than the perpetual boner he had for the female species. So he did this really sweet candlelit dinner on the beach where he apologized and uttered his undying love for me. It was very happily ever after."

I gag.

"Oh don't worry. We still want to strangle each other on the regular."

We go silent for a minute and then she looks at me.

"Is this where I start singing Avril Lavigne?"

I throw a pillow at her and hit her square in the face. She doesn't even miss a beat.

"So how about it, fucked up Stephanie? Will you be my friend? I promise to be just as fucked up as you." She bats her eyelashes.

"Check yes." I say. Jessa just falls on her back and throws her arms up toward the ceiling and squeals. When she's done, she sits back up and stares at me with a goofy smile. I stare back.

"Does this mean I get my friendship bracelet now?"

## CHAPTER SEVEN

Jessa hasn't convinced me to leave the hotel room yet, but she did convince me to eat. We ordered from a Chinese take-out place down the street and after she got back from picking it up, we spread it out on the bed. The scent of pork fried rice, General Tso chicken, snow peas, pot stickers and mushroom and leek wontons fill the air. My stomach growls.

"I am so hungry right now."

Jessa laughs between bites of rice. "You think? When's the last time you ate?"

I pick up a pot sticker and pause. "I really can't remember. It might have been the pizza place in San Diego."

Her jaw slackens. "I would have cut a bitch already."

I laugh as I lick my thumbs. She points at me. "You think I'm kidding. I apologize in advance for anything I may say while hangry."

She stabs her fork in the snow pea leaves and clears her throat.

"So."

I glance up at her in between bites of pork and vegetables. "So." I echo.

"While I was out getting food, I got a phone call from the guy who's investigating that kid at the building."

I put my fork down and curl my fingers around my knees.

*Damn shaking.*

She watches me for a second.

"He wants us to come in to give a statement."

My eyes widen.

"But…I thought you guys talked with them back at the hotel?"

She shakes her head.

"Remember? The building almost blew up?" She tilts her head. "Have you seen anything on the news about it? They've had some coverage off and on of the case. Apparently it's a big deal."

I shake my head. "I haven't watched TV in days."

She takes a bite of a pot sticker and picks off the piece of lettuce that fell on her shirt.

"Oh. Okay. So, we totally walked into this human trafficking plot. Crazy, huh?"

I push my food away, no longer hungry.

"Crazy." I whisper.

*Shit. Shit shit shit.*

She nods. "Right? So, they caught the kid—Oliver? And he squealed. These guys really did beat him up pretty good, but then told him they'd pay him this god-awful amount of cash if he helped them out with this plan they had. That building we found…"

"The building *you* found…" I correct her.

She laughs. "Yes. The building *I* found is actually a really popular place for prostitutes to go and uh…" she raises her eyebrows. "You know."

I swallow.

"Yeah."

"So these guys left Oliver there for a few hours hoping that someone—a druggie, a prostitute, kids looking for a hangout spot—would come and find him, get into his story, and then get brought into the fold. I still don't understand how they think it would have worked. I mean, did they think people wouldn't call the police?"

*I wouldn't.*

"Huh."

"Don't you get it? We totally could have been kidnapped." She smiles and brings the top her hands up to either side of her chin, resting it in her fingers.

"I told Ren he was our knight in shining armor."

I snort. "Because he called the cops?"

"They found their getaway car stashed in the woods, Stephanie. There was rope and tape in the trunk. Enough to tie up multiple people." A slow grin spreads across her face. "We could totally be in a movie one day."

I wipe my nose with one of the napkins and move to get off the bed. I'm anxious. Nervous energy begins to flow through my veins.

"I can't eat anymore."

"Oh I know, I'm *stuffed*." She closes the containers and wraps them in her arms, stepping off the bed and walking toward the fridge. I make my way to the bathroom and lean against the counter, staring at my reflection in the mirror.

*Just breathe, Stephanie. Just breathe.*

I can feel the thrumming of my heartbeat in the nail beds of my fingers and behind my eyes.

Jessa calls from around the corner.

"So? Should we make our way to the station?"

I drop my elbows onto the granite and rest my forehead in my hands.

"I don't understand why they need our statement if they already know what happened."

I hear her lean against the frame of the door.

"I don't know. Hey. You sure you're okay? You look pale."

"I'm fine."

I glance up slowly and catch my eyes in the mirror again—they look haunted.

I walk past her and start opening drawers, trying to find something to wear.

I turn and look at her.

"What's the weather even like outside?"

"You live in LA now. It's either hot and 80 degrees or freezing and 55. And what are you, a vampire? How do you not know what the weather is like? Jesus. How long have you been in this hotel room?" She looks around and notices the double curtains shut. Walking over to the window, she flings wide the curtain and turns to look at me with a grin.

"See? Sun." She frowns. "You're not sparkling."

"You're ridiculous."

"I tend to rely on the term *creative*."

.:.:.

Thankfully, the police station looks nothing like the one back home. Jessa called the investigator on the way here so he's waiting for us when we walk in the door.

"Jessa. Stephanie. So glad you guys stopped by. I talked with Ren earlier today." He holds out his hand and Jessa takes it. He smiles. "I don't know if you remember my name. It's Max."

He turns toward me with his hand out and I just stare at him until he awkwardly pulls it back. "Alright then. You can come back here."

He motions for us to follow him and we walk down the hall and into a small office. His desk is stacked with papers and folders and there's a mug half full with what looks like greasy coffee. I fight the nose curl and sit in a chair next to Jessa.

Max sits down in his chair and pulls his leg up and over his knee.

"So I'm sure by now you've heard the news. We know everything there is to know about what happened that night, and we believe you guys really were at the wrong place at the wrong time."

"So why are we here?"

Jessa elbows me and I look at her. "What?"

Max chuckles and pulls a file folder out from under the stack. "Well, since you want to get on with it, I guess we can start. There's a fugitive attached to the case and we've been looking for him for a few months. Goes by the name of Joey."

"I just moved here."

Jessa turns toward me and whispers out of the corner of her mouth. "Give him a break, Steph."

Max pauses from pulling out a piece of a paper and studies me. "Okay. That's fine. But do you know what he looks like? Maybe you saw him that night and you don't remember."

He hands the paper to Jessa and she looks at it and shakes her head.

"I don't know this guy."

She looks at me and shows me the picture, but I already know what he looks like. I saw it as soon as Max pulled it out of the folder and have been working to keep my face void of any reaction. I flick my eyes down to the picture and back up to Jessa.

"Nope. Don't know him."

I take a deep breath and reach for my purse. Turning my gaze back toward Max, I raise an eyebrow and push off my legs to stand.

"Is this all you needed sir?"

He leans back against his chair.

"You didn't really take a good look at the picture, Stephanie. Are you sure you don't know Joey?"

I stare at him. "Blue eyes. Black hair. Stubble on his chin. Scar on his right eye. Gap between his bottom two teeth. I saw the picture, and I don't know anyone who fits that description." He pulls the picture out of Jessa's hand and checks. Looking back at me, he squints. "How did you see that scar? I didn't even catch it."

I shrug. "My dad taught me to be observant."

*Not a complete lie.*

I scratch my nose and glance at Jessa. "I'll wait for you outside. It's hot in here."

Before she can object and Max can ask another question, I walk out of his office. Another thing my dad taught me how to do? Lie. Cover my tracks. Breathe through the interrogation. Only when I'm outside and sitting on a bench do I look down at my hands, trembling in the sunlight. I look around and shove them under my thighs and wait for Jessa, fighting the chill that radiates through my bones. I hate cops. Always have and probably always will.

But who could blame me? How would anyone begin to trust the very people who allowed justice to fall between the cracks? I'd rather take care of myself and fight for what I know is true. And right now, the only thing I know is that the man in the picture isn't Joey. It's my father. I wrap my arms around my chest and bounce my feet on the pavement below me.

*What is taking Jessa so long?*

My eyes dart to the left and right and I force myself to breathe in and out—in and out—until I can feel my pulse begin to slow. I think of his mugshot, taken days after Kevin found me in the shed and I pointed them to his hideout on a lake nearby our house. That scar on his right eye? I gave it to him. Cracked a beer bottle against our table and threw it at his head to keep him from charging at mom. If Max would have looked close enough, he would have seen a matching one that covers my entire hairline, courtesy of my father of course.

I sigh and cradle my head in my hands. These people don't know who they're dealing with—how is he out of prison? Thoughts and questions fill my head as dread fills the spaces in between my bones. I can hear the silence crackle in the distance and I fight to push it away. I don't want this—I ran away from this to find a new beginning.

Now look at me. Tweaking like a drug addict outside of the precinct and looking like a nervous cat.

I have no idea how I'm going to make it out of this alive.

Jessa walks out and sits down next to me.

"We're going to need to work on your social skills."

My feet are still tapping on the cement and I pause just long enough to look at her.

"I don't like cops."

She snorts. "You think? But could you make it a little less obvious? Right now you seem a little more *skills of a misspent youth* and less *functional human being*. Good ol' Max was suspicious. I could feel it. Hell. I was suspicious. You bolted. Guilty people bolt."

"So do innocent ones. Especially those who hate cops."

She shakes her head. "Whatever." She glances down at my feet, now bouncing out a cadence, and nudges me with her shoulder. "Hey want to come over to my place? We can paint each other's toe nails, perm each other's hair—"

I ignore the teasing lilt of her words and throw a look of disgust her way.

"Do you even know me?"

"I'll make you that friendship bracelet…"

"You wouldn't."

"I have a rainbow loom in my closet."

I stare at her for half a beat before allowing a giggle to escape. "What the fuck is a rainbow loom?"

Her eyes widen. "Only the single most important piece of equipment for kids twelve and under." She adjusts her skirt and looks back at me. "I keep it on hand in case I need to babysit."

I purse my lips and nod. "Sure."

She rolls her eyes. "So are you coming or not?"

I shrug. "It's either hang out with you or go back to the hotel and watch another episode of America's Next Top Model so…"

She grabs my arm.

"Is there a marathon today?!"

I peel her fingers away and give her a sideways glance. "….no."

"You're lying."

"I'm saving you."

"Whatever. You're saving yourself." She stands up and begins walking, side-stepping a guy meandering down the street toward the front door of the station. You can smell the bourbon coming off of him in waves. Curling her nose, she turns back over her shoulder and catches my eye. "Let's get out of here. This place is starting to creep me out."

I hop-step to catch up to her. "It's all the cops within a square mile. You're douche-meter is probably off the charts right now." I shudder. "I know mine is."

She lifts her pointer finger and keeps walking. "You have *got* to stop saying stuff like that." And then she pivots and turns in a complete circle, checking corners and all areas surrounding us. "You're gonna get yourself in trouble."

"Oh I'm already in trouble, Jess," I respond, matching her gait and rummaging through my purse for my sunglasses. "The question isn't if but when and how much."

.:..

"When you said we were going to your house I wasn't anticipating a sprawling estate."

We turn the corner into the driveway and I lean my head out the window. Palm trees line the gravel drive.

"Well, to be fair, it's a condo."

"And you own one of them?"

She pauses.

"No. No, my dad owns all of it. He gave me one when I turned 21."

I stare as she places her car in park for the valet to take over.

"Thanks, Victor."

"No problem, Jessa."

I open the door and stumble out, trying to look as unaffected as I obviously am—it's not working. Smoothing my hair, I look around me and see fancy cars, high-end shops, *the beach.*

"Wait. Wait. You said your dad was a counselor."

"I did. He is."

"So…."

She walks around the front of her car and toward the double doors leading into the lobby. When we enter the building, a bunch of people sitting in chairs and couches positioned for meetings and lounging look up and smile at her. She returns the favor.

"My grandfather bought this place in the 40s. I think it was a warehouse or something?" She points to exposed brick walls in the hallway to our left.

"Yeah?" I turn my head from the brick and take in the wall-length windows facing the line of bougainvilleas hanging from a crest in the outer wall. Everything is natural light and dark oak and absolutely beautiful. Her eyes flicker toward me and she smiles.

"You like the flowers? That was my mom's idea." Her smile fades for just a second before continuing. "My dad had a moment after her death where he wanted to take them down, but I refused. Told him the pop of color made things a little less dreary."

I nod. It doesn't surprise me that Jessa would fight for color. Today she's wearing a bright orange off-the shoulder t-shirt with an electric blue mini-skirt. Her rainbow wedges click against the wood floor as we make our way toward the elevator in front of us.

"Anyway, It was one of those deals where my grandfather bought it for super cheap before anyone ever really thought of California as this place to be extravagant. It was just coming into its own, you know? And so he bought the property, flipped it into a leasing opportunity and started renting out condos."

She grabs the latest newspaper, sitting in a basket in the middle of the lobby, and I look around.

"So how did your dad take over?"

"My grandpa died the year my mother found out she was pregnant with me. My dad took over at first to pay his way through graduate school. It's actually turned into a hobby of his; he loves it so much."

"Your dad is a landlord as a hobby?"

She rolls her eyes. "I know, right? He's fucking brilliant." She waves her hands. "All this? It's how mom and dad paid for my education. Private school isn't cheap."

Walking past the person working the front desk she waves. I follow her, my head moving left and right, stalling at the line of framed photos on either side of the elevator doors.

She pushes the button signaling that we're going up and then looks at me.

"Oh. Right. Those are the movie stars who have lived here at some point."

My eyes grow wide.

"Whoa."

"Yeah, unless you consider that *when* they lived here they were probably just trying to survive—I think the only people who lived here when they were in movies were like the ones from Old Hollywood. All the ones who have lived here in the past decade move out as soon as they get a movie deal worth a month's rent somewhere else."

The elevator dings and the doors open. Jessa steps in and then turns to face me. "Next stop Casa de Jessa!" She waves a card in front of the buttons.

"What are you doing?"

"Oh. Dad gave me the penthouse. The elevator opens up to the condo, but I have to use this card. It's like my key." She glances back up at me, still waiting outside, and she raises an eyebrow. "You coming?"

I startle into movement, shaking my head as I walk into the elevator and take my place beside her.

*This is my life now,* I think. But I don't believe it. It hasn't settled deep enough. I remember the tendrils of fear earlier today when Max pulled out my dad's picture. I grip the bridge of my nose in between my thumb and index finger and squeeze.

*Just breathe, Stephanie.*

"You okay?"

I feel Jessa's hand lightly brush my arm.

"I'm fine. Just a headache. I think I need some water, that's all." I look her in the eyes, keeping the worry at bay. But it only lasts for a second. I look away again, resting my head against the wood behind me.

Hope always has this way of lingering—toying with my emotions and tickling my senses. But I'm constantly ripped back into reality. Unease ripples its way into my skin and I breathe through the tightening of my chest. Friendship is great, until they realize how fucked up you really are—how you're just going to bring them down with you and your problems. Chinese take-out and pretending your life lacks the twists and knots of nights spent tied up in a shed only lasts long enough to remind you of what you *don't* have: freedom. Because like hope, freedom tangles. It's all just a mirage, and I'm the idiot who believed I got away. I suck in a breathe and let it out slowly, the realization inching into every pore.

*It's only a matter of time before this all comes crashing down.*

## CHAPTER EIGHT

The elevator doors swing open and I gasp.

"Holy shit. Jessa, this is amazing."

She laughs. "Thanks."

I pause before crossing the threshold, just taking in what's in front of me: windows that stretch the entire wall and face the ocean.

Seriously. I'm staring at the ocean. That's what pushes me over the edge and into her apartment. *I have to stand by those windows.*

I see a sitting area to my left and make my way toward the leather couch, falling against the coolness and noticing how the sun warms my limbs through the glass.

"That's where I people watch."

I shift my head up and see Jessa grabbing something from her fridge. She opens a cupboard and glances at me.

"Strawberry lemonade?"

I swallow, noticing how dry my throat is, and throw up a thumbs up. "That sounds amazing, actually."

I turn back toward the window.

"I would sit here and read."

I hear her walking over to the couch and she sits by my feet, handing me a glass complete with chopped strawberries. She pulls her legs under her and shakes her head.

"That's where we're different. I like to watch all the life happening—there's a lot of it there, you know?"

I nod.

Her face lightens. "Oh. Watch this."

She reaches her arm for a remote on the table next to her. Hitting a button, the top of the windows crack open and the sound of waves come crashing in around me.

"Shut the hell up."

She giggles and settles herself deeper into the cushions. "I know, right? Thanks daddy." And then she closes her eyes and falls asleep. I know I'm not far behind her. I feel my eyelids getting heavy and I rest my head against the pillow. Closing my eyes, I hear the waves and the belly laughter and the gleeful shouting of lovers and kids and friends.

*She's right.* I think to myself as my breathing gets deeper and deeper and I relax into the cushions around me. *That is the sound of life. But what about those other sounds? The ones of hidden sheds and sterile hospital rooms? What do we do about those?*

There's no one to answer my questions though, and as I drift into sleep I try to focus on the sun shining in my eyes instead of the clouds trying to take over my soul.

.::.

Within the hour, we wake up and find ourselves with massive cabin fever and munchies. Jessa makes her way into the kitchen to throw together dinner—a Mexican feast, she calls it.

I'm still stretching out my nap-muscles and watching the waves.

"Want to go take a walk?"

I breathe in and out a few times before answering, just watching the movement beneath me.

"There's a lot of people down there." I turn and walk back into the kitchen, sitting on a stool while she peels an avocado for guacamole. "I don't do well with lots of people." I grab a chip and dip it into the queso, enjoying the way the cheese melts its way into the crevices before I drop it into my mouth. She keeps peeling and chopping, this time turning to garlic and onions and tomatoes.

"Well. It *is* Santa Monica." She shrugs and shoots her eyes up to mine before darting them back down so she can pay attention to the knife slicing through onion. "Kind of a tourist attraction around here. There's even that god-forsaken song." She rolls her eyes. "But we don't have to do the pier. We can just take the route to the beach. It's getting to be sunset anyway; people will be leaving."

I turn my head around and watch the tiny people skirt around each other. Even from here I can see the umbrellas staking claim and the kids running to catch waves before turning around and skipping back to shore. I think about the feeling of waves around my ankles and smile.

"Sure. Let's do it. I'll help you put everything away and then we can go see."

She tosses me a lime. "Perfect. Cut that and then squeeze a few drops into the guacamole." She pivots and grabs the salt from above the gas stove. She places it in front of me. "Throw a few dashes of salt on top for me. I'm going to go change into my suit." She stands back and looks me up and down. "Wanna borrow one? I bet we're the same size."

I choke on a tortilla chip and move my arm up by my mouth, covering it with the crook of my elbow. Tears come to my eyes and I shake my head, and she reaches for the water. I grab it from her hands and take a sip. Taking control of the wheezing, I look at her.

"Sorry. No. I'm fine. I'll just go down in this." I flick my hands down and up, over my standard leggings and over-sized shirt.

"Okay. Let me know if you change your mind. It'll be hot out there."

I call after her as she walks into the bathroom.

"75 degrees is *not hot,* Jessa."

She answers by throwing me her middle finger and then slamming the door in my face. I take the knife and cut into the lime, squeezing the juice over the bowl. Jessa's out of the bathroom and completely changed before I can grab the salt.

"Okay. I'm ready when you are." She leans against the counter and rests her chin in her hand.

I grab the bowl with both hands and swing around to the refrigerator, put it on one of the shelves, and then turn to face her. Her bikini is bright orange—a big surprise—and her cover up reveals what her mini-skirt did not: another tattoo of a lion with a mane made of flowers on her upper thigh.

"Whoa. Nice piece." I point to her leg and then blush when she giggles. "I meant your tattoo. Not your ass. Although, you do have a nice ass. It's just…" I can feel my face shift into ten shades of red so I stop. "Never mind. I like your lion. That's not a euphemism is it?"

Jessa laughs. "No. But I'm sure we could make it one."

Groaning, I walk past her and grab my phone out of my purse. "Okay. Now that I've sufficiently embarrassed myself, I'm ready."

.::.

The late afternoon is hazy with a marine layer blowing in over the shore. We walk down the street, passing a teal building with yellow trim, the various tourist groups with matching t-shirts, and a man attempting to convince people that he's opening for Usher in his concert next week.

"Come on, man! Help a brother out. I just need gas money." He turns his eyes toward us and smiles. "Hey ladies. You want to help me make my dream come true?"

A growl escapes my lips before I can stop it and Jessa just walks on by, not allowing him any attention. However, she does stop at a guy who sits at a table with a typewriter. A poster board on the front of his table flaps in the wind - WILL WRITE POEMS FOR DONATIONS.

She pulls a twenty out of her wallet. "Hey! Will you really write a poem for me?"

He nods. "I will. Just give me the topic and it'll be done in about thirty minutes."

She doesn't hesitate. "Write me a poem about emotion."

He looks at her. "Emotion?"

"Emotion."

"Any specific one?"

"No." She shrugs. "Just emotion."

He glances at me. "Do you want one, miss?"

"Um. Sure." I look through my purse and pull out a five dollar bill. "This is all I have. Sorry."

He flashes a smile and shrugs. "No worries. What word do you want me to focus on for your poem? I can do anything. Anything at all."

I think for a moment and look around me for inspiration. Nothing comes. I bring my hand up to my forehead and shield my eyes from the sun. I think of the silence and how it burns, and the abandoned building going up in flames, and the fear that one day all this good around me will fall to ash.

"How about burning?"

The poet is already writing down words and phrases for Jessa's poem when I speak up. His eyes flicker up to my own.

"Burning?"

"Yes. Burning." I feel the heat of attention settle deep in my chest and radiate down my arms. I only have a few minutes before my arms feel like lead so I look away, avoiding eye contact. My gaze meets Jessa's and her eyebrows are raised in approval.

"Okay then. Burning and emotion. Should be easy." He claps his hands and moves his face down toward the paper, jotting down notes and ideas. For now, we've lost him. He's in a completely different world.

Jessa nods her head. "So uh…we'll see you in about thirty minutes?"

He answers with just the raising of a solitary finger, pointed to the sky. Jessa and I look at each other and shrug and then move toward the pier.

"If you look to your right there's a pathway down to the beach."

I find the side path and make my way to the steps.

I'm halted by her sudden hand on my wrist. "Stephanie! Look!"

I follow her gaze. "What? I only see an older lady with horrible fashion sense."

She snorts. "That's who I want you to see. Look closer. Don't you recognize her? It's Diane Keaton."

"That's Diane Keaton."

We're ear to ear now, standing side by side and staring at someone not four feet from us. "We look ridiculous."

Jessa laughs.

"*She* looks ridiculous. I have to text Ren. He won't believe it. He gets so angry because I'm always the one seeing people. Just yesterday I saw Severus Snape filling up at a gas station."

I laugh, still caught on Diane Keaton wearing what is hopefully a horrible disguise. "Wait-wait-wait. That's Diane Keaton. Wearing a dog collar and floppy hat? Oh my god. She's wearing *a dog collar?!* And what's with that guy she's talking to—he's like, 20-something. Fucking cougar."

We dissolve into a fit of laughter, wiping our eyes.

"Oh, Santa Monica." Jessa sighs. "You never disappoint." She looks at her phone. "Twenty minutes until our poems are done. Let's go catch the beginning of the daily diaspora of tourists not wanting to hang out after dark."

We rush down the wooden stairs, side-stepping families with two or three bedraggled children in tow. As soon as our feet hit the sand, Jessa takes off her wedges and I maneuver out of my socks and boots.

"Hey Canada. You live in California now. You can stand to purchase a pair of sandals or ten."

"I'm not from Canada. And I happen to like these boots."

"Yeah. If you want to kick ass. Your name isn't Buffy." She pauses and I shake my head.

"No, Jessa. Just no."

We reach the water within a few minutes and start walking opposite the pier.

Jessa glances my way and clears her throat.

"So what are you going to do about Kevin?"

I pause mid-step and then continue, hoping she didn't see my falter.

"What do you mean?"

She spreads her hands wide. "Well. It's been established that he's here and wanting to talk." She looks at me. "He seems pretty torn up, Steph."

"Like hell he does." My words are short. I can feel the anger building and I clench and unclench my fists. I blink and his face fills my memory.

*Dammit.*

"So what happens if he just shows up? What are you going to do?"

My pulse races and I sink my feet into the sand. "You didn't." I look around. "He's not coming here, is he? Jessa, I can't see him." I start shaking my head and my eyes grow wild.

Jessa walks a few steps ahead and then stops to turn. She reaches her hand out to calm me. "No. God, no." She rushes over to me. "He's not here. At least not by my invitation."

I find my breath again.

"He knows where you work now." She shrugs. "It's only a matter of time before you see him. Have you thought about how you're going to handle it?"

I run my tongue across the ridge of my teeth. The thing is, I have thought about it. I've thought about it every day since pushing him out of my hospital room. I thought about it when I ran out and found a bus home and when I found the cash my mom stashed and when I decided what to bring and leave behind.

Every step of the way, I expected him to intercept me. I never imagined he wouldn't fight.

I glance at the cliffs in the distance. If I saw him, right here—right now—I'd want to grab hold of what he took from me and find a way to put it back together again. I'd want to kiss him. I'd want to punch him. I'd want to run away. I look at Jessa.

"I have no idea."

She nods.

"When Ren came back to apologize I spent the majority of that evening wanting to lick every inch of his skin as well as twist his balls."

A laugh bubbles up and out of my mouth. "That's fucked up."

She sighs. "I know."

"I kind of love it."

We walk for a few more minutes. A toddler comes running up to us with a beach ball, her mother calling for her a few yards away. Jessa laughs, throwing it back to her mother. She squeals and runs after it, jumping into her mother's arms. The woman waves at us and hollers a thank you. Jessa just turns to me and pushes her hair out of her eyes.

"How long are you planning on staying at the hotel?"

I raise an eyebrow.

"Full of questions tonight, aren't we?"

She points to me. "Captive audience."

"I don't know. Until I have enough money to move somewhere else? I was able to grab some cash from my mom before I left, but I'm saving that for school."

"I thought you didn't know where your mom was?"

I wince. "I don't. This was cash she left behind." I bend down to pick up a shell and then toss it back to the waves. "I may have known where she stashed it and considered it serendipitous."

"So would you consider moving now if you found a place?"

"I'd consider it if I had money." I throw her a side-eye. "Where's this going, Jess? I thought you didn't need my story? Feels like you're fishing."

"I'm not fishing. At least not for skeletons. I just…I get lonely here and I kind of want a roommate." She chances a glance in my direction. "Everything is already paid for, Stephanie. We just need groceries."

*Is she serious?*

I think for a moment about living with someone else. I have to swallow just to keep the fear at a reasonable level. It doesn't really work. The burning flickers and catches at the base of my throat. The nightmares—the random flashbacks—not being able to sleep without the bathroom light on—the mornings I don't want to get out of bed. Too many things I would have to explain.

*There's no way this would work.*

I stop and cross my arms over my chest. "Remember when I told you that I was all kinds of fucked up?"

She nods.

"I wasn't joking. I've never lived with anyone other than my family and well—that didn't turn out well."

She stares at me and then shrugs.

"If I don't take my anti-depressants I go ape-shit."

"I have nightmares."

"…I do too."

"I may try to push you away."

She pulls a strand of her rainbow hair forward and runs her fingers through it.

"I've been labeled clingy."

"I have a very deep need for perfectly clean living spaces."

"I haven't cleaned my bathroom in three months." I blanch and she laughs. "My dad has a cleaning service come once a week. Relax."

Rubbing my hands over my face, I peek at her in between fingers.

"I can't believe I'm actually thinking about this."

She throws her hands up in the air and squeals. Before I can say another word, she does a back flip—a *back flip*—and then rushes at me with a hug. A group behind us lighting a bonfire starts whooping and hollering and applauding. I just stand there, awkwardly patting her back.

"I knew you'd say yes!"

"I actually haven't yet? And you have to stop. I think those people assume you just proposed."

I feel her laugh vibrate against my chest. She pushes away and holds on to my arms. "Oh no. No. You can't get out of this one, Stephanie. You're staying in a hotel and I just offered you free room and board and a kick-ass friendship and no. No. You're not turning it down." She starts shaking her head and I laugh.

"Is this where the clinginess comes in? Because…"

She gives me her middle finger again.

"I'm becoming well acquainted with that finger today. Shall I name it?"

"It means I love you."

"Oh really?"

She nods. "Yep." Reaching forward, she grabs my hand. "Now come on. We have poems to discover and a condo to decorate."

We walk back toward the stairs, a chorus of *congratulations!* following us. Jessa throws her hand up and waves at them.

"Thanks! She's going to be the best roommate *ever.*" She responds.

I let my hair out of its ponytail in order to cover sections of my face otherwise exposed. I look back at the group and they've moved on past our conversation and are huddled together under blankets, roasting marshmallows.

I focus again on the path in front of us and whisper.

"Okay, Jess. If we're going to live together, you need to know I hate attention. Like....*hate.* I'd just rather be invisible."

She scoffs. "Nonsense. Everyone needs to be the center of attention now and again." Smiling, she tucks strands of hair behind her ears. She moves to link arms with me and I welcome the exchange of hands for arms.

Much less personal.

"Shall we go get our poems?" She asks as we make our way through the crowds of people leaving before sunset.

"Check yes." I mutter, suddenly anxious to get back to the condo and behind a window. Having a see-through barrier between me and this mass exodus seems really appealing.

# CHAPTER NINE

Poet guy is just finishing up a piece when we arrive at his table. He looks up and smiles, handing us each a sheet of paper.

"These were fun to write. I'm glad you stopped by today. I was having a bit of a block with some of the other words."

Jessa returns the smile and takes her paper. I grab mine from his other hand and read the words. My poem is short, but packs the punch of a thousand decibels.

*My heart is a golden burning*
*reaching toward the wild unknown*
*of longing.*
*Liberty? Freedom?*
*Perhaps maybe one day—when the darkness*
*closes around me and the night*
*hides even the brightest of prayer.*
*Until then, my heart is a golden burning,*
*reaching toward the wild unknown.*

I look up from my paper, eyes blinking furiously to keep the tears from falling.

"This is beautiful."

Jessa grunts her agreement. "Listen to mine." Her voice fills the silence around us, melodic and falling into rhythm immediately. My eyes flicker to the poet and he has his eyes closed—a faint smile gracing his lips.

*What does an emotion sound like*
*when it cracks and burns?*
*The faded hope left unwanted*
*and buried in the heap of dreams*
*jangling from the wolf's mouth.*

*What does it sound like when*
*Fear grows feral and snarls quick*
*and fierce, snapping at love in the*
*jagged way of grief ripping*
*at wounds?*

*What does an emotion sound like*
*when it believes in the fairy tale—*
*swooning and gorging on the fields*
*too empty to roam?*

*Maybe it sounds like the rat-tat-tat*
*of the keys when typing or the*

*slap-clap-slap of the haka warrior*
*banging on his knees*

*Or maybe it's just a whisper,*
*quiet on the breeze.*

She clears her throat and blinks away the tears collecting within her own eyes as she glances up and offers the poet a slight shake of her head. Placing her hand on her heart, she whispers quietly.

"This is perfect. I mean it."

She sniffs and wipes at her cheeks.

"Do you have any work up at the Poetry House?"

His eyes light up and he slaps his knees.

"I do! I don't know very many people who know about that place. You go there often?"

"It's my boyfriend's favorite spot. He likes to take me there for inspiration in song writing. What's your name? I'll try and look for your stuff next time we're there."

"My name's Fitzgerald. You'll note the poems by the *Fitz* at the end."

Jessa looks at me. "The Poetry House is this place where poetry is written on the walls. Every once in a while there will be a concert there or some type of massive pot-luck picnic. It's an abandoned building. Total antithesis of what we saw the other day. Every time I go it leaves me breathless."

I nod. It's really the only thing I can do, my mind still stuck on the words of these poems and the ache billowing inside.

"Anyway." Jessa folds her paper and sticks it in her purse, giving Fitz a slight wave before turning away. "You ready to head home?"

"Yeah."

I swallow. Put one foot in front of the other. *My heart is a golden burning* on repeat like the worst kind of broken record vibrating against my bones.

We walk for a few minutes, passing buildings that look haunted with the glow of the sun behind us. I can feel the darkness snaking its way through my veins and know that it's only a matter of time before it takes over completely. I need to be alone.

"Hey—you know what? I'm beat. I think I'm going to go back to the hotel."

Jessa stops. "What? Are you sure? We can move your stuff over if you want. It's not too late."

"I'm sure. I'm fine. We can move everything over later." I smile and shift my steps to the bench at a nearby bus stop. "Promise. I just need some quiet tonight. It's been a long day."

She's not convinced but there's nothing I can do. I realize it's too late —I'm already falling. My vision blurs and I stumble on a crack in the cement.

"Shit, Steph." Jessa grabs at my wrists and misses when I jerk away.

"I'm fine! I'm fine."

My dad's voice thrums with a ferocity between my ears.

*You're not worth it. You'll always be mine. She won't ever believe you. I'll make you pay, stupid bitch.*

I suck in a breath and scratch my forehead to keep from banging my palms against my ears. What is happening? Kevin's voice joins the chorus and I fight a moan.

*I won't ever leave you. Why did you run from me? You know I love you. Let me help you find that piece of sky you lost.*

My heart races and I lick my lips. Desperation is calling. I don't even look back when I turn and walk the other way.

*I have to get away. I have to run. I have to leave.*

I leave Jessa behind, confused and looking around to see what could have possibly set me off. That's her mistake. It's never my surroundings.

It's always the inside.

That's where I'm most broken.

"What the hell? Stephanie. Come back. Don't do this. Not at night. It's not safe." I laugh under my breath.

*She doesn't know what the fuck she's talking about.*

Jessa hollers after me but I refuse to answer. I keep my eyes straight ahead, my heart bent on one thing: walking until the voices stop.

Until my eyes find focus.

Until the roar in my bones lessens to a dull whimper.

I walk down streets and get on buses and turn corners without thinking. The tears fall down my cheeks and no one even stops to ask if I'm okay because it's painfully obvious I'm losing my mind.

*I'm too messy. Too fucked up. My past will always be my future.*

And when I turn a corner and see my hotel in the distance, I only let the relief of finding my way back last for a second before falling back into the shadows.

I don't look when the man at the desk calls out good evening.

I say nothing to the couple in the elevator trying to make conversation.

And when I get to my room and there's a piece of paper taped to the paneling of my door, I simply rip it off, crumble it in my hands and pull out the card to let me inside.

It's not until I'm safe in the comfort of the hottest bath water I can muster that I grab for the crumpled paper on the floor beside me. Opening it up, I begin to read, my blood reaching fever pitch before I finish the first stanza.

*Betrayal*

*the kind that reaches in and rips
the necessary bits to shreds —
this is what you did to me.*

*Revenge
the kind that fills your blood
with determination and hatred —
this is what I'm after.*

*Lollipop, I will not stop until your
breath reaches mine and
falters with regret and doubt.*

*I will not be satisfied
until that faltered breath
dies out*

I can't even keep the paper straight my hands are shaking so bad. I notice the small indentations of certain letters and know without a doubt this poem was written with the same typewriter as the one used by Fitz earlier today. Whoever paid for this poem was there watching us.

I imagine my father, watching us from a distance, that smirk of celebration on his face. He knew he had us—*had me*—and chose to show it with a fucking poem. I squeeze my eyes shut and then open them again, my gaze falling on the nickname of my childhood.

*Lollipop.*

I moan as memories of my father whispering that name in my ear resurface.

"It's because you taste so sweet, Lollipop."

I breathe in and out and in and out and it's not working and I pitch forward for one of the candles and without even thinking set the paper on fire and watch it burn until the flames singe toward my fingers. When the ashes have floated down into the water I sit there and push my hands into my eyes as deep as they will go. I see red and it's perfect because I *feel* red. I feel red and hot and the fear overtakes me. I let myself sink into the water and the tears mix with the ashes around me. My hair floats above and behind me and everything makes sense in this moment where I'm both suspended and numb. The water closes in on me and I breathe in one last time through my nose and sink even deeper.

How easy would it be to just end it here? To take one last breath and then never another, allowing the water to have its way? Would I even be missed?

I close my eyes and wait until my lungs burn for air. I smile.

Sometimes the golden burning is what feels good. And this? It feels sublime.

I feel the strength leave me. I'm floating. I open my eyes under water and the redness around my vision turns yellow and blue and brown—the oxygen dying out slowly. My lids flicker shut and I know the choice is mine.

I think of escaping—*really* escaping. I think of living a life without my father. I think of ridding myself of him for good.

Is it even possible this side of existence?

I startle awake.

In that last moment—the breath between here and there—I gasp and suck in the air above me. I let my head fall into my hands and I rub the tension still pulsing in my temples.

Sometimes the burning is what feels good, but giving up? That wouldn't be escaping. I know that now. Giving up would just give my father the glint in his eyes to move forward and find another victim. Giving up would let him get the best of me. I punch the water and let out a silent scream.

*Fuck no.*

I lean forward and blow out the candles and flip open the drain, watching as the ashes swirl and disappear with the water. The anger and fear and brokenness merge together and morph into a dangerous resolution brimming underneath my veins. I step out of the tub and shake off some of the water. Grabbing a towel, I pat myself dry and run the towel through my hair still dripping with crystal beads.

I make my way to the mirror, staring at my reflection.

I look different.

I raise my chin and push back my shoulders, the hatred taking root. I think of my father, laughing and reveling in the way his evil heart pounces for the kill. It's not going to happen anymore. I look myself in the eyes and see a life lived in turmoil and fear and desperation.

Not anymore. Tonight? I'm taking back my life for good. The rage lights my face and gives me purpose. I can hear whispers of Emma and Jude, talking about forgiveness and the way anger turns into a bitterness that echoes those who wound us, and I smirk. Fuck forgiveness. Eighteen years of fearing for my life. Eighteen years of learning how to bend to the will of others.

Forgiveness has no place here.

Let him follow me. I'll set traps and watch him fall.

There is no way in hell I'm going to let him win.

## CHAPTER TEN

I get to work the next morning when the sky is still the color of freshly poured tar. After last night, I'm barely functioning.

I had so much pent up energy after finding dad's poem that I went running.

Running. At like, midnight.

I never run.

Walking through the door, I see Jessa pouring herself a large glass of iced toddy. I yawn and stretch my arms over my head. I know I will have to explain myself about yesterday—but I don't want to, so I choose ignoring the situation.

"Want to pour me one of those? Or five?"

She looks up at me and raises an eyebrow.

"Did you get my text last night?"

I sigh.

"Which one?"

*You sent about a million of them.*

"Any one of them." She sets her glass on the counter. "What the hell, Steph? I was worried about you. I mean…" her eyes dart back and forth and she throws her hand up in the air. "How was I supposed to know you weren't dead in a ditch somewhere?" She picks up the towel near her and begins wiping down everything in sight behind the bar. "It's the second time you've just up and left with no reason. You can't just leave like that…"

"I'm not dead. I'm here."

She throws the towel at me and I dodge in just enough time for it to hit the door behind me. I pick it up and walk over to a stool across from her.

"I told you I do weird shit. That's the weird shit I'm talking about—I get nervous, I run away. I'm always okay. Promise." I shrug. "I just don't like people sometimes."

"Whatever, Stephanie. That's more than just not liking people. You've told me, remember? We know you're fucked up. We know you come from some troubled past. But guess what? We all do. I've told you about me and yet you've said nothing outside of your dad being in prison. If that's it, and there's nothing tying you down to what happened before, it's time to move on. Start over."

The anger from last night ignites within me.

I tilt my head sideways. "You don't know shit about me."

"Seriously?" She shakes her head. "You know what? You're right. I don't." She points at me and I see her freshly painted nails glittering in the overhead above us. "But that's not because I don't care, it's because you won't tell me a damn thing. How do you expect me to act?"

I sit there staring at her.

"What do you want me to say, Jessa? I don't get it. I didn't think friendship meant you needed to share your deepest, darkest secrets. I thought that was reserved for elementary sleepovers where you tell ghost stories over the fireplace."

*Even though I never had one of those, I know a few girls who did.*

"I don't know how many friends you had back home…"

*None.*

I don't say anything.

"You have to understand, Stephanie. This is a two way street." She motions from her chest to mine. She starts counting off her fingers.

"What I know about you: you hate when people touch you. Something weird happened with the poem yesterday. I think you may want to be my roommate. You love the ocean. You fucking *hate* the cops. You wear black but you want more color in your life—I see you staring at my outfits all the time." She pauses and rests her hand against the counter. "And this is all from observation."

I shrug.

"And?"

I still don't know what she's looking for—and I'm starting to feel antsy. My feet bounce on the metal rings underneath me and I pick at my chipped fingernail.

*This is why I don't do friendship. Like ever. How do you even act?*

She falls back on the heels of her feet and crosses her arms. She stays like that for a few minutes—looking everywhere but in my eyes. Which, for Jessa, is really weird. Normally I'm the one who is fighting eye contact. Finally, she takes a step back toward the counter and rests on her elbows. She looks right at me.

"I had a friend once in middle school."

"Really? Just one?"

A shot of anger flashes in her eyes and I pinch my lips together.

*See? I have no clue how to act right now.*

"Her and I connected immediately. At least, I thought we did. Anyways, we did everything together. She'd spend the night at my house. We'd go to the mall or the beach on the weekends. I would go over to her house to do homework and talk about boys and dream about getting into the Fine Arts academy. Her dad was always there. Always watching us. I never thought anything of it, just chalked it up to over-protection, you know?"

I nod.

"Slowly, she started changing. She cut off all her hair—" she runs her hand around her head, "like shaved it all off. Started talking to me about these voices she was hearing. When I freaked about that and told her we needed to find someone to help her, she stopped answering my calls. Refused to eat with me at lunch. It was the weirdest thing. One minute we're inseparable and the next, it's like she's avoiding me." She looks down and plays with the beads of cloth hanging off the towel.

"We both got into the fine-arts academy. I never saw her because she was in fashion design and I was in music but I missed her—a lot." She wipes her cheeks and I close my eyes before opening them again, forcing myself to focus on *her* but not focus on the wetness building in her eyelashes.

*God I hate crying.*

Jessa shakes her head swiftly and closes her eyes tight, standing straight for half a second so she can breathe in deep. "Shit. This was so long ago; I don't know why I keep crying over it."

I pinch my tongue in between my teeth to keep from saying anything.

"I had my dad drive me to her house one day. We were pulling up and I got out to walk to the front door. I remember walking up the sidewalk and seeing her dad's truck in the front lawn and wondering how the hell he decided it was a good idea to park *there.*"

She looks at me. "My dad still talks about watching me walk up those steps and seeing the curtain flutter before the door opened and Genevieve came running out."

She stops for a moment and the air around us hangs damp with the weight of knowing.

I swallow and feel the pulse in my neck growing heavier and heavier. I think I know where the story is going—and I'm trying really, really hard to maintain a level posture. My fingers grip the sides of the stool where the metal railings meet the cushion.

"She looked so different. Like she wasn't herself anymore. Her eyes, Stephanie. Her eyes were *dead*. It was like I was looking at a zombie."

Jessa hides her head in her hands and speaks into her fingers.

I feel my nails digging into the palms of my hands.

"She told me to run. Had this crazed expression on her face and kept talking about her dad—how he had been drinking and was yelling and freaking out inside and she needed to get back, needed me to leave."

She sniffs and straightens up, throwing the towel behind her in our canister for laundry. She twists her lips and then looks me in the eyes.

"That was the last time I saw her. The next week, there was an announcement at school that her body had been found in the ravine. Within a month, her dad was arrested." She shakes her hands in front of her. "Stephanie, I've done a lot of stupid shit in my life. A lot. I know what it's like to want to just end it all. But that? That was different. That was *evil*. It has a smell, did you know that?"

*One—two breathe, Stephanie. One—two breathe.*

She levels me with her gaze. "I've never forgotten the scent of hopelessness and despair that took over Genevieve when her father gained control. I smell it on you. You hide it well. You know how to laugh and joke and carry on like nothing's wrong and every once in a while the spark takes over your eyes and it's like you're alive." She hiccups and wipes her eyes again.

"But most of all there's this emptiness and it's like having Genevieve with me all over again. And I don't know what kind of evil you've seen—what hell you've brushed up against. But I smell it. And I want to help. Please let me help."

I'm quiet for half a beat and then I clear my throat. I don't even look at her, I just stare at my hands shoved in my lap. I can feel the muscles in my neck stretch as I let the weight of everything fall on my shoulders.

"I can't really talk about it."

"Why?"

Silence.

"I don't know how."

She sniffs. "I don't know what to say—open your mouth. Say something. Anything. What's going on? What happened yesterday? Why is your dad in prison?"

"I wouldn't know where to begin."

"How about at the beginning?"

I laugh. "The beginning? Would that be where I lost the ability to trust anyone? Or would that be when my father discovered poker? Or would that be when my mom took to Nyquil because dad took all the money to the local bar?"

She watches me and I feel the burning take over—starting in my gut and spreading out into my limbs. It's too much. It makes me jumpy. I hop off the stool and start pacing, clawing at my jacket and trying to wrap it tighter around me.

"You want to fucking know me? Then you should probably know this: I've had one person I've met within the last two years that I thought could possibly be a friend because she seemed to know what I'd been through—knew my thoughts before I even said them. Turns out? She knew my thoughts because my dad fed her my fucking journal so she could get on my good side." I glance at her and her eyes are wide.

"Stephanie…"

"Yeah. How's *that* for fucked up?"

I'm on a roll now, and out of the corner of my eye I see the darkness of night edging away to the blues and pinks of dawn.

And well, that just pisses me off even more.

"What about my brother? Should I mention how I watched his skin build scars the size of polka dots because my mom didn't know how to take her anger out on anyone except for him? Or how a few months ago he was taken from me in our house and I had no idea where he was or if he was safe?"

The rage is building and I can feel my face turn the deepest shade of red—the color that filled my vision last night as I waited for life to finally leave me.

"Or how about the fact that I can't even see a fucking sunrise anymore without thinking about the one person who was supposed to love me—the one person I trusted—the one person who reminded me of hope and new beginnings and getting out from under my dad's thumb alive? Huh? That's an amazing story. Because he was fucking using me as a *job*." I wipe my arm across my nose and let the sobs rack my body into oblivion. I stop trying to pace because it's no use. I'm doubled over now, my arms wrapped around me, my hands gripping my elbows.

That's when I hear the door open behind me.

"Stephanie."

My hands fall to my knees and I blink to keep from collapsing. I would know that voice anywhere. I stare at the linoleum square right underneath my foot and try to make sense of what's happening. Nothing is coming to me.

*He's here. Ohmigod he's here. This can't be real.*

My breathing turns erratic and I close my eyes, shaking my head. I straighten up and turn to face Jessa, my eyes still closed.

*If I keep my eyes closed it won't have to be real.*

My hands come up to meet either side of my face and I'm crying and begging someone to do something because I have to be crazy—he really can't be here—I really can't see him right now and my heart is breaking because *why did he have to follow me* and *why does it hurt so much to hear his voice* and *why do I want to fall into his arms and let him take away the pain.*

I breathe in deep and wipe my eyes and look at Jessa. She nods.

I don't know how I find strength to turn around, but I do. My legs feel like cement. My hips feel like magnets for the linoleum beneath me. My head wobbles like a helium balloon.

*I don't want to do this I don't want to do this I know I have to do this.*

I breathe in, and turn.

I breathe out, and stare.

My voice cracks.

"Kevin."

## CHAPTER ELEVEN

Jessa clears her throat behind me. "Um. I'm going to go get something…"

"Don't you leave me." I turn for half a second, my heart about to break through my chest, and I plead with her. "Please. Don't leave."

Her eyes widen and she freezes, arms akimbo. As I turn back toward Kevin I see her reach for her phone in her pocket.

*Probably texting Ren.* I think as I stare at the ground, Kevin's shoes, the sky turning orange and pink through the window.

This moment—right here—is one I've waited for and feared for months. I want all of the things at once: I want him to wrap me in his arms and remind me that I am okay. I want to taste his lips, his throat, his everything. I want to punch him. I want to scream. I want to cry. I want to laugh.

"Stephanie." His voice cuts through the silence and I fight the urge to fall into his arms. It's an all together different sensation to both desire something and dread it at the same time. I hate it. I clench the fabric of my jeans.

"Are you going to look at me any time soon?" I open my eyes and see his feet take a step toward me. I stumble away. My dad's voice roars in my ears again.

*Stupid bitch. Of course he didn't love you. Don't let him get closer.*

"Kevin…"

"Listen. I know I screwed up. I know I should have told you…"

I put my hands over my ears. "Please….stop."

All of the voices grow so loud I don't know who I'm talking to anymore.

"I didn't know I'd fall in love with you when I agreed to help Jude…"

"Stop." I repeat, a little louder than the first time.

He ignores me, reaching for my arm. I breathe in quick and snatch it away from his grasp. A wail escapes me and I put my hands out in front of me as a barrier.

"Don't. Touch. Me."

He flinches.

I think of the poem left on my door the night before and the journal last week. Something crystallizes. A ball of cement centers itself in my gut.

*He led him to me.*

"How long have you been following me, Kevin?"

"What do you mean? I've been looking for you for…"

"Answer me." My voice is poison. I can hear it. I can *feel* it. My skin sets fire to the anger and I'm undone—I look at Kevin.

"Since you got here." His voice has dropped to a whisper. He's the one looking down at the floor now as I let the truth sink in: I've never been free. Not once.

I feel the vein pulsing in my neck.

"You fucking *asshole*. I told you to leave me alone. I told you! I told you. I sat in the hospital bed and pushed you away and you're still here — you followed me. You *freak*." I walk toward him and for a moment, see a glimmer of hope in his eyes.

My voice grows so quiet only he can hear me.

"My dad is here—did you know that?"

He grimaces and I know. I know he's still on the job. I laugh and shake my head.

"What were you going to do Kevin?" I spread out my arms. "Were you going to come in and rescue me? Am I the fucking damsel in distress?" I put my hands on my head. "Oh god, where's my knight in shining armor now?!" He shakes his head and looks away from me but I walk around him to make sure we're eye-to-eye.

"Were you going to be the one to save me from the evil Sam Tiller?"

He places his hands in his pockets and shoots a glance toward Jessa.

"I don't give a fuck who knows anymore, Kevin. You've ruined me. I don't trust anyone."

I can feel myself losing control and I throw my head back and laugh again. It feels good to not care—to lose yourself to the flames threatening to burn away everything around you.

He frowns. "Stephanie, just…can you listen for a second?"

I drop my head and look him in the eye. "Are you fucking serious? You want me to listen to you? You want me to hear your story?" I shake my head. "No. No you don't get that. You don't get to tell me your side." I press my finger into his chest. As soon as it hits I know I've made a mistake.

Contact.

Bit-by-bit, the armor around me cracks. I stare at my finger and scowl.

*Traitor.*

My head drops and the sobs come deep and fast. He wraps his arms around me and pulls me close. I don't even try to fight it because I can't—I just melt into him, inch by fucking inch.

"Shhh. Stephanie. It's okay. It's okay. I'm here." His breath falls hot on my ear and I wince.

Clarity.

I choke on a sob and push myself away. I point at him again, this time staying far enough away where touching is impossible. Out of the corner of my eye, I see Ren walk in from the back. Jessa leans sideways and whispers in his ear.

"I need you to leave."

Kevin blinks.

"Go, Kevin."

"Stephanie..."

"I said go!" I'm yelling so loud now my entire head feels as if it may explode. "You are not *here* for me, Kevin. You're here for a job. You're here for some type of hero-status. Just leave. Leave. FUCKING LEAVE."

I don't even know when I start to hit him but I'm throwing punches and kicking and and scratching and he's trying to get control of me but it's not working because he won't ever have me—never again. The anger builds and builds and builds and I throw one final punch to his shoulder before wiping my cheeks with the back of my hand. Only then do I realize I'm crying.

Ren steps in between us and faces me.

"Steph. Why don't you come with me. Take a breather." He turns around and looks at Kevin, still rubbing his shoulder from where I hit him. "I think it would be best if you listen to her, brother."

Kevin laughs. "Who are you?"

I reach for him again, so tired of his arrogance and assumptions, but Ren grabs my hands and twists me around and maneuvers me toward Jessa.

"Ren, let me. I'll take her. I know where to go."

She's waiting with my purse and her keys.

I blink.

"Where are we going? What about the shop? Who's going to run it?"

She shrugs and grabs my hand when Ren passes me off to her and turns to square off with Kevin who's shouting in the background about strangers and trust and knowing who I'm leaving with—I place my hands over my ears for the second time and groan.

"Make him stop, Jessa."

"Come on." She looks at me and offers a small smile. "I know just the place."

∴

We get into her car and she pauses before putting her keys in the ignition. Glancing at me with a side-eye, she turns on the car and backs out of the parking space and toward the road.

"That was intense. Are you okay?"

I wipe my cheeks and shake my head. "I'm sorry—I-I don't know what got into me there."

She puts her hand briefly on my arm and then pulls it away. "Stop. Don't even think about apologizing. Just put on your seatbelt for me?"

I nod and click the latch into place and rest my head on the window, gripping my hands together to keep the tremors from being too noticeable. My father's voice is loud and clear in my head and I close my eyes to get away from him. It doesn't work. I can hear his laughter and the way his words stumble into each other after drinking. I can see his snarl and the way his hand reaches up to push me against a nearby wall.

*No one's ever going to love you, you little bitch.*

I flinch and jump and open my eyes.

We're at a stoplight and Jessa's staring at me with a concerned look on her face.

"Are you sure you're going to be okay?"

"I'm fine."

She knows I'm lying, but simply nods and looks back to the street.

"Okay." She whispers.

I'm still shaking when we make a turn on a side street. We haven't said a word the entire drive and I have every belief Jessa now knows how certifiable I really am—it's only a matter of time before she stops talking to me completely.

*She probably said not to apologize because it's too late.*

I look out the front window. I haven't even been paying attention to the route we were taking. We're oceanside, the sun casting reflections on tide pools up and down the sand.

"We're back at the beach?"

Jessa turns and glances at me before putting the car in park.

"Kind of." She motions for me to follow her. We get out and find our way to a path in the brush and I take in our surroundings: seagulls crying in the distance, surfers catching the morning waves, our feet making indentations in the sand. She points in front of us.

"Do you see that?"

I squint against the rising sun and notice a shady outline of what looks to be a house.

"This is the poetry house I was telling you about—I come here on days I just need to decompress."

"It's...colorful." It's the only thing I can think to say because the only thing I see is color.

*No wonder Jessa loves it here.*

Each window's trim is outlined with a different shade: indigo, pink, teal, orange, yellow, red. The porch is stained purple. The chimney sticking up from the roof is magenta.

Jessa laughs under her breath and opens the gate. I notice a sign barely hanging on to the fence that's been transferred from *Absolutely No*

*Trespassing—Violators Will Be Prosecuted"* to *"Absolutely Trespass— Violators Will be Hated.*

"It's...quaint."

Apparently all of my words have blown away with the sea breeze and I'm left with descriptors.

We walk up the stairs leading into the front of the house and immediately I'm struck by the amount of words written on almost every square inch of plywood. My feet are not my own anymore. I rush over to one of the walls and trace my fingers along the wood and peeling wallpaper.

"Whoa." I whisper.

Jessa laughs. "I thought you might like it."

My eyes scan the living room. "The entire house is like this?"

She nods. "The entire house. Rumor has it that Jack Kerouac was the one who found the place and him and his friends would have these beat parties here—writing on the walls and then reading them out loud for anyone who would show." She points to the wall. "That poem with the circle around it and JK underneath? Everyone thinks it's his."

I walk over to the poem.

*The mad ones beat to a rhythm of their own
while the sane ones beat on like drones.*

I laugh. "Jessa. This poem could literally be written by anyone. It's only two lines." I turn and look at it again, noticing the obvious age of the lettering. You could barely see the words anymore. It'd been there a while.

She shrugs. "Well it's been there as long as I've known about this place, so it's kinda cool to think about it that way."

"You're such a romantic."

She throws up her middle finger at me.

I smile sweetly. "I love you too, Jessa."

She turns away and finds a spot on the wall to begin spilling words and I pace the floor for a while before walking down the hallway. I find handwriting that looks vaguely familiar. I lean in close and begin whispering the poetry engraved into the grooves with sharpie.

*I believe in the symmetry of time*
*and how it rolls back onto another*
*like waves crashing against waves*
*the bedrock smooth after nights spent*
*with storms beating the sharp pieces down—*
*the distant beam of light ricocheting off blue*
*and pointing ships back home*

*I believe in the gold of a new day spreading*
*out-out-out*
*caressing the blue-dark and*
*weaving her fingers through iridescent clouds*

*Seconds build*
*to the next*

*minute*
*-expectant-*
*ripe with the hope of maybe then*
*turning into now.*

I look for an author but am distracted by the poem sitting crooked next to it. The first line jumps out at me: S*ometimes, my words lose themselves in the pieces of you.* I whisper them out loud and hear Jessa call out from the other side of the room the line that follows.

"…in those eyes that light up a room…"

I turn around, see her writing on the wall, and then glance back at the poem. *How'd she know what the next line was?* I shift my eyes down, the poem forgotten, and see her name scratched beneath the words.

*That's why the handwriting looks familiar. I've seen it on the chalkboard in the shop.*

"You wrote this." I turn and look at her again, pointing to the faded sharpie behind me.

She catches my eye and then focuses again on the words flowing from beneath her pen.

"Yeah. It was in response to that other one you read out loud—the one about the hope of then turning into now." She shrugs. "I wrote the first one right after Ren broke up with me. I was convinced we'd get back together."

I raise an eyebrow.

"You were right."

She caps her sharpie and then walks over to where I stand.

"Yeah but, like, three years off." She points to the poem. "Finish reading this one. I wrote it after a particularly painful episode of missing him and screwing things over."

I stare at her for a few more seconds before turning back to the poem, reading her words quietly under my breath.

*Sometimes, my words lose themselves in the pieces of you*
*in those eyes that light up a room*
*my sentences fall flat—the rise and fall of semantics forgotten*
*in the way your finger brushes against her cheek*

*I remember when I was the center of your world*
*when my phrases were the ones you repeated back to me*
*and my hand was the one you reached for on nights*
*when no words were necessary.*

*Now I see worlds disappearing within one glance*
*the stories we shared falling away like dust*
*as a new chapter unfolds with a better character*
*waiting for your return.*

I look at her questioningly, trying to remember the story she told me a few days ago in my hotel room.

"Is this when he sent you pictures of him with other girls?"

Jessa smiles. "No. This was after—when I received one of those pictures and went a little nuts." She presses her hands on the wall behind her and lowers herself to the ground before catching my gaze. "I went to New York after he left to shoot that series. Followed him around and did some creepy shit because I just couldn't wrap my brain around him and me not being together anymore."

I widen my eyes in mock horror. "You? Invasive and creepy?"

She swats at my shoe and I side step her, smiling for the first time all morning.

"Old habits die hard, I guess." She wraps a few strands of pink hair around her finger and looks out a nearby window toward the waves. She bites her lip and looks at me.

"I followed him to a club one night where he was celebrating a pretty good day on set with everyone." She laughs and shakes her head. "I was pathetic, Stephanie. Sitting behind this big-ass man and trying to act interested in what he was saying when really I just needed him to block me from Ren's view. But then I saw him with her and I flipped."

"You flipped?"

Her eyes grow wide. "Yeah. Threw my drink against the wall behind them and climbed on top of the table to kick everything off." She places her head in her hands. "I still get embarrassed thinking about it."

"Shit." I whisper.

Her shoulders shake and she peeks out from her fingers. "Yeah. Shit." She points at herself. "See? Fucked up. Right here." Shrugging, she tosses her hair behind her.

"Needless to say, that's when Ren filed the restraining order. On my way home I nursed my wounds at this small bed and breakfast off the coast. I walked the beach every morning for like a week—it didn't solve everything, but it sure helped me stay sane right after the bottom fell out from under me." She toys with the hem of her shorts. "I wished even then that I would walk down that beach and see him running after me."

I clear my throat. "Why are you telling me this? Why did you bring me here?"

"I think I understand Kevin. Understand why he would do something creepy like follow you here after you guys obviously broke up."

I laugh and she puts her hand up to stop me from interrupting.

"At the bed and breakfast, they had these massive trees that looked like a solitary branch until you got to the top and everything was gnarled together. Walking the coast you could see where the wind whipped them into where they grew—the branches, the leaves, the shape—everything bent into one direction." She gets up and walks to the window and places her hand on the frame. She's not even looking at me. I squat and find a place to sit.

"One morning I went out to catch the sunrise before my flight left and the owner of the bed and breakfast followed me. Told me she'd seen me walk the same path every morning and could tell I was nursing a heartbreak," Jessa laughs. "She told me that in her experience, extreme heartbreak often came out of one or two things: a great love or a great addiction." She looks at me and then back out the window. "Anyway. I told her a bit about Ren and how I screwed everything over and then we just walked the shore for a little while, with neither of us saying anything. And then, out of nowhere, she pointed to those trees standing guard in between the ocean and her place. Told me they were called storm-wood. That they bend with the wind so that they don't break." She wipes her cheeks with her fingers and looks down.

"That's when I realized that even though Ren and I had a great love, I was treating him like an addiction. I had to lean in to this pain—had to let it cut off all these dead pieces inside so I could grow and be better for it. I let him go, then. I never texted, never called. I just waited."

She turns and walks over, kneeling in front of me and grabbing my hand.

"I don't know what happened with you, Stephanie. But you gotta learn how to be storm-wood. You gotta learn how to bend so you won't break. It's the only way you'll really survive. Kevin screwed up. From what it sounds like, he had a great addiction that morphed into a greater love. He just didn't know what to do with it. Let him fix it. I think he can if you let him."

She squeezes my hand and moves to sit next to me. We sit there in silence for a few minutes.

My heart beats a rhythm I'm not familiar with—one begging me to say something, to speak, to offer some type of response.

I clear my throat.

"I don't really know how to trust people."

Jessa nods and cracks a smile.

"So you've said."

I pick at my nails and refuse eye contact.

*She won't ever believe you.*

I hear his voice loud and clear.

*Stop.* I beg him—silently, I'm not to the point where I'm verbalizing my conversations with the voice of my father in my head—but I still feel crazy giving him attention.

*You'll always be mine. You'll always scare people away. I own you, Stephanie.*

I'm barely breathing. I close my eyes and imagine myself pushing the voice over the edge into oblivion. When the chatter stops, I look at her.

"I think it's time you know my story," I whisper.

## CHAPTER TWELVE

I begin slowly, still fearful of the voices coming back with a vengeance. I stare at the floor the entire time, too chicken to catch Jessa's eyes. I'm almost positive what I would find—rejection, horror, repulsion—would send me over the edge.

"You have to understand. I don't tell anyone what really happened to me because no one would believe me."

Her voice cuts in, barely a whisper. "I'll believe you."

I sigh. "You say that now. You don't really know me. You only know that I claim to be fucked up and come from a rough background."

Her silence serves as an invitation to keep going. I watch her hands—still toying with the strands falling from the hem of her shorts.

"My father sold me, Jessa. I was his pawn in this wicked game he played with the authorities back home. Everyone was in on it. Including Kevin."

I hear her breath catch.

"Kevin?" she whispers, her voice pained.

I nod. "Kevin. He knew the entire time—even before I told him. I had this teacher who befriended me and kind of took me in—we were super close. Her husband had this mysterious job and I never knew what he did until just recently. He studies trafficking patterns. Watches perpetrators and those he suspects are in the business of sex slavery."

*Breathe in, breathe out.*

"He'd been watching my father for at least a year. Pulled Kevin in on the case after hearing about him from some friends within the local unit. Kevin watched me for months before introducing himself at a coffee shop."

"Why Kevin?"

A sob catches in my throat and I shake my head.

"Because he was accused of raping a friend at a party. He was the only one who came forward to give information and then the authorities turned on him. Sticking your neck out for other people is kind of their modus operandi."

I wipe my nose with the back of my arm. The only thing you can hear in the room is our breathing.

In and out. In and out. Almost in unison.

"How long did he do this, Stephanie?"

"Since I was twelve."

She's quiet again for a few beats.

"How can someone possibly get away with selling their own daughter?" Her voice is tinted with disgust.

"He involved the authorities. His biggest customer was the sheriff."

She gasps.

"No wonder you don't like cops."

"…yeah."

"Fuck." It's barely audible, her response.

I nod.

*Fuck.*

She reaches for my hand and wraps it in both of hers.

"Stephanie. How the *fuck* are you still breathing?"

I laugh. "Trust me. I've tried. You'd be amazed at the system and their blind eye toward familial dysfunction." I glance at her for the first time and notice tears streaming down her cheeks. "Last year I was hospitalized after a particularly brutal evening with a few men." She winces and I continue, gaining strength as I share.

"For a while, we were able to keep my father out of the loop until they realized I was underage. Because of local legislation, if authorities found out that I was technically a prostitute, even though I was forced, I would be sent to juvie. We were stuck. Of course, this was before I knew everyone was involved—Kevin, Jude, Emma. All of them knew." I pick at a piece of fuzz stuck on my shoe.

"We decided to keep the story under wraps and stick to the reality of it being a gang rape. They called up daddy dearest and he had the entire floor charmed."

One of her hands squeezes mine.

"Shit, Stephanie. I mean. We're all damaged, right? We can't get through life without the metaphorical bumps and bruises to our psyche. But you? You're sitting here, telling me this as if you're reading from a newspaper. I don't understand."

I shrug.

"Denial? It's amazing what we can forget about if we force ourselves to just not think about it. I just don't think about it. Some days are better than others. The bad ones are the ones where I hear my dad's voice louder than the rest." I push a strand of hair behind my ears. "We all want to be normal, you know? It just takes some of us a deeper sense of pretense."

She lets go of my hand. "Wait. You told Kevin your dad was here."

I stare at my hand, now hanging limp off my leg, and don't respond.

"Stephanie."

I bring my gaze slowly to hers.

"He's here."

She exhales. "Double fuck."

I twist my fingers and let out a derisive laugh. "I thought I was done with him. I thought I would never have to see him again—it's bad enough his voice won't leave my mind. He has to follow me too?"

"How the hell did he find you?"

I grow silent for a moment. "I don't know. I have no idea. I thought…" I breathe in and roll my shoulders, stretching my neck. "I thought I was done."

Jessa stands and starts pacing. "So. Your dad is here. Following you."

"He left a poem from Fitz taped to my door."

She pauses and looks at me, wide eyed.

"He…what? He left a poem? From the same guy we got poems from? Stephanie. That's like….really close to where I live."

"…I know."

She starts pacing again—this time with quicker steps and big gulps of air. "I need you to know I'm trying really hard not to freak out right now."

"You hate me. I get it. I should have told you."

She turns to me. "No. No I did not say that. I mean, yes. I wish you would have told me your father is some psycho fuck who is stalking you and coincidentally, stalking me but…you know." She shrugs. "Details."

I crack a smile.

"I don't hate you though, Stephanie. I'm just….I'm trying to wrap my brain around this." She leans her back against the wall across from me. "Is there anything else I should know?"

I swallow and bite the corner of my thumb and just stare at her, my heart still beating an erratic rhythm.

Jessa crosses her arms. "Stephanie. I know that look. What."

I drop my hand. "My dad's name is Sam Tiller."

She nods. "I caught that in the coffee shop."

I look at her. "He's going by the name of Joey."

For the past few minutes, she's had her foot propped up behind her. It drops with a thud and dust flies up into the air.

"Joey." Her hands fly up to her mouth. "Ohmigod. The guy. That picture! You *did* know him. Is that why you freaked?! Why you ran off?"

I hesitate.

"My dad was at the abandoned house, Jessa. I don't know how he did it. I don't know how the hell he knew we'd go down that road on the way home. Maybe he didn't. Maybe it was some crazy-ass scheme of his to continue to make money while looking for his deranged daughter and we just happened to stumble into it like a nightmare. But that was him. I knew it the second Oliver started telling us his story."

Jessa walks over and sits in front of me, grabbing my hand. I try not to notice how much her fingers are trembling.

"My dad used to always say things like *if you run away, bitch—I'm always gonna find you.* Oliver said the same thing. He said his kidnapper told him if he ran away that would be the least of his problems."

"Shit."

"Yeah. And that's not —that whole story? I knew it. I knew when the SWAT team ran up the stairs that Oliver wouldn't be there. I knew the whole thing would go up in flames. I knew it all because my dad used to talk about this amazing fool-proof plan he had in relying on the kindness of strangers."

She tilts her head. "The kindness of strangers?"

"If Ren wouldn't have been there, and you and I would have waited just five more minutes in calling the cops, they would have ambushed the place and we would be in some shed right now—waiting for our next customer."

Her breath grows shallow and I continue.

"And, who knows—if Ren would have waited, they still may have ambushed and just killed him or maimed him or something severe enough to ensure he never messed with them again. They did that once to a guy working with Jude." I grimace. "I saw the pictures. It wasn't pretty."

She rubs her face with her hands.

"Stephanie. What the fuck are we gonna do?"

I laugh. "We? Last time I checked *I* was the one who was in this situation…"

Her head jerks up and she points at me. "No. No." She shakes her head. "You don't get to do this." She finds my eyes and stares me down.

"You will not run from this, Stephanie. I won't let you."

My voice falls to a whisper. "You're kind of scaring me, Jessa."

She rests her hands on her knees. "Good. Because you've been running from the second I met you." She reaches into her pocket and pulls out woven thread with a small key attached to it. "I brought this with me to work today to give you." She hands it to me and I take it and run my fingers over the thread.

My eyes grow wide and I struggle with the words.

"It's a…it's a friendship bracelet. You actually gave me a friendship bracelet. I've never had one. Did you make this?"

She nods and smiles.

"There's this poem I love that talks about being key droppers instead of cage dwellers. It seemed like you needed reminding that the key to your cage is within your reach." She lifts her wrists and I notice a similar one hanging delicately from her arm.

"We're twinsies."

I laugh and sniff and wipe my cheeks with the side of my thumb.

"I need you to know that I'm trying really hard not to be scared shitless right now."

She grabs my hand. "See? That's what so great about friendship. You can be scared shitless. I just get to hold your hand through it all. You can't run forever, Stephanie. No one can. The past has a way of catching up with us."

I watch the way the key grabs the sun peeking in through the windows, creating a dance of light on the ceiling.

"I don't want to run anymore. I just…"

She reaches for me and for once, I don't back away; I just lean in and rest my head on her shoulder.

"We won't run, Stephanie. We won't. I'll stand with you. So will Ren. We'll stand with you and we'll fight. Bastards don't get to have my friends."

I snort through the tears and she gives me a squeeze before leaning back and looking me in the eyes.

"Okay. First thing. Ren is having a get together at his place tonight. Do you want to come?"

I stare at her for a few beats.

"You're seriously inviting me to a party?"

She shrugs. "Why not?"

"I don't know…I just…maybe I thought we'd do something different. Like watch the ocean or something."

"…watch the ocean?"

"Yes."

She sighs. "You're such a transplant. Listen. While I absolutely agree that facing those demons and *not running* is of the utmost of importance, sometimes you just need to remind yourself that you *can* have fun."

"Fun…"

She nods. "Yes. Fun. It's this thing that forces belly laughter to rise from the center of your gut?" She runs her hands in circular motions in front of her crop top and I crack a smile.

"Is it like…a crazy party?"

She throws back her head and laughs.

"Hardly. Ren is like…three steps away from teetotaler. Seriously. We just eat, drink a few drinks, chat, and see where the evening goes from there. Deal?"

I chew on the inside of my cheek for a few seconds before responding.

"Okay. Fine. Deal."

We hear footsteps behind us and we look to see Ren peeking around the corner. Jessa motions him over and he scratches his head.

"How long have you guys been here?"

Jessa and I look at each other before she turns back to Ren.

"I don't know…maybe an hour? Two?"

He blinks and looks at something behind him.

"Did you hear anything at all?"

We shake our heads.

Jessa stands and walks over to Ren.

"What's going on? Besides the occasional seagull, I heard nothing."

He points to something and Jessa goes white.

"Stephanie. I think you need to come here."

I can't breathe again, my heart pounds in my chest and I feel my pulse everywhere: my fingers, my eyes, my toes, my scalp.

"What is it?" My vision is already growing blurry with the preparation of something grotesque. I walk over to where they stand and peek my head in between their shoulders.

The first thing I see: Kevin leaning over something written in the dirt.

The second thing I see: scrawled in front of the door, less than ten feet from where Jessa and I sat and talked, words that make me see red all over again.

*Lollipop,*
*I will not stop.*

Kevin lifts his head and meets my eyes.

"Your dad."

I nod and look toward the ocean, the waves crashing over each other, and clench and unclench my fists.

"I know."

*Breathe in. Breathe out. Breathe in. Breathe out.*

"He could have…" I close my eyes and grab for Jessa's arm. She reaches up and rests her hand on my own.

Ren's voice cuts through the silence. "Help me out here? What does this mean?" I open my eyes and look at him pointing at the message in the sand.

I sniff. "It's part of the poem he left on my door the other night. The next few words are *until your breath reaches mine.* And then he threatens me." I point to the words. "This is a threat. He sat here and listened to us talk and decided to send me a message instead of doing something immediately."

I rub my hands through my hair.

"He's toying with me. Trying to get me scared—normally his threats make me run after him in fear."

"No more running." Jessa whispers.

I shake my head. "No more running. I'm sick of this. Sick of the fear. Sick of him controlling me." The anger from the other night thrums wildly through my veins and I draw in a shaky breath to try and contain it.

Kevin notices.

"Steph…"

I hold up my hand.

"I'm fine." I shoot him a glance letting him know that even though his presence is accepted, it doesn't mean anything's changed. Not yet. He lowers his head and nods.

I push through Ren and Jessa, and Kevin steps away from the words, giving me room. I kneel down and start running my fingers through the dirt. Standing up, I brush my hands together and look at Jessa, ignoring Kevin's frown.

"Let's go, shall we?"

She smiles and nods, walking over to where I stand, my response to my father directly in front of her. Grabbing my hand, she motions for the boys to follow and they take one last glance before we walk to the cars.

I imagine my dad is watching us somewhere, waiting until we leave to follow us. For once, I'm ready. I have people in my life who know me —all of me—and are still willing to stand. When he walks up to see what I wrote, he'll read a different Stephanie than the one who ran out of the hospital months ago.

*Come and get me,* I said.

And I mean it.

I really want him to try.

I've tasted freedom now and there's nothing he can do to scare me away. This right here? It's not living. Not really. And I'm ready to change that.

I hear the distant rumbling of his voice begin in my head and I ignore it, choosing instead to focus on the view in front of me: Jessa letting her rainbow hair loose in the wind and Ren chasing after her down the path. I smile.

*Come and get me, dad. Just try. I promise you're in for the fight of your life and you just might not make it out alive.*

## CHAPTER THIRTEEN

We hang out at Jessa's place for the rest of the day. I sit on her patio, the wind whipping my hair around, and stare at the people below us on the shore. For a brief moment, I wonder what would happen if I were to decorate a poster with *Hi, Dad!* and post it on the railings.

I know he's out there. I know he's always only a heartbeat away.

For once, this only ignites anger and action, boiling and certain. There is no fear anymore. My kingdom for his head. On a platter. With lots of people around to watch the fall of a monster.

The only conflicted feelings I possess deal with Kevin. I frown. If only he weren't so…*sexy*. Seriously. I have a strong suspicion this whole thing would be a lot easier if, I don't know…he had a combover or something.

*Ugh.*

On our way from the Poetry House, Kevin stopped and asked what I planned to do—said something about me being a hazard because of these mood swings he kept witnessing.

"I'm just worried about you." He said.

"Mood swings? You're witnessing mood swings?" I said.

"Well, yeah Steph. You go from okay to livid in like, .3 seconds. It's scary."

I'm not sure where I got the gumption, but I stepped within millimeters of where he stood, breathing in his scent and fighting the memories threatening to overtake me. Leaning close, just close enough to where he fought his own study of my lips, I looked him the eye and whispered.

"You want a mood swing? Keep following me. You'll get to see what it's like on the other side of my hatred."

He had blinked then, and stepped back from me before turning around and asking Ren for a ride back to his car.

Then, I only felt a fraction of guilt.

Now, I'm shaking with questions of whether he's right.

Maybe I am going off the deep end.

Jessa appears at the sliding door of her porch in gold pants and a black hi-low shirt with a see through back. I glance down at the capri leggings I threw on for work that morning and twist my lips.

"Hey. You want to borrow some of my clothes?"

I squint and put my hand above my eyes to look back at her. "Um. Sure?"

Her face breaks into a glow.

Apparently she wanted me to answer yes.

"Come on. I already picked a few possibilities out…"

I laugh under my breath. "Why am I not surprised?"

She answers with a flip of her hair and we walk down the hallway into her room. She points at an empty one on her left.

"By the way. That's your room when you finally move in."

I peek in and try to hide my surprise.

"It's…huge. Wait. Is that a *patio?* Off the *room?*" I look at her in confusion.

"I still haven't even said yes—are you sure you just don't want to find someone who I don't know…is more stable?"

Jessa winks and says nothing before walking into her room. I follow her and sit on her bed as she shuffles through some clothes on a nearby chair. She pulls up a flowered skirt with a look of satisfaction.

"There! Found it. What do you think?"

I take a look at the pattern: bright pink background with colored flowers. And it looks about three inches shorter than anything I've ever worn before. I reach for the bottom of the skirt and try to find words.

"That's…pink."

She rolls her eyes. "It's pink *and different shades.*" She points to my leggings and black shirt. "You know. Color."

I look down.

"I like color. Just not…always."

She stares. "That didn't even make sense, Steph."

I shrug and she drops the skirt against her bed. Looking back at me, she scrunches up her eyes.

"You sure you don't like it? It has pockets."

I perk up. "The skirt? It has pockets?"

Her eyes brighten. "Yep. And you could wear these wedges. And this shirt." She leaves and comes back with a t-shirt that has screen-printed words in grey font across the chest.

FAMOUS CAUSE WE PROGRAM WORLD WIDE

"Aren't those…Tupac lyrics?"

She laughs and holds the shirt out for me to grab. "Yeah. It's awesome isn't it? I found it online."

I finger the lettering and am surprised at how well it goes with the skirt.

"…I kinda love it."

I grab the shirt and skirt, and throw a dubious glance toward the wedges. I point down at my well-worn red chucks.

"Actually, I think I want to wear these. They go with that bright red rose that will be plastered on my thigh."

Jessa cocks her head and then nods.

"I approve." She raises an eyebrow. "But next time, we're getting you in a crop top."

I shake my head vehemently. "No. No crop top. No unnecessary skin."

"But those *abs* tho!"

I blink and walk away and she just calls after me.

"You'll think differently when it gets above 80 in the summer!"

"That's not hot!" I respond and she just grunts.

"You don't know California heat, love. Just wait. You'll be walking around in a bikini in no time."

I show her my middle finger, nestled above my head, and she giggles.

"I love you too, Stephanie. Now go change. We're gonna be late."

.:::.

As soon as we walk into Ren's house we're bombarded with noise and laughter.

"Nah man. Claire is the best companion. You know this. Not only is she well-spoken but she *knows things.* You know? And like, she can totally hang with the Doctor."

Whooping and hollering and a "no way! No way. It's Rose. Rose beats every other companion out of *principle*" are thrown out into the atmosphere before we walk into the room with a bunch of guys sitting at a table.

I widen my eyes at Jessa.

"Nerd talk?" I mouth.

She nods and purses her lips in confirmation. Her eyes scour the table covered in Pokemon cards and what looks like an abandoned game of Settlers of Catan. She wrinkles her nose.

"Nerd talk. It's about time we got here. Things could have gotten scary."

She breaks into a smile and grabs my hand, lifting our arms above our heads and forcing us to walk further into the room.

*Oh god oh god center of attention don't look at me I may puke.*

I mean, those are my general thoughts. I can't be quite sure because *everyone and their fucking mother* is staring at me. I put on my brave face and struggle with lifting my lips into what looks more like a grimace than a smile. I throw a withering glance toward Jessa and then wiggle my arm free before crossing them in front of my chest.

Social interaction: check.

Friendly acceptance: Baby steps.

Jessa doesn't miss a beat.

"Gentlemen! The party has arrived. Let's um…clear the table, shall we? Unless of course there's vodka and juice somewhere. Then you can get me to join you. I may even contribute to this um…riveting conversation you guys were just ending."

I lean over and finger the bottom of my skirt and whisper in Jessa's ear. "They're still staring."

She nods and looks at me grimly.

"We're gonna need a bigger intervention."

She motions for me to follow her and she begins opening cabinets in the kitchen and pantry, looking satisfied when she finds a stack of red plastic cups.

"Hey Rasco! Where's your alcohol?"

A booming voice echoes down the hallway. "Left cabinet. Behind the soup."

"Behind the soup? I can't even…" Jessa mutters under her breath before answering. "How about you organize your shit once in a while, huh? Liquor does not a tomato soup make my friend."

I blink.

"Jessa. I can't drink. I'm underage."

She's reaching for something on the top shelf, standing on her toes and grunting. She pauses and falls back on her heels.

"Oh Steph. This isn't for you. You can have, I don't know, Kool-Aid? I have no clue what the boys have here outside of water and liquor."

I wrinkle my nose.

"That's lame. And boring."

She lifts her finger. "Oh wait. Wait before you judge my friend." She pivots and opens the fridge, grabbing the freshly squeezed lemonade.

"Here. Here's juice. Oh! And coffee. Coffee?"

She holds a pitcher of iced toddy behind her and I grab it, pushing the lemonade back toward her.

"A pox on you for handing me juice over coffee. And yes. Coffee I will most definitely have…"

She carries the vodka, lemonade, gin and whiskey in her arms back into the room with the boys. I follow with the pitcher of coffee and a glass full of ice.

We put all of the glasses and drinks on the table, now clear, and Ren widens his eyes.

"Jesus, Jessa. That's a lot of booze. I'm not looking to get wasted tonight."

"Oh no, Ren. No tapping out tonight." A wicked grin crosses her face and she pulls a timer out of the waistband of her pants. I scratch my head.

"When did you put the timer in your pants, Jessa?"

The boys chuckle and Jessa offers a wry grin. "Well. Considering Ren over here has been tripping over his feet for a few years, I'd say about that long." And then she winks, and my face grows crimson. I'm sure there's no difference between my skin and my hair.

Ren hides a smile behind his hand and jerks his chin toward the drinks.

"So…what are your plans, Jess?"

She punches a few things on the screen of her phone and places it on the table in between everyone.

"I figure it's been a while since we've heard this song, yes?"

A twinkling sound comes from her speakers and almost every single person in the room throws up their hands at the mention of something about *lazy hooks*.

I say *almost everyone* because I'm not yelling something about good shit. I have no idea what's going on here.

"GOOD SHIT!" They all scream and then begin pounding on the table with their fists.

"GOOD SHIT. GOOD SHIT. GOOD SHIT."

The song shifts into a driving beat and Ren belts out the chorus while Jessa breaks out into a sultry dance around a nearby chair.

*You know it when you see it.*

*You know it when its there.*

*Like Michael Jackson's Thriller,*

*like Farrah Fawcett's hair.*

I don't even know what's happening. Should I laugh? Cry? Run far, far away from whatever the hell is happening? I don't know. Because I have *no clue* about anything right now other than some weird techno voice keeps talking about him (her?) liking when someone plays with their hair. When Andre 3000 comes on and starts talking about American Apparel ad girls, I get really confused.

*What in the actual fuck is happening here.*

I raise my hand and try to lift my voice above the bedlam happening in front of me. Coincidentally, the song ends right as I start hollering and the room grows quiet. Like a damn movie.

"Can someone please explain what the fuck is going on?"

Jessa breaks into shaky laughter, breathy from dancing. Flipping her hair as she sits down. "Whoa, Steph. No need to holler…"

"I was just…nevermind." I grab the seat next to her.

She picks up the timer.

"So a few years ago, when we were all in high school and doing things high school students shouldn't do, we came up with this game." She eyes me. "A drinking game."

I study her. "I gathered that." Pointing to the timer, I raise an eyebrow. "So what are the rules?"

Ren jumps in, "at the time, we just called it FUN SHIT, because we would go around in the circle and list well…fun shit we liked to do…"

Jessa nods.

"Right. And we would keep going until the timer stopped. The rule is, if the timer dings when it's your turn, you finish your drink."

Ren leans in, "and if you've done what someone says, you take a sip." He glances at Jessa. "We never really last very long."

Jessa shakes her head and giggles. "Yeah. Yeah we only last about three rounds before we have to stop."

I frown.

"So what does this have to do with that song you guys just flipped out on?"

Ren raises his eyebrows. "You've never heard of Capital Cities?"

"….no?"

"Huh. Well. Anyway. That song—Farrah Fawcett Hair—became our unspoken opener to the game. It talks about good shit people like. We've since renamed the game."

"Good shit." I respond.

"Good shit." He nods.

I rest my back against the chair and take a sip of my iced coffee. "Okay. Okay this should be interesting. I'm suddenly very thankful I'm disqualified based solely on my age."

Jessa shakes her head and grabs my arm. "Oh no. No. You're not disqualified. You're on my team. I will drink for you."

I pause mid sip.

"Jessa. That's a lot of alcohol."

She smiles at me. "I can handle it. Promise. I'm kinda known for my alcohol tolerance."

Ren nods.

"Yeah—she's got the fortitude of a camel. It's ridiculous."

"…okay?"

Jessa slaps the table and looks around. "Are we ready?"

Everyone nods and she turns the timer, the ticking of the tiny second hands filling the space around us.

"I go first. Good shit: this girl right here." She jerks her thumb toward me. Ren takes a sip of his drink and the other guys raise their glasses before sipping out of their own cups.

"Am I…are we supposed to drink to that? I'm myself and…" I frown and point to the other guys. "You guys don't even know me."

A tall lanky guy with curly hair shrugs. "Jessa's stamp of approval. Not many have that so you're in as far as I'm concerned." He breaks into a slow grin. "Plus you're kinda cute."

Nope. Just kidding. *Now* my skin matches my hair color.

"Um…thanks?"

Jessa puts her hand up in front of her.

"Off limits for multiple reasons, boys. No explanation needed. She needs friends, not male pheromones."

I hide my face behind my glass and drink half of my coffee before feeling safe enough to set the cup on the table. Jessa turns to Ren.

"Your turn."

"Gidget." Ren responds and Jessa blushes. I roll my eyes.

And we continue on and on and on for the next few minutes—answers like *JRR Tolkien* and *Battlestar Galactica* and *Beyonce's ass*.

I go for easy ones: coffee, the ocean, new journals, my little brother.

Jessa answers back on one turn with "staying up all night to catch the sunrise" and motions for a cup tap in recognition. I shake my head.

"I'm not big on sunrises, remember?"

Her face clouds with recognition. "Oh yeah. Right. Sorry."

I shrug and listen in, that round full of answers like *dancing to Justin Timberlake* and *meeting Alec Baldwin* and *filming my first commercial*.

When I was able to share again, I look at her.

"Watching the sunset off Sunset Cliffs."

Her eyes brighten and she takes a sip of her drink.

*"Good shit."*

On our tenth or so round, when the timer is slowly coming to an end, I sense a slowing down of people's responses. Some guy mentions the way the wind rustles the leaves of trees and I take a sip of coffee to make him feel better but really? It could be the lack of spirits in my drink and the up tic of caffeine in my system, but this game is getting boring.

"I ran from a train once. Almost got run over before I jumped off the cliff the tracks were on. That was pretty fun."

*Blink blink. Stare.*

The timer dings and no one even notices.

"I'm sorry." Ren is the first to speak. "Did you say you ran from a train? Like on its tracks?"

I nod. "We thought they were inactive. At least—until we were on the bridge and we heard it rumble and felt the tracks shake."

Jessa's eyes grow into saucers.

"Shit." She mutters.

I keep my face straight. "No. *Good* shit. It really was amazing. Thrilling. Scary as fuck when it happened but still exhilarating." I point to her drink.

"Drink up, Jess. Timer went off."

Ren throws up his hands and does the robot.

"Timer went off!"

Jessa starts laughing and grabs her drink, then thinks twice and sets it down before grabbing my own. Within two gulps the rest of my coffee is gone and Jessa is slamming the cup on the table.

"Another pox on you for finishing my coffee before I could!" I grab my cup to refill it. "Remind me not to go out with you when I turn 21." I refill my glass and then reach for the timer, turning it all the way around before setting it back down in front of me.

"Now, Ren. I believe it's your turn. Where for art thou good shit?"

## CHAPTER FOURTEEN

The game lasts for another forty minutes and only stops when Jessa puts her hands up in surrender.

"I call it." She groans.

I'm only slightly disappointed. Although it's obvious Jessa is having difficulty staying on her chair by herself, I was becoming more and more amused by the answers they were willing to throw out the more they drank.

*Riding down a hill on your stomach with a skateboard* and *skinny dipping in the ocean* and *playing the will it blow up game* were some of my favorites.

Ren scratches his chin. "Yeah." He looks at his almost empty glass and frowns. "I'm not sure vodka was a good friend to me tonight." He looks at Jessa. "This isn't going to be pretty. I have to open tomorrow."

She places her hand on his arm.

"Is it okay if I leave my car here overnight? Stephanie and I can take the bus home. I won't be driving."

He reaches for her keys still dangling out of her nearby purse.

"It's more than okay. You're not leaving here with these."

"Good thing I don't really need a house key, huh?" She leans over and pecks him on the cheek.

"See you tomorrow some time?"

He nods and smiles at her, briefly touching the tip of her nose with his finger.

"Tomorrow," he promises. "I'll call you after my shift."

She turns toward me. "Are you ready?"

I nod and move to stand, helping her up and holding out my hands to make sure she doesn't fall. She brushes me off and stands on her own, not even flinching or wobbling when she leans over and grabs her purse.

"You are far more mobile on your feet than I anticipated."

She smiles and motions for the door.

"This is where my talent for handling my liquor mixes with all of the dance training I had in school. Grace is an under-celebrated skill when one's inebriated."

I watch her place one foot in front of the other with ease and I raise an approved eyebrow.

"I'm feeling slightly better about accompanying you down the street, now."

She grabs a glass full of water on the counter on our way out and finishes it within a few seconds.

"Hydration, Stephanie. Remember that. It's all about hydration."

"Noted," I reply, and we say our goodbyes and walk out into the windy coastal air.

She lifts her hands slightly and lets her arms float in the breeze.

"I love nights like this, where there's the hint of summer in the wind. It doesn't have that bite anymore—the one that makes you reach closer around you? It's more of a caress. I can feel my muscles relax."

I look at her.

"Sounds like a poem right there."

She does a little spin in my direction. "Ooooh. You're right." Fumbling for something in her purse, she pulls out a Sharpie.

"How about we not get arrested for defacing public property."

She laughs.

"No. Not public property." She lifts up her arms and writes down the words in what looks like rivulets down her arm. When finished, she holds it up for me to see.

*The bite is gone now,*

*the hurtling reminder of winter's grip.*

*What's left is the sun's caress,*

*her whispers of life in the wind.*

I make a circle with my index finger and thumb. "It's perfect."

She looks down again and nods in agreement before dropping her arm and pointing for us to take a left.

We turn and immediately run into a huge crowd of people gathered around a guy dancing to music blaring out of a nearby boom-box.

Jessa breaks into a grin and walks faster to join the crowd, leaning forward on her toes to see the moves. He pop and locks and points to someone else in the crowd and she puffs out her chest as if he's pulling her toward him, moving with the beat and walking into the center of the group. They choreographed a routine before this, because soon their feet are matching the thrum of the music.

*And there's no stopping us right now.*

I nod my head in appreciation—this song is a favorite of mine. I'm caught by the movement, though. The way their limbs synchronize and pulse as part of the song. I've never been able to let myself go long enough to enjoy dancing. I'm all left feet and elbows. Kevin tried once to teach me how to line dance and I just tripped through the song before giving up and begging for him to just carry me home.

The music shifts and five more people from the crowd jump and maneuver their way to the center, now moving down the sidewalk. Jessa claps her hands.

"Ohmigosh. Stephanie. I heard about this. These guys are a dance crew and go perform roaming dance parties."

I glance around. "All of these people?"

She shakes her head. "No. Some of them are just bystanders—people on the street when that guy first started dancing." She circles with her hand toward the growing group in front of us dancing. "Sooner or later, they'll move down the street to their next spot—the last one went all night long before they decided to end it—the crowd was just getting too big." She turns her wide eyes toward me. "Can you imagine? Dancing all night? That's amazing."

I watch the crowd for a little while before responding.

"That's...yes. Amazing. Amazing is what it is...are we staying?"

She's not even listening anymore. Janelle Monae's *Dance Apocalyptic* comes on the speakers and she squeals, beginning to bounce with the beat. A guy nearby grabs for her hand and twirls her around before breaking out into a kick-hop-swing movement of complicated dancing. Jessa answers back with her own hips moving in ways I never knew joints and bones could work together. I lose her somewhere in the crowd, but every once in a while see her rainbow hair bouncing above the rest. I smile.

*She really is her own individual earthquake.*

A guy comes close and holds out his hand. I widen my eyes in shock and put my hands up.

"No thanks. I'm just watching."

He smiles.

"Come on. I saw you move those feet every once in a while. Just let go."

I study him for a few seconds and he just waits, arm akimbo.

I could do a lot of things here.

I could run, because the amount of human energy pressing into my own is nothing short of overwhelming and electric.

But…the atmosphere is haunting. Alive. It's pulsing with the beat of this growing crowd's heart and I kind of love it.

*No more running,* Jessa had said earlier.

I'm tired of saying no to everything.

I'm tired of thinking that life is not for me—that these experiences are kept close to the chest of those who live a privileged life of hope and continued promises coming true.

I look toward the sky and hide a smile. It's moments like this I breathe in the ache of missing Kevin. I wish he could see me now. I wish he could experience *this* Stephanie instead of the one who hid with fear and wonder at everything that came her way.

I already know what I'm going to do. I think I knew the second I lost Jessa in the mass of people.

I glance at this stranger's eyes and see nothing but kindness and life and adventure and I don't know what's gotten into me but I don't think—for once I just don't think about anything—but I smile back and place my hand in his and then we're moving with the music and I'm laughing and throwing back my head and watching the stars above and turning with the beat and letting everything fill my senses as the songs keep coming and we keep moving and the scenery keeps changing.

.:.

The roaming dance party ends somewhere in the middle of downtown after more than a few people recognize a brief appearance of a well known DJ. The whispers and attention break the spell, if just for a moment, and that's enough for the original crew to thank everyone for coming. A hat passes around the crowd for donations and by the time Jessa and I get it cash is overflowing.

"I think I missed my calling," I whisper and she giggles, grabbing my hand and pointing to a nearby garage. We say bye to our new friends and walk over to the ledge overlooking the Pacific. The blue-dark of night is still winning—the light of morning only a mere hour away. If you look close enough, you can see the first hints of orange over the horizon where the water meets the sky.

I suck in a breath and watch the line become hazy.

"This is one of my favorite views." Jessa breaks the silence.

I look at her and sniff.

"Pavement?"

She swats at my arm and points in front of us. "That. That line." She motions around us. "These buildings. It's all sharp edges set up against the softness of the ocean. Mesmerizing."

I sit there, not responding, just watching the stars slowly disappear.

"I miss him," I whisper. I'm not looking at her—we're both still sitting on the ledge facing out toward the Pacific.

I'm prepared for her to grab me and shake me and tell me that I shouldn't be moaning over a boy.

I'm prepared for her to reach for my hand to squeeze it and tell me how she knows and she's sorry and she's been there.

I'm not prepared for what she does next.

Jessa jumps off the ledge and starts running toward the stairs.

I frown and stare after her for a second. When I realize she's not coming back, I call after her.

"Jessa, what the hell?"

"Just follow me!" She says, a silly grin on her face.

"But…where are you going?"

She stops and turns and gives me a serious look. "Have I ever led you somewhere horrible?"

I sigh and remember the last time she asked us to follow her.

"This better not be an abandoned building, Jessa."

She laughs and winces at the same time.

"Just come. No abandoned buildings. Promise."

I jump off the ledge and chase after her across the parking garage. We race up flights of stairs, her muttering "hurry, hurry, hurry" under her breath as her feet slap against the pavement. I'm beginning to regret the running last night because my thighs have turned into a single flame.

We get to the top and I lean my hands on my knees.

"This way." And she grabs my hand and pulls me toward the ledge. I halt.

"Jessa…"

She turns and her hair blows up and around her face in the early morning wind.

"Just trust me?"

I'm exhausted now, the night catching up to me and hitting me like a square brick in between the eyes. I watch as she climbs up on the ledge and reaches her hands around the metal bar.

"A few years ago, when I was in the middle of all that therapy, my counselor mentioned I needed to work out my anger." She balances on her feet and spreads her arms wide in front of her. She turns her head and smiles at me.

"This became my therapy."

Leaning forward, I see her take a deep breath and then she screams.

"What the fuck?" I mutter under my breath and begin to look around to see if anyone hears us. Of course no one will—we're in the middle of downtown LA and twenty stories up from ground level. This is as separate from the flow of traffic and busy-ness as you can get.

And also like, ass-crack early in the morning. Or late. Whatever.

She screams again. This time her arms stretched out beside her, her head tilted back. She looks ethereal. Turning around she catches her breath and smiles.

"You joining me or what?"

"In...screaming? You brought me up here to scream?"

She holds out her hand. "Steph. You got all this poison pent up inside. All this anger. You need to release it—remind yourself what it means to feel alive."

"I think I know what alive feels like." I put a finger to my pulse on my neck and then point below us. "I'd rather not tempt fate."

She laughs and motions for me to join her.

"Come on. You'll love this." Her gold pants shine in the lights of the garage and I'm sure if anyone happens to glance up, they'll wonder about the colored pinwheel glowing up above them.

I climb up the ledge and position myself next to her. She grabs my hand. "Count of three?" She looks at me out of the corner of her eye and my breath catches.

So this is friendship.

Too close. She's getting too close.

Slowly, my life is turning beautiful because of this fire cracker standing next to me. It scares me. I return her smile, only slightly faltering. I answer back in a whisper.

"Count of three."

My heart is pounding in my chest. I'm not sure I will know how to scream. I think that's when I remember that outside of a few moments with my dad, I've never screamed before. Not like this. Not from the gut. Not without fear of anyone listening.

She starts to count.

"One…."

My breath shortens and I close my eyes.

"Two…."

Slowly, I lean forward to where my chest is up against the metal bar.

"THREE."

I open my eyes and see the world before me. I open my mouth and let the fear and hurt and anger and sadness leave me in a rush. My scream seems quiet at first, reserved. But I just keep screaming—building up breath only to release it again. Every scream is louder and more guttural. I see the poem taped my door. I see Kevin walking into the coffee shop in the middle of my breakdown. I see the poetry house and think of Pacey and Emma and the way my body melted into Kevin's in the field watching stars and the way my pulse jumped out of my skin when he kissed me in the rain and with every breath—every scream—I feel the weight of a hundred men fall from my shoulders.

When we finish, I'm shaking and there are tears streaming down my cheeks. I wipe them away before Jessa can say anything.

And that's when I see the sunrise.

It's the first one I've seen since moving to California. All this time, I've avoided it because of the memories. Sunrises remind me of the life I lived. They remind me of him. And now, staring at the soft pink light creeping its way across the blue-black sky I begin to wonder why it took me so long. The pink echoes off the water below it and glows in every direction.

I see Jessa's eyes on me and I turn to look at her, this time not bothering to wipe away the tears.

"I love sunrises," I whisper.

She smiles and squeezes my hand. "I know."

We stay there, hand in hand, watching the sun's rays shoot forward and point to the moon still hanging in the sky, and I can almost hear the day tell the night that its time is over. When there's more light than dark and the sun is cresting over the buildings, she turns and motions toward the car.

"You ready?"

I nod.

We hop off the ledge and begin walking back toward the stairs when I turn to look at her again. "Why did you bring me up here again? Why did you want me to scream?"

She laughs. "Oh I didn't know we were going to scream until I realized just how far up we were—I came up here to catch the sunrise."

I stare.

"If there's one thing I've realized, Stephanie, it's that boys are great but we don't need them for romance. We can find romance in other ways. Chasing the light of day with a friend, screaming at the top of our lungs twenty stories in the air, joining a dance mob through the streets of LA—beauty and romance can happen at any moment. We just have to open ourselves up for it." She looks at me again. "You don't need a guy in order to live a life full of beauty. You just need people. Those who will go to bat for you and stand by your side when things get shitty. You need those people to remind you of the good. There's always another day, you know? It's what I love about sunrises. The way the rays crack the night sky wide open. Kind of sentimental."

Something inside me shifts as I listen. Without even thinking, I wrestle her into a hug and she starts laughing.

"I didn't think you were one for hugging."

My voice cracks and I spit out a mouthful of purple hair.

"I'm not. I'm so not. But you have a way of pushing through all my defenses, dammit."

She throws up her arms with my own still wrapped around her neck and she lets out a squeal.

"I did it, Universe! I did it! I cracked the impenetrable Stephanie Tiller. My life is complete."

She quiets then and wraps her arms around me and squeezes.

"Now. Do you happen to know the bus route back to your hotel? I'm picturing showers and a hell of a nap before moving all of your stuff to my place."

I slowly step away and wipe the tears off my cheeks and swallow my laughter.

"Jessa. We've been through this. I haven't said yes yet."

A slow smile spreads across her face as she walks away from me.

"*Yet*. Only one small, insignificant letter off from *yes*."

I call after her.

"Do you even know where you're going? I have the bus route, remember?"

She pauses in the doorway and I laugh.

"Who needs who now, huh?"

And she loops her arm in mine, and we make our way down the stairs and out into the sunlit street as the night lamps turn off above us.

## CHAPTER FIFTEEN

About ten minutes into the bus ride, Jessa decides to reroute and grab her car.

"It's not that much longer of a wait, we're already here, and it will save me a trip later which will save *you* a trip later since you'll be with me."

I raise an eyebrow. "Oh I will?"

"You will."

We get to the bus stop right around the corner from Ren's apartment and walk the rest of the way as the city wakes up around us. We pass the spot we found the dance crew the night before and I smile. Before I can stop myself I'm whispering lines underneath my breath, dropping cadence with my feet as I walk.

"Bones crack against the rhythm of your memory / who knew the feeling of a beat / within my veins / would be the thing to get you out of me."

Jessa pauses and looks at me.

"Damn. I like that. Is it a song? Who wrote it?"

The smile spreads across my face.

"It's a poem. I wrote it. Just now—remembering the roaming dance party last night."

Her lips form an O and she widens her eyes.

"That's the first time you've shared poetry with me."

I nod and she grabs my wrist.

"Stephanie. *Stephanie.* We really are besties!"

I roll my eyes. "Okay stop. You ruined it. None of that…"

She hides a smile.

"Do you want to be blood sisters next? I have a needle…." She sticks her hands in the pocket of her golden pants and I shake my head, laughing.

"Ohmygod. *Stop.* Ridiculous. I'm never sharing a poem again."

She keeps walking, both of her hands now tucked into her pockets. She's slightly in front of me and only now am I seeing just how high her stiletto heels reach. She's practically walking on her tip-toes. And not falling. She turns her head and winks at me and I throw my hands up in the air.

"How the hell are you not falling on your ass right now?"

"Practice. You'll learn. And you'll share more poems with me too. It's what best friends do."

She points to a parking lot on our left and we cross the street, walking to her car. When we get inside she closes her eyes and rests her head on the seat behind her.

"Just a little nap?"

I slap her thigh. "No. No. Wake up. You fall asleep and we'll be here for hours. Let's go. King-size hotel bed with crisp linens await you."

She jerks her head up and nods.

"Yes. That's right. King size." And she turns the ignition.

.::.

We see the flashing lights as soon as we turn on the street for my hotel.

"Shit." Jessa mutters under her breath. She looks at me and I squint to get a better view.

"Maybe there was an accident in front of the hotel. Maybe they aren't actually *at* the hotel," I offer. But I know better. I know my luck. And with my dad just hours away from scratching a menacing message in the sand, I have a gut feeling he's got something up his sleeve.

When we pull in to the parking lot and see the roundabout blocked with cop cars, I groan.

Jessa's phone rings and she answers it. "Yeah. We see them." She glances at me and nudges the phone toward me.

"It's Kevin."

I widen my eyes.

She answers with a pinch of her lips. "Relax. He's calling from Ren's phone." She shakes her hand and I grab the phone from her, placing it against my ear.

"Hello?"

Kevin's voice breaks through and I roll my eyes at the butterflies careening against my ribcage.

"Steph. Wait for me, okay? Don't go in there alone…"

I laugh and scratch at my neck, feeling antsy.

"Wait for you? Kevin…I shouldn't have to *wait* for you…"

He interrupts me.

"Stephanie. You don't understand. Jude's been tracking your dad and…"

I sigh.

"I don't…you don't…" I can feel the pressure rising in my chest and I swallow it down before I explode. I turn my voice to a whisper.

"I am not your fucking job anymore. Got it? Hitch a ride with Ren. Show up places where you know I will be—do whatever you need to do to satiate that conscience of yours. *But leave me alone.* God. I can't…"

The words for my frustration leave me and so I just hang up the phone and motion for Jessa to take it.

She raises an eyebrow.

"Everything okay?"

"It's fine. Let's just go. Get this over with." I unbuckle my seatbelt and lean forward to open the door. Jessa grabs my wrist.

"Steph…are you sure?"

I turn and look at her.

"No running, right?"

She nods slightly, biting her lip. "Check yes." She answers. She points to the window. "But I don't know if you really have much of a chance right now…"

I turn and see a uniformed police officer at my side, leaning down and motioning for us to unroll the window. I startle and look closer, noticing that it's Max.

*Act casual, Stephanie.*

I roll down the window. "Hi Max," I choke. "Long time no see."

He wrinkles his nose and pushes up his sunglasses before placing both hands on his hips, pushing back his jacket to where his gun shows. I hide a smile.

*All he needs is a porn-stache to round out this look.*

"We had an anonymous tip about some illegal activity going on in this hotel. When we checked the records, the claim was attached to your hotel room, Stephanie." He looks down on me over the top of his sunglasses. "Would you know anything about this?"

I mimic him and point to myself.

"Wait. Me?" I arch an eyebrow and shake my head. "I've done nothing."

He looks toward the hotel for a second before leaning his elbows against the window sill. I shift my weight to my left hip and try making eye contact.

It lasts for about two seconds before I puff out my cheeks in frustration. He's not saying anything, just watching us.

I shoot a glance to Jessa who is studying her fingernails.

*Well this is a heavy dose of awkward.*

I twist my hands palm up.

"Soooo…."

Max looks at me. "You really have no idea?"

I widen my eyes and shrug. "Aside from the extra lime I stole from the hamburger joint last week, I literally have no idea what I could be charged with…"

He grabs his notepad out of his back pocket and flips open to a page in the middle.

"Aiding and abetting known criminals and engaging in prostitution." He shuts his notepad and glances at me, chewing the inside of his cheek.

*I will always find you. You bitch. I will always find you.*

My dad's voice begins to echo louder and louder and louder and I close my eyes and open them, hoping for some type of relief. It doesn't help much.

Suddenly all I see are hands.

Max's hands, shoving themselves in their respective pockets.

Jessa's hands, now strangling the steering wheel, turning white at the knuckles.

My hand, up against my chin, my fingers strumming my lips like a guitar. The other hand is underneath my thigh, the shaking invisible to prying eyes.

And in my mind, the hands of what seems like a hundred men, grabbing pieces of me that don't exist anymore.

Max shifts his weight and squints at the surrounding cars in the parking lot and then back down to me.

"Well? Do you have anything to say?"

I stare at him for a second too long. He shakes his head.

"Stephanie…"

Static fills his radio and a man's voice interrupts what I imagine was going to be a not-so glamorous conversation.

"We have a situation we think you'd be interested in, sir."

I frown and look at Jessa.

Max listens to the codes given and points his finger at me. "Stay here," he orders as he turns and runs back toward the hotel.

Jessa and I look at each other again.

"I'm not staying."

She shakes her head.

"Yeah, eff that. Let's go."

I pause mid-reach for the door handle and laugh.

"Um. Since when we are we censoring ourselves?"

She shakes her head and points toward Max's retreating figure.

"Since he scared the hell out of me by appearing out of nowhere. He fucking took all my words from my mouth. Just…" She makes a sweeping motion with her hands up her chest and under her mouth. "Just gone. All of them."

She holds her hands out in front of her and I notice the tremor. "Jesus. I'm still shaking." She presses her hands against her legs and closes her eyes, breathing deep before turning to look at me.

"Okay. I'm ready. Let's do this."

And we jump out of the car and follow Max inside.

.:::.

There are a few things I notice as I walk into the lobby.

The guy at the front desk is leaning forward and whispering with an officer. Words like *strange* and *quiet* jump out at me from their conversation.

Across the room a maid answers questions with another officer.

And right by the elevator, blocking our entrance, is the woman from the other day. She's clutching at her pearls and looking with earnest at an officer taking notes. Once we're within earshot, she glances toward us and startles.

"Oh! There she is officer! Right there." She points and Jessa stops in her tracks, reaching for my elbow.

"Steph…"

"I'm fine," I whisper out of the corner of my mouth and manage a smile and slight wave.

"Hi," I mutter.

The officer turns toward me and then back at the lady, surprise dripping off his face.

"This is the girl who had a meltdown in the elevator and threatened you?"

I widen my eyes. "Wait. Wait. What? I didn't…"

Pearl Lady sniffs with disdain and raises her nose. Like…*actually raises her nose* and reaches for her pearls again before grazing the officer's elbow with her fingers. I raise my eyebrows.

*Fancy.*

Her voice is now weaker—more subdued—no withholding of the dramatic. "And *yes*. Officer. She threatened me. Told me that if I didn't help her get out that she would rip me to shreds like she did that journal she tore to pieces."

*Ren would give that a standing ovation.*

I hold up a finger.

"Wait. Wait. Um. *I'm right here,* first of all, and so you can ask me questions if you want." I shrug. "And second," I point at the lady. "Where do you get off saying that? I freaked. Yes. I tore up my journal. Yeah. *Because someone was stalking me.* But I did not threaten you." I wave my hand at her, brushing her off. "Seriously. I think you can quit the theatrics."

I wrinkle my nose in disgust and she gasps.

Jessa leans into my shoulder. "If you ask me, you were pretty generous with which finger you chose to point in her general direction."

The officer looks between her and me and his notepad and clears his throat. With a quick glance around I notice that we've attracted a whole lobby full of curious onlookers casually sitting on couches that were previously vacant and gathered in groups that look like riveting "discussions" — but I know these crowds. I grew up with them. The only difference between them and the ones that gathered in my neighborhood was the familiarity of faces. Here, there was no chance of running into someone I saw in the shed. Or at school. Or down the street.

Turning back to the officer, I motion toward the elevator.

"Do you mind if we run up to my room?"

He hesitates for just a moment before answering, his eyes flickering to the double doors of the elevator and back at me.

"Ma'am I think it'd be wise for you to stay here…"

I throw up my arms and turn and roll my eyes at Jessa.

"Just relax." She scratches her nose and whispers under her hand. "If you don't act suspicious he won't think you're suspicious and spoiler: you're acting suspicious."

He glances quickly in our direction and then jots something down in his notebook.

I whisper back, not trying to hide anything I say. "I'm fairly certain people know when you're whispering about them, Jessa."

She catches my eye and smiles, this time leaning in to whisper in my ear.

"I'm fairly certain you're giving this lady a fair amount of glee and gossip this afternoon."

I snort and look at Pearl Lady who has taken to dabbing her forehead with a handkerchief and blinking her nonexistent eyelashes toward the officer.

A chime goes off and my eyes shoot to the elevator. The numbers are counting down: fourteen, twelve, eleven…

And I remember—my room is on the fourteenth floor.

Nine…eight…seven….and the atmosphere of the entire lobby has shifted—everyone focusing on those steel double doors, waiting to see who will appear.

The numbers fall and I feel that strange rumbling in my gut when I know something is about to happen that I will wish I could blink away. But I can't stop it—I never can. I have a fleeting thought that I should have listened to Kevin—because if I listened, if I waited, he'd be here with me.

I set my shoulders back.

I know now I can make it without him. I just don't know if I can take the pain of living without him.

I take a deep breath and reach for Jessa's hand.

The chime goes off again and the officer turns toward the doors, moving out of the way.

And when they open, I see a man in a suit talking on a cell phone and holding a guy at arm's length. A sapphire gem glows in the artificial light, bouncing off a ring the guy is wearing. I blink and my heart does a double take.

*I know that ring.*

My knees give way and I lean into Jessa because I'm not sure which one I'm more surprised to see: the guy in a suit or the guy with the ring.

Jessa grabs hold of me and pulls me closer.

"Stephanie. What is it?"

The man in a suit catches my eye and breaks into a huge grin. He motions with his free hand and another immaculately-dressed man and standing a few feet away reading a newspaper runs to his side and takes over with handcuffs.

"You have the right to remain silent…" His voice carries over the lobby and people part like the red sea as he walks the guy with the ring out the door. I follow them with my eyes, still trying to make out if that guy handcuffed is really the one I saw sitting in a booth in Americana. The one who sat next to me on the bus.

It looked like him. The eyes. I remember the eyes. And the ring.

But I don't think about it for very long. Suddenly I notice that all eyes are on me. I look around and feel Jessa's finger tap my shoulder.

"Stephanie. Hey…Steph. He asked you a question."

"Yeah? Who?" My voice comes out breathy—I blink and realize where I am again.

I turn my head slowly and meet the only eyes sharp enough to have seen my pain and known its depth.

"Hi, Jude," I whisper.

He smiles and holds out his arms. I realize I'm still holding onto Jessa's fingers. She squeezes my hand and I let go and walk into his embrace, breathing in the woodsy scent of his cologne.

He voice booms within his chest. "I really didn't know if I'd ever see you again, kid."

I laugh and step away from him, suddenly all twisty inside about how I should be feeling.

Happy? Sad? Excited? Pissed? Relieved? I decide on ambivalent and just shrug.

"Well…you didn't really give me a choice now, did you?"

He drops his head for a moment and then catches my gaze.

"You know Emma and I would do anything for you, right?"

*Seriously? No like…"hey the weather sure is nice here" small talk? Let's just jump into the deep stuff? Alright. Fine. Two can play.*

I nod and cross my arms over my chest. "I know this—you guys have told me this before numerous times. And, I want to believe it. I do. But…I just don't get *why*. Why you waited. Why you asked Kevin to join you. Why you never said anything—anything at all."

He twists his lips and looks away for a split second before reaching forward and tweaking my arm.

"You always did have all the questions."

I raise an eyebrow. "And you always knew how to be evasive and not answer them."

I feel Jessa take a step toward us. Behind her, I hear Kevin hollering for Jude. I turn my head and see Ren running to catch up.

Kevin reaches us and I shy away from his hand that makes a move toward my own. Jude notices and frowns.

"Jude. Good. You found her. Did they get the guy?"

I look at Jude. "What guy?"

Jude nods at Kevin. "We did. But…he was tied up in her room, which means we'll need to answer questions about that…the authorities will want to know how he got there."

I shake my head, confused.

"What? Wait. A guy was in my room? Tied up?" I look toward the door where one of Jude's men ushered the guy with the ring. I point. "Was it that guy with the ring?"

Jude follows my gaze. "He had a ring?"

I turn and look at Jude. "A sapphire. It's huge. How'd you not see it?"

Jude shrugs and looks at Kevin.

"Not an important detail, I guess."

"Well. It's an important detail if you've seen him before. And I have. I saw him a few weeks ago. At Americana. And then before that he was on my bus on the way to work. He sat next to me." I chew on the corner of my lip. "I may have kicked his junk for being a smart-ass."

Jude hides a smile and I hear a sharp intake of breath from Jessa.

"Ohmigod." She whispers. "He was sitting in the booth next to us when I stopped you from leaving. I remember." I look at her and nod. She pales a little and then looks at Jude, her voice quiet.

"What's is going on here?"

I bounce off her question. "And how'd he get in my room?"

Jude scratches his forehead as if he's trying to figure out a puzzle.

"It's complicated, Stephanie."

"Complicated my ass. Check who you're talking to and try that again."

Kevin opens his mouth as if he's going to say something and then, catching a look from Jude, shuts it and turns away. I pounce, the frustration growing to code red levels.

"Wait. What was that? I saw that look. No secrets, you guys."

*Fuck this shit.*

I grab for Kevin's wrist for the first time since seeing him. His eyes grow wide and I lower my voice. Once I have his attention, I let go of his arm, my fingers still tingling from where we had contact. I have to clench my jaw to keep my voice from trembling.

*I really, really, really hate emotions.*

"No secrets, Kevin. I'm done with those."

Jessa clears her throat and raises her hand.

"I'd like to know what's going on, too."

Ren nods in solidarity, even though I have no idea if Kevin filled him in on anything on the drive over here.

"It would be nice to have an inkling of why I played chauffeur today to a teenager with a federal ID."

I raise an eyebrow and Ren looks at me, thumbing his hand toward Kevin. "This guy just shows up at my place early this morning demanding a ride over here. Said it was 'of the utmost importance.'" He jerks his head back. "Who talks like that anyway?"

A breathy laugh escapes and I glance at Kevin.

"You really told him nothing? Just demanded a ride?"

"I had to come, Steph. I wanted to make sure you're safe."

I say nothing. There's nothing to say to that kind of idiocy.

Jude blinks and notices Ren for the first time. He points at him and Jessa.

"Who are you?"

"They're my friends. And you don't get anymore information until you answer questions."

He studies my face and then nods, rubbing his chin with his fingers. I notice the stubble.

*Emma never lets him get away with stubble—always complains when he gets lazy in shaving.*

"How long have you been here?"

He closes his eyes for a split second before looking at me again with a slight smile.

"Steph. I promise. I'll answer your questions." He glances around and that's when I see two things: there are absolutely no officers left in the lobby—and I have no idea when they left—and the men in suits sprinkled around the lobby are acting inconspicuous but eyeing us. There really is no difference between surveillance on both ends of the spectrum. I remember noticing the men watching me at all times back home—the men my father hired to keep tabs on me. They held the same stance as these men, the good guys.

Always suspicious. Always watching.

Jude gives a slight hand motion and the men disappear slowly and methodically. Pointing to a room off to our left, he looks at me.

"Come on. We can talk in here."

I follow after him and Kevin, Jessa and Ren by my side.

"Wait. Jude. Where's Max?"

He holds up his hand and shakes his head.

I purse my lips and sigh. I know that signal too. I give Jessa the side eye.

"His wife used to do that in the classroom," I whisper. "We called it the STFU hand." I shake my head. "He just doesn't get it, though. I'm not shutting up about this. I want answers."

She nods. "I know, girl. You deserve them." She grabs my hand and makes me slow down to lengthen the distance between us and them. "I mean it, Stephanie."

I look at her and frown. "What do you mean?"

She sets her jaw. "Don't let them officiate you into being quiet or doing something you don't want to do or believing something you know in your gut is a lie. This is *your* life and even though they may love you—that doesn't mean they'll always do right. Trust *yourself.* Remember? Storm-wood."

I swallow.

"Storm-wood." I respond, before turning around and walking toward Jude and Kevin, waiting for me down the hall.

## CHAPTER SIXTEEN

I pause at the door to the room and look around. There are surveillance cameras, laptops, wires—a set up that's been weeks in the making…at least. I zone in on what the cameras are facing and recognize the curve of my hallway, our coffee shop…

…Jessa's house.

"Whoa," Ren exclaims behind me.

I start breathing a little heavier and point a shaky finger at the screens.

"What is that."

Jude and Kevin just glance at each other and do their best to turn off the monitors before I can see everything. A slow iciness spreads across my skin.

"You guys have been watching me."

Jude leans against the table and crosses his arms over his chest. When I start backing away, Jessa grabs my arms and leans in. "No you don't. No running. Besides, I gotta hear this." She motions quietly with her chin. "That's my condo."

"I know," I whisper back.

Jude moves to clasp his hands in his lap. I throw up a hand.

"Well?"

He exchanges a look with Kevin.

"We've been following you this whole time, Stephanie."

I breathe in quick and shake my head.

"I told you not to…I said to leave, to not follow me…what part of that did you not understand?"

He nods. "I know. But you have to understand you were in jeopardy. You were completely unaware of Sam's men watching you at all times."

"That's not true. They haven't been following me. Only him. He's the psycho."

He places his head in his hands and mutters into his fingers.

"Did you even know one stayed right next door to you? It was a couple. We found them a few weeks ago. Brought them in. They're in custody now."

My limbs grow heavy with memory—they were the ones I stole the champagne from—the ones who told me they moved from Portland and were staying there while their new home was built.

I shake my head. "That's impossible."

Kevin jumps in and I bristle with the way my breath catches. I hate that he has this effect on me.

*Why can't he just go away.*

"It's true, Steph. You know it, too. That guy at the Americana? He followed you guys there. He was tracking you before then—you said so yourself. He sat next to you on the bus."

My insides empty out into a puddle on the floor. I feel hollow—numb. This can't be happening. I shoot a glance at Ren and Jessa, frozen in place. Jessa blinks and furrows her brow.

"So what does this mean?" Pointing to the camera, she looks at Jude. "How long are you going to be watching my place? Isn't that some kind of invasion of privacy?"

Kevin chuckles and Jude throws him a warning glance. He opens his hands. "Unfortunately, for cases as intricate and complicated as this, you don't really have a say."

"Like hell we don't." Jude looks at me in surprise. I can feel the anger boiling to the surface again and this time, I don't push it down. I step closer to Jude, keeping my eye on Kevin. I know his pattern. Now would be the perfect opportunity for him to run in and save me from myself. He's done it before. My anger always surprised him.

"For months, I've believed I was starting fresh. I allowed the lack of answers because I was here and you guys were there and I felt a separation." I motion to Ren and Jessa. "I made new friends. *Actual* friends who weren't just using me as a job." My gaze lands on Kevin before falling away.

"They had no idea who I was until dad starting showing himself again. And when they found out? They didn't run. They didn't go behind my back to try and save me. They're showing me that I can do this myself."

Jude winces. "Steph...please."

I hold my hands up. "No. YOU NEED TO LISTEN TO ME. For once. I want answers, Jude." I stab my finger into my palm. "I'm tired of being the blind one when this? All of this?" I turn and point to all of the intricate wiring. "It's about *me*. And I had no idea it was here." I wrap my arms around my chest and feel my heart beating wildly.

"It's time to talk, Jude." I point to Kevin. "And you? You stay silent."

Jude studies me and then cracks a grin.

"Emma warned me this would happen."

I feel my head jerk back. "What?"

He stands and moves to a nearby chair, placing his hands on the back of it. He smiles and looks off in the distance and shakes his head. "From the very beginning, she told me it was a bad idea, hiding this from you. I just couldn't risk your dad finding out and then running away with you. We had to get you out." His eyes turn serious. "It was a risk I was willing to take. Even if it meant you not understanding."

Jessa pokes me in the back with her finger. "That's fucked up." She whispers. I hide a smile.

"You need to know Emma fought for you. From the very beginning, she hated that you didn't know." He sits down and motions for me to take a seat across from him.

"I'll tell you everything I know."

"Jude...." Kevin's voice cracks the silence and I look at him.

Jude sniffs and looks down at his hands. "Kev…you know how much I respect you. I think though, for this conversation, it would be best if you leave."

Kevin stares in shock and Jude shrugs. "You know what I'm going to say. Nothing will be left out. She's right. She needs to know."

Kevin sighs and runs his hands over his face.

*He's stressed.*

Grabbing his jacket, he glances at me for just a moment before walking out the door. My vision blurs. I clench my fists.

*Shit.*

Just then, when he caught my gaze, I didn't see fear. I didn't see the righteous indignation or anger I'd come to recognize in the baby blues. I saw love. Regardless of what he did and the reasons behind it, I knew now the foundation—at least in this moment—was love.

I think of what Jessa told me the other day, how sometimes, we do pretty shitty things to the people we love. And if I could do anything right now, I would run after him. Make it right. Find a way to start over from this crazy twisted nightmare.

Because even though I *know* he loves me? I still can't get it out of my head that I was his *job*.

Jessa squeezes my arm.

*She saw it too.*

I blink and look at Jude, trying to hold my composure. I sit down and straighten my back and look him in the eyes.

"From the beginning." I say. "Tell me everything."

.:::.

Jude studies his hands.

Ren and Jessa have taken seats next to me.

"We started watching you a little over a year ago."

"Who is we?"

Jude looks at me. "Me. Kevin. My team."

"Why me? How did you know?"

He tilts his head. "We didn't know, actually. We just knew your dad had some suspicious behavior. We'd see him with younger girls; he was constantly being called into the precinct; we had rumors of dirty cops—and then of course, Emma reporting your family to CPS."

I flinch, remembering when they took Pacey.

He opens his hands. "Stephanie—we never knew anything for sure until Kevin found you in the shed that morning."

"But why Kevin? He was still in high school. Why drag him into this mess?"

Jude sniffs and grows silent.

"There are a lot of things I wish I could go back and do differently. At the time, the way he handled the rape case involving his friend caught our attention. We knew pimps were beginning to drop placements within the schools to gather girls who were particularly susceptible to attention." He glances at me and then looks away.

"We thought maybe we could beat the system. Have our own person on the team that could infiltrate the ranks and watch for us while roaming the halls."

He points at me.

"He found you, you know."

I blink.

"What?"

"Kevin. He found you. Noticed the bruises on your arms and the way you avoided eye contact with almost everyone." He wipes the corners of his mouth with his fingers. "He saw you talking with Emma in the hallway. Said you looked familiar. Remembered you from a run-in at the corner store when your dad caused a scene in the parking lot."

He smiles and shrugs. "Started watching you before we even knew Sam Tiller had a daughter."

I look down at my hands, not sure what to say. Kevin saw me before Jude told him to follow me?

My voice is quiet. "I always thought you pointed me out to him. That I was his job first."

Jude shakes his head. "No. He noticed you before. Started keeping tabs on you. Said you reminded him of Jamie after the rape—timid, scared, walking around like a wounded animal." He plays with his cell phone on the table. "When I approached him with your name, his whole face lit up—said he knew exactly who you were. That he'd been following you for about a month."

He finds my gaze.

"He even knew your favorite coffee place."

Jessa snorts.

"I don't know whether to be thoroughly creeped out or swooning right now…"

Jude chuckles and Ren turns to study Jessa.

"Creeped out? You mean you don't understand Kevin's infatuation with following Stephanie to the ends of the earth?" He smiles and winks and nudges her arm before leaning in for a kiss. Jessa scowls but offers her cheek. Jude just offers a confused expression before I jump in with more questions.

"So Kevin saw me before you had him tail me. And you guys didn't fill me in on knowing what my dad was up to because you were scared he may call your bluff and leave town. But why follow me? And why let Kevin go all creeptastic and leave those journals everywhere?"

Jude widens his eyes. "We did *not* know about those journals. I'll be talking with Kevin about appropriate protocol—especially in this line of work. And we followed you because of one reason: we had people watching, and we noticed activity among your dad's men. They started buying plane tickets to California. Started mini-cells along the southern coast line. Knowing this state's history with trafficking and the direct access to Mexico, we needed to make sure you were safe."

"And my dad got out of jail."

Jude nods.

"A minor technicality and a horrible judge was the cause of that—I'm still raging at the judicial system back home because of it. Something about evidence." He shrugs. "There's nothing we can do about it except watch and wait for him to make a dumb move. Like today."

"Today?" I feel Jessa's eyes on me and I turn and look at her. She looks just as confused as I am—what part of today? The creepy message? The poem? The weirdness that happened at the hotel?

Jude leans forward. "It was your dad who sent in the anonymous tip to the cops. Had Pierre waiting in your room, tied up with false evidence. Thankfully, we beat the cops and were able to have them at arm's length due to jurisdiction. This is one of those few moments where we can push them away."

"Which is why Max disappeared."

Jude nods. "He got sidetracked by another cold case that just happened to fling wide open."

I stare. "You guys planted something."

"You're quick, kid."

I lean back into my chair. "So what's next? What do we need to do? Obviously I didn't have Pierre tied up in my room. How can we fix this?"

Jude takes to twirling a pen and looks off to the side.

"Well—there's no *we*. You don't need to worry about anything. We can take care of the local authorities. Let them know it was a simple misunderstanding. Wrong hotel room, that sort of thing."

I see Jessa clench her fists under the table and I widen my eyes at Jude.

"You don't want me involved?"

He shakes his head. "Not at all, Steph. This — this whole case — it's just too volatile."

I laugh.

"Too volatile. Jude. My whole fucking life has been volatile. What makes you think this is any different?" I rise to my feet and the chair jerks back and crashes to the ground. Ren and Jessa glance up with surprise. They stand with me.

"I'm going to the police station, Jude."

Jessa sucks in a breath. "Steph…are you sure?"

I look at her and then look at Jude. "Positive. My whole life, I've been afraid of authority. I've hidden and expected the worst." I bite my lip.

*Am I really doing this?*

"Pierre is in custody?"

Jude nods. "But Stephanie…your father…"

I put my hand up and I notice it's shaking, but this time it's not because of fear. The anger rolls deep. I harness it and look Jude in the eyes.

"Screw him. I'm done not being able to live my life because he is calling the shots."

Jude just stares at me and rubs at an eyebrow.

"I'll be safe, Jude."

He closes his eyes.

"You have to trust me."

When he opens them I see a sliver of confidence. "I know. And I do trust you. More than you know." He smiles. "You can talk to the police, Stephanie. But let me go with you. Let me at least be there so I can field any legal questions they may have."

I study his face for a moment and then nod.

"Deal."

I turn and look at Jessa and Ren.

"Listen. You guys have been amazing. You don't have to come—I can do this on my own. I'm sorry—I know I've ruined your day."

Ren frowns and Jessa balks.

"Are you kidding?! I'm not leaving you." She lifts her wrist and the bracelet dangles, the key catching the light above us. "I'm in this." She winks. "Besides. This totally beats having guys hit on me at the coffee store."

Ren rolls his eyes and then catches my gaze.

"Ren?"

He shakes his head. "I'm in too, Mystery Girl." He looks away and then a slow grin spreads across his face. "Besides. How could I miss out on all of this character study?"

I groan and grab my purse, walking away from them.

"What?" Ren calls after me. "It's only truth. Stephanie. You're like… fucking friends with Jack Bauer."

Jude, now walking beside me down the hall, hears that and crinkles his eyes.

"Jack Bauer?" He mouths at me.

I shrug.

"What can I say?" I nudge him with my elbow. "My friends have a thing for the mysterious hero and the over-dramatic."

Jude laughs and I look down at my hands and smile.

When I look back up, I blink away the tears. I can't fall apart now—even though inside is a raging storm begging to be released. That will come at another moment—another day. Now? I sigh and square my shoulders.

Now is a moment for facing the monsters.

## CHAPTER SEVENTEEN

I don't question my decision to talk to the police when I get into Jessa's car and she tells me for the bajillionth time that she doesn't mind coming with me.

I don't question it when we turn the street corner and the precinct parking lot is twice as full as when we visited the other day.

I don't even question it when we run into Jude, Kevin and Ren at the front doors.

But when we walk into the police station and I see Max in a corner office talking with a guy, I suddenly freeze.

*What am I doing what am I doing what am I doing?*

"I can't do this. I lied." Jude turns toward me in surprise as I turn to leave. Jessa shakes her head and steps in front of me.

I motion my hand for her to move. "Jessa. I'm done. I can't do this. It was a dumb-ass thing for me to come here."

She nods. "I get it. I do. But, do you want GI Jude and his man-boy talking for you?" She points to Kevin and Jude and I crack a smile.

"You said man-boy."

She snaps her fingers in my face and I focus my gaze.

"Repeat after me: not all cops are bad."

Ren snorts.

I whisper and roll my eyes. "Not all cops are bad."

Ren mutters under his breath.

"Tupac is rolling over in his grave….but no big. You guys just keep doing you." He runs his hands through his hair and then glances back outside to a guy with piercings in his cheekbones.

"I uh…I'mma go talk to ol' dude out there. But Stephanie, she's right. Not all cops are shady douche wads." He points his thumb over his shoulder. "So I'm gonna go talk to this dude, and you're gonna go talk to that dude, and maybe we'll both make some surprising friendships today. Deal?"

Jessa throws him a look and I just sit there staring.

"I don't really know what you just said, Ren but…sure."

Jessa waves him off and he walks away, whistling Macklemore.

She turns and looks at me and grabs my shoulders. "You can do this. Your story matters. Your voice matters. *You* matter." She shifts me around and I see Jude and Kevin, waiting for me, a curious look on their faces.

I close my eyes. The distant rumble of my father's voice echoes in the quiet space and I just push them away.

*Not here.*

I open my eyes and smile.

"Okay. Let's go."

The truth was, I *could* do this. I know what it looks like to fake it until you feel a little bit of normalcy. So I push away the sadness and the fear. Max glances up from his stack of papers and sees us. He points in our direction and motions for the man sitting across from him to wait and then walks out of his office, calling attention to a nearby officer.

"Hey Rob? Would you finish up with this guy? I just need his signature on those papers. Thanks."

He walks over to where we're waiting.

"Stephanie. Jessa. I'm surprised to see you here."

I nod and step in front of Kevin and Jude.

"Could I maybe talk to you about something?"

He falls back on the heels of his feet and sticks his hands in his pockets. "Sure." He throws a glance at Kevin and Jude.

"Do you know these guys?"

I hesitate for a split second and then nod. "I do. That's why I need to talk with you, actually."

He frowns and then motions us to his now empty office.

"Here—take a seat." He quickly glances at the crowd we've brought and shrugs. "I only have two—I apologize."

Jude quickly moves out of the way for Jessa to grab the second seat and him and Kevin position themselves between us and the door.

Max sits down and leans his elbows on the desk.

"So what brought you in here today?" He rubs his hands over his face. "Sorry about the confusion earlier—our tip turned out to be a dud. But, we still got a lead on a cold case that we'd almost given up on so..." His palms turn upward. "It all worked out, it seems."

I clear my throat. "Actually. There was a guy in my room."

He pauses and stares at me. "Come again?"

"There was a guy in my room. And he was tied up. And, he was involved with illegal activity." I bite my lip and breathe in, glancing down at my hands.

"I just didn't bring him in—I was set up."

His eyebrows lower.

"Why would anyone set you up, Stephanie? And we checked your room—there was no one. If there was someone there, where did he go?"

I turn my head and glance at Jude, standing with his hands clasped in front of him. We make eye contact and he nods slightly. I look at Max.

"Jude took care of it—and I imagine you guys will talk through it all later, but the important thing is not how the guy got into my room. It's who put him there."

Max swallows and runs his thumb underneath his lip.

"I'm listening."

I breathe in and out and look at Jessa. She smiles and grabs for my hand.

"My father put him there, Max." I stop and wince and look around the office for any chance of escape because now I'm shaking and I don't know if I can continue.

"Your father?"

*You bitch. You'll pay for opening that mouth of yours.*

I startle and close my eyes—wishing the voice away. I feel Jude's hand on my shoulder and I slowly find Max's gaze.

"Max, my father is Sam Tiller."

His eyes widen in recognition.

"The guy in prison for trafficking? But how…"

I lean forward. "Have you ever seen a picture of him without a beard? He looks different. An awful lot like a guy named Joey."

I wait for the pieces to fall together for Max. He falls back in his chair.

"Fuck me."

He places his elbow on the arm of his chair and leans his head to rest on his hand.

"You knew. When you two came in earlier last week…you knew."

I hold up my hand. "I knew. She didn't." I point to Jessa and then look at him again.

*Please understand. Please hear me.*

"Max, my father is conniving. Smart. I don't understand how he's here but he is—and he's *dangerous.* You have to understand. He had the entire police force back home eating out of his hand. Some of his biggest customers—" I falter and choke back a sob.

He straightens his back.

"You were one of them. You were one of the girls he sold…"

I nod and wipe at my cheeks.

"The first," I whisper.

"Bloody fucking hell." He moves to the edge of his seat and starts rifling through papers on his desk.

"Max…listen to me. If he's here—chances are he's already working on grabbing some of the guys here. In this precinct. He thrives on bait and switch—manipulation—bribery."

He points at me. "Not on my watch. You hear me? *Not on my watch.*" He points to a framed picture on his desk. "You see her? She's my daughter. Born just two months ago." He shakes his head and his eyes search for something to focus on before they land on me again.

"I can't imagine what kind of monster…"

He can't even finish his sentence without clenching his fists.

Jessa leans over and brushes up against my arm.

"Hey. I need to use the restroom. Will you be okay? I'll be right back."

I find her eyes and nod.

"I'm fine."

She stands up and slides in and around the chairs and desk and walks out of the office almost running into Ren on his way inside.

I turn my attention back to Max. He's still rustling through papers. Finally, he finds what he's looking for and pulls out the picture of my dad from his stacks of files. He looks up at me with darkened eyes.

"We're going to find this bastard, Stephanie. I promise."

I hear Kevin shuffling behind me and whispering to someone. Turning to see what's going on, I notice Ren peeking over my shoulder at the picture on the desk.

"Wait. Who's that guy?" He asks.

I turn and look at him.

"That's my dad, Ren."

Ren pales and looks at me and then Jude and Kevin and then back to Max.

"That's your father." He points to the picture.

I nod. "Yeah. Why?"

He steps back and his eyes go wide.

"He was outside. I was talking with him." He wrinkles his nose. "He noticed you guys—was asking why I was here and who you all were...I didn't say anything. I swear. He-he even followed me in here because he said he needed to check on a buddy of his..."

He glances at me. "I had no idea..."

My skin turns to ice. My hands wrap around the arm of the chair.

*Jessa.*

I feel faint.

"Kevin...Jessa. We have to..." I can't even finish the sentence before he's out the door. Jude breathes deep and places his hand on my shoulder.

"She's probably fine, Stephanie. The restroom is right around the corner."

My heart starts pounding and I rub at my chest to calm it down.

*My dad is here. He found me again. My dad is here.*

I feel a vibration in my pocket and pull out my phone.

"It's an unknown number."

Max acts as though he's reaching for the phone and then pulls back his arm. Resting his chin in one hand he taps his desk with the fingers on his other hand. His eyes grow wide and he shifts to lean against the back of his chair. He motions at me, waving his hand.

"Answer it."

I already have though. The phone is to my ear and all I hear is heavy breathing. There's a struggle on the other end of the line and I hear flesh slapping against flesh.

A cry.

"Stephanie! Stephanie I'm fi- " I hear what sounds like a punch and I close my eyes, avoiding those in the room. That was Jessa. My dad has Jessa.

"H-hello?"

"Lolly. I've missed you."

"What are you doing, dad. Bring her back. You can't do this. Not to Jessa."

The line goes quiet for a moment and I see Ren out of the corner of my eye frantically pacing back and forth on his cell.

"No answer." he mouths to Max. Max runs out of the office and I hear him hollering for back up. Everything around me is chaos but I am frozen. A statue. I close my eyes and pray this is just another nightmare. My dad's voice breaks the silence.

"Oh but why? She's so perty. And those golden pants look mighty nice. I like her hair too. She seems feisty." He growls again and his breath deepens.

"We haven't had feisty since Marisol."

My spine turns into a flame.

"Anyways. I'm glad you're sharing your friend with me. What's her name, Jessa?" He laughs. "Such a beautiful name." His voice fades and I can hear whispering in the background along with moaning. My dad grunts.

"You stupid bitch. I told you not to fight."

Another slap.

*No. No. Shit-shit-shit-fucking-shit.*

"Stop! Stop. I'll do whatever you want. Whatever you want, dad. Just…just leave her alone. Let her go."

"Let her go? Well that's no fun." His words slur in on each other and I wonder how much he's had to drink today. "You never liked sharing anyways. How about we make a trade? You come and meet me at the parking garage and I'll give back this pretty girl." He chuckles. "Maybe."

The line goes dead and I'm left holding the cell phone in my shaking hand. Kevin's saying something but I can't hear him because I'm somewhere else—I'm back in the shed, the men above me and my soul below—and everything darkens until there's nothing left except for this broken piece of hope.

## CHAPTER EIGHTEEN

I'm doubled over in my chair when I feel Kevin's hands wrap around my wrists. I don't even know my eyes are closed until I hear his voice.

"Steph. Steph. Hey Steph, come back."

I blink my eyes open, see him kneeling in front of me, and drop my head even further.

"My dad has Jessa, Kevin. He has her."

His eyes look into mine.

"We found you, didn't we? We'll find her. We'll get her back. I promise."

I start shaking my head vehemently, rubbing the snot from my nose on my sleeve. I gingerly touch my fingers to my cheeks and notice tears streaming down my skin.

"Don't promise, Kevin. Promises aren't for keeping."

He looks away for a moment and then grabs my head in his hands. I pull away for just a moment before resting, remembering my exhaustion and how amazing his fingers feel on my skin. I close my eyes and lean into him.

"Look at me, Stephanie."

I look at him.

"I've made some mistakes. I'll be the first to admit that. But you need to know that every single moment I've lost my shit these past few months—every single moment pointed to you knowing how much I love you. You are not a job to me anymore. I tried telling you this in the hospital." His hands fall to his knees. "I've been off the case since before Thanksgiving. Everything I've done has been behind the scenes with Jude."

I blink again, the words falling together and not-quite-making sense in the wake of knowing my dad's hands are touching Jessa's skin.

"You…quit?"

"I quit. I told them I couldn't do any of this without you knowing. I was going to tell you that day we went over to Emma and Jude's—when you found out about Pacey." His face darkens. "Then my mom called and ruined everything."

I smile.

"I'm not your job."

"You're not my job. You never were. From the second I saw you walking down that street I knew something had shifted. You changed me. I was different. And when we met in the coffee shop, well—that sealed the deal. I was done."

He takes my hands in his.

"Listen. I don't know everything. But I know I love you. I know I will do anything for you—lose my shit if that means you're safe. Maybe that's not normal. Jude says I have a hero complex." He shrugs. "I don't know. But I know I never feel myself unless I'm looking into your eyes."

I study him for a moment, unsure of what to say. In my worst nightmares, my father comes back with a vengeance and sets fire to everything I've ever loved. In my wildest dreams, Kevin and I are together and all of this is just a distant memory.

And right now, in this fraction of eternity, I'm on the edge of both.

"…I don't know what to say…"

His lips curl into a slow smile.

"That's okay." He nods, his eyes glancing over to where Jude is now standing in the corner of the office talking on his cell. "It's okay. You take your time." He leans forward and kisses me softly on the forehead. Before he stands up and walks over to Jude, he winks. "I'll wait forever if it means I'll have you on the other side."

I shake my head slightly as they talk in hurried whispers.

What is even happening?

Max walks back into the office and rubs his face with the palms of his hands. Grabbing the coffee cup on his desk, he downs what's left in two gulps and sets the cup on the nearest ledge. Unhooking the gun on his belt, he opens a drawer and then looks at me before slamming it shut.

"We need a plan."

Jude looks up from his phone and stares.

"We're working on one. My men and I are highly trained in this area—you can't just bust in and expect nothing to happen. You have to treat these situations as though everything will go wrong."

Max blinks and Jude continues.

"You let a fugitive walk through this station and kidnap a girl. Your first priority? Tighten those lips. If the media gets wind of this…."

Max smiles. "I think you underestimate the professionalism of my men."

Jude just shrugs. "We'll see." Turning to Kevin, he points at me.

"Stay with her until we get to the parking garage. We'll have men surrounding the area in civilian clothes. Two men will be posted as homeless on either side of the street." He turns and looks at me. "Stephanie, you'll walk in alone. We'll be watching you and within gun-shot range."

Kevin crosses his arms. "Where do you want me to go after we drop her off?"

Jude glances at Kevin and thinks for a moment.

"Out of the way. We need certified officers dealing with this raid. You can stay in one of the convoy vans and be one of our eyes and ears."

Kevin twists his lips and I know he's disappointed but he swallows it and offers Jude a smile.

"Okay. I can do that." He reaches out his hand and taps my arm.

"Please be careful?"

I smile slightly and lift my chin.

"Of course."

Jude looks down and then back up at Max. "At my signal—and only my signal—we'll rush Sam and get both Jessa and Stephanie out of there alive." He studies all of our faces and a shadow crosses his eyes.

"His life isn't really a priority at this point."

Jude turns to walk out of the office and Max rushes to stop him.

"You can't mean that you're wanting him shot. That's not the way we do things…"

Jude smiles slightly. "You really don't know what this guy is capable of, do you?"

Max frowns. "Apparently I'm going to find out."

I study my fingernails and feel the stress beginning to gather in my chest. *I'm going to see my father. I'm going to see my father.*

Jude continues to debrief the gathering team and I sit alone at the desk, thoughts running wild through my mind. Everyone is scared of my father. Everyone seems to know what he's capable of—what lengths he'll go to in order to get his way. Of course, this does nothing to ease the anxiety and anger building blocks of solidity in my veins.

Something catches in my mind and I glance up, my eyes locking on Max's desk drawers. I swallow.

Jude said nothing about me being armed when I faced my father. But I know Sam Tiller. I know the tricks he plays. There's no going in prepared for what he may do because there's never any knowing. There's always something more—it's never over.

I know that now.

I also know the depth my hate.

I take a quick glance at the men who've migrated into the hallway and in one fluid motion I lean forward, open the drawer and grab the gun. My breath lets out in a rush. I can't believe he didn't lock it. I feel the weight in my hands and something ticks inside. Benefit of living with a deranged psychopath for most of my life: I know how to use a gun. I check the safety and surreptitiously make sure bullets are locked and loaded.

A slow smile spreads across my face. Holding the frigid metal against my skin sparked life to the anger within these bones. I slowly set the gun in my purse and stand to make my way over to where the men are circled.

*I'm coming, Jessa.*

Jude catches my eyes and studies me.

"Are you ready for this, Stephanie?"

I am peace and anger and decisiveness.

"I'm ready."

Kevin smiles at me from the periphery and I smile back.

A few months ago, he carried my broken and bloodied body out of a shed. Tonight, I will know what it feels like to be pieced back together by revenge.

## CHAPTER NINETEEN

They drop me off down the street—away from any visibility my father may have from the garage.

Jude steps out of the car for just a moment and puts his hands on my shoulders.

"Remember, Stephanie. Just walk in, try and stall him for a few minutes, make sure Jessa is okay and we'll be right behind you. You're wired so we'll know at any second if things go haywire."

I look up at him.

"This is my dad we're talking about—chaos is just part of the game. You should know that by now."

He nods and kisses me on the side of my head.

"Please be careful. You don't have to be a hero here. Just talk—ask questions. You know what will set him off."

I sigh and turn to walk down the street, my hands clenching and unclenching against my legs. I breathe in—one beat, two beats, three beats—

and then breathe out—one beat, two beats, three beats.

I pass a homeless guy and look at him out of the corner of my eye. I know Jude has men everywhere, even in places I wouldn't think to look, and so part of me wonders. I note his disheveled beard and clothes that barely hang on to his frame. There's a shopping cart resting next to him with crusty blankets and miscellaneous belongings I'm sure were found in some dumpster. The man catches my eye and gives me a slight nod. I keep walking and fight the urge to turn around for a second look.

The parking garage looks different in the daytime. Gone is the dreamy quality of the early morning. It only fits, really. Sunrises are meant for hope—for new beginnings and friendships and cold bleachers snuggled against someone who loves you. Sunsets are for endings. I squint up at the sun and draw my arms closer around me.

My skin still feels on fire but I'm shivering.

I wonder. Is it possible for a heart to freeze when the flames lick around it?

I find the entrance to the garage and swallow, nervously fingering the gun hiding in my purse. I need to find a way I can grab it easily. I can't just waltz into this situation with my hand stuck in my bag. My dad knows me too well. He'd know I was up to something. I swing my bag around toward my back and in the same motion manage to sneak the gun in the waistband of my skirt.

When the metal touches my skin, I sigh.

This I can handle.

I take one last look around before walking into the garage. When my eyes adjust to the shadows, I pause. I take a step and hear a crunching beneath my feet. When I look down, my vision blurs.

Broken lollipops line the ground leading to the staircase. My breath grows shallow as I realize how long it took him to do this and what it means.

*Lollipop I will not stop.*

The path looks like a shattered rainbow—all torn and ragged, the pieces of hardened sugar jutting up and out like CandyLand's worst nightmare. I move slowly and methodically, each step bringing me closer to a monster.

.::.

I hear my dad before I see him.

"Are you sure you don't want a lollipop? I have a few that match your hair."

"You are such a sick bastard. Step one foot closer and I'll stab you with these stilettos again."

Laughter.

"Oh I'd like to see you try, sweetheart. I'd like to see you try."

I smile and wince at the same time. If anyone can handle my father, I know it's Jessa. But even still: knowing she's *there*—dealing with *him*—it makes my heart fold in on herself. No one should have to deal with him. I peek around the corner and see my dad's back. He's pacing and looking over the ledge beneath him. Jessa is standing against a nearby pillar, tied with rope.

Her left eye is blackened, her lip is swollen, and her shirt is torn.

"Motherfucker," I whisper.

Jessa leans her head against the concrete behind her and squeezes her eyes shut. I can see her trying to breathe—her mouth is a small "o" and her chin is quivering.

*She's hurt.*

I take a step and the candy crunches underneath my footing. The sound is barely noticeable, but Jessa's eyes move quickly in my direction and a flash of recognition crosses her face. She glances at my father, still staring over the ledge, and then slowly moves her eyes toward the wall to my left.

"Have you taken enough pictures yet, sicko?"

My breath catches. There's someone else. I move back behind the corner and press against the wall, waiting for a response.

"Not even close."

My knees weaken and my hand flies up to my mouth. I bite down on my index finger to keep from making any noises. I would recognize that voice anywhere.

It's my mom.

"You know, when Stephanie was growing up she always wanted a sister. Would come up and ask me if she could have a twin—as if that was something I could just do for her."

I close my eyes and fight the dizziness.

"Then, she goes off and gets our little boy taken from us. And then she takes my money. Moves out here as if she could start a new life without any recognition of what we did for her. Ain't that right, baby?"

I hear my dad grunt and I sink slowly to the ground, too confused to even move. Jessa sniffs.

"Stephanie said you were in jail. She said both of you were in jail. How'd you guys get out?"

My mom laughs and my dad spits his chew on the ground nearby. I bite my lip when I realize he's moved closer to where I am hiding.

"Stephanie says a lot of things, Jessa girl. You'll learn to only believe about half of what comes out of her mouth. Now turn toward the light. There you go. I want to get that beautiful chin in this next shot."

I hear my dad's boots kick stuff around and he throws out a string of curse words.

"Where's that fucking girl? She's late. She should be here by now."

"She'll be here, Sammie. You know she will. She's always wanting to be the hero. She won't be able to stand Jessa girl stuck between us."

"That's a stupid thing to say and you know it." I hear a slap and wince. My mom cries out.

"Well dammit, Sammie. How am I supposed to know? You never said nothing to me while you had this thing going. Made me guess it all by myself."

"Just shut up, wouldja? I don't want to hear anymore of it. Just be glad I got your sorry ass outta prison."

She snorts. "Oh you did nothing of the sort. You just made a big fuss with your boys at the station and they did the dirty work. They always do your dirty work."

Jessa coughs. "Is anyone else slightly uncomfortable with the conversation?"

A glass crashes against the wall behind me and shatters. Mom gasps. Jessa jumps in.

"You know what? I would have to agree, Mrs. Tiller. After all. If he didn't get you out of prison you wouldn't be able to practice those horrid photography skills right now. And this party! We wouldn't have this amazing party." Jessa *tsks* under her breath. "Pity, don't you think?"

My dad's boots beat a path across the garage and another slap echoes across the vacant lot.

"Shut that mouth, you hear? You have just as much sass as my daughter and it bugs the hell outta me. Thinking you can just come in here and do what you want."

I chance a look around the corner and catch him pressed up against Jessa, her chin in between his thumb and fore-finger. I grimace and slowly slide my way up the wall. I'm not sure how much time Jude and the men have given me to stall my father, but it seems as if I've waited long enough.

Everything pauses, and then moves forward at once.

I reach behind my back and grab hold of the gun.

At the exact moment I reach for the gun, Jessa starts screaming.

As soon as I register Jessa screaming, someone sets loose a string of firecrackers in the garage.

But of course, it isn't firecrackers, it's bullets.

As I'm diving for cover amidst the broken rainbow beneath me I hear gargled breathing and then nothing but silence and I bite my lip because *ohmigod if he just killed Jessa I will fucking cut him alive.*

.:::.

My dad's voice is the first to shatter the emptiness.

"Come out, come out, wherever you are...."

My shoulder is touching the corner of the wall. All I need to do is pivot my left foot and I will be able to see him. But I don't want to do anything now. I don't want to see what he just did.

He laughs.

"I know you're here, Stephanie. I can *feel* you. I can always feel you. I know you."

I strain to hear something—anything—from my mom or Jessa and it's nothing but radio silence on either end. I close my eyes and remember.

The nights I spent running.

The mornings I spent hiding.

The bruises I covered up.

The men I pretended not to know.

Being pulled by the hair and being tied by the wrists and being made *something* out of someone who should have known everything.

I remember the heavy breathing. The weight of it all pressing on my chest because that's where the weight of the men would often land.

I remember the bottle of pills. I remember the pictures of Marisa's body and the way Chad's face was broken on my behalf.

I remember nights spent in the parking lot of Dilsey's Pub waiting for him to finish so I could drive him home.

I remember Valerie and the faces of the girls he's found and made into his play-things.

I remember it all and every moment, every instant, pulses in my veins to one single rhythm of hate.

A cough settles on the breeze—soft but distinct. I raise my head and listen closer. It's muffled, as if the mouth is covered by a cloth.

"Ohmigod. You killed her."

A small smile rests on my lips. I don't even have time to process the lack of grief I feel for my mother. In this moment, one thing matters: Jessa's still alive.

It's the permission I've been waiting for all along.

Slowly, I twist my foot and take the first step into the clearing, raising my arm with the gun. He's standing right in front of me, cleaning his gun with the rag I assume was used to gag Jessa. Her eyes are wild, looking between me and my father.

He glances up and sees me standing there, the barrel of my gun pointed at his chest. His hands hold the slightest tremor and stop mid-swipe of the gun.

His pause is just enough for my confidence and anger to boost through the roof.

I smile.

"Hi, daddy."

## CHAPTER TWENTY

"Stephanie. Baby. Put the gun down."

I laugh.

"Put the gun down? Not a chance."

"What are you gonna do? Shoot me?"

I look him in the eye and then focus on his chest. Right there—the money spot. Right where the ribcage meets the lungs.

"If I'm lucky."

Aiming for his heart wouldn't do any good—he doesn't have one.

I want his lungs. I want him to know what it feels like when your breath is taken from you.

He focuses on me as if trying to figure out whether or not he can call my bluff. Lifting the gun, he points it at Jessa. My heart stutters and stops before racing to life.

"Don't be stupid, sweetheart. You may have that gun pointed at me but it only takes a second for me to pull this trigger." He glances at my mom's body.

"I would hate for you to be the reason for two deaths today."

I narrow my eyes.

"You're seriously pinning that on me? You pulled the trigger. You've been wanting to do it for a while."

"But *you* were late. Cons-u-quences, darlin."

His speech turns to a staggered lilt and weariness settles in my bones. My dad under normal circumstances is a loose cannon. With alcohol, he's a monster waking up hungry.

"How much have you had to drink."

He reaches for a flask in his jacket and tips it over. A solitary drop falls on the cement beneath him.

"I'd say about this much."

Shots are fired in the distance and I jerk my head toward the ledge opening to the street below. My dad smirks and rocks back on his heels.

He's calm. Too calm.

"Looks like you brought company, even though I told you not to....what are we gonna do about that, now?"

He takes a step toward me and I stumble backward, just enough to lose my sight with the gun. My feet get tangled and I feel myself falling and I hit the ground with a thud, my hands landing hard on the shards of candy and the gun bouncing out of my grasp.

*Shit.*

A slow smile spreads across his face and Jessa's face is full of horror. I can't think straight because the only thing I'm thinking is fear. Fear and anger. My blood is vibrating and my legs and arms are shaking and I'm ignoring the pain shooting up my arms and pushing myself away from him.

There's nowhere else for me to go.

I'm pressed up against the wall and all I see are his boots coming closer and closer and closer.

They say at the end of your life, you become hyper-aware of everything. I've had enough experiences to know this just isn't true. All I know in those moments comes to me in flashes of understanding.

The look on Jessa's face as she's screaming for help.

The way my mother's blood glistening in the shadows isn't red but black.

The evil taking over my dad's eyes as he lifts and points the gun at me.

The way he whispers "Lollipop I will not stop."

And then....

explosions.

I see Jude and his men burst through the door on the opposite side of the garage and they storm the level toward Jessa. My dad, gun already primed and ready, turns quick and shoots off three shots toward the men running. Within the blink of an eye, Jessa's untied and picked up and taken out another door. I hear her screaming my name the entire way.

I blink again and see Jude reach for something in his jacket.

But then he stumbles and his arm drops and there's something red on his hand and it's on his shirt but it's spreading and *ohmigod Jude no not Jude no - no - no* and I can't tell if I'm screaming or if I've been shot or if it's just the way your heart feels when it cracks in two.

He slides against the cement wall, leaving a stain behind that won't ever go away. Half of his men surround him and call for backup, the others cover the perimeter and point their guns at my father, hollering at him to surrender.

He won't surrender. They should know that. You'll have to carry him out in a body bag if you expect him to leave.

I see them carry Jude out the door, and much like Jessa he's calling my name as he disappears.

I turn my focus to my father, ignoring the men yelling at him to stand down, chewing on a cigarette and laughing in Jude's direction.

My anger bursts into flame.

I see the gun in my peripheral vision. It's sitting there right where it fell when I tripped earlier. I grab it and turn, pointing it straight at my father's chest. The evil spreads from his eyes to his mouth, curving it upward in recognition and pride and then it drips to his chin and lifts it in a dare.

"Go ahead, baby doll. Shoot me."

I breathe in and out and notice the men on standby around the garage. They've gone silent. At this point it's a matter of who will make the first move.

"I hate you."

This is the moment I've waited for—the moment I've rehearsed in my mind too many times to count. I open my mouth to speak, but nothing comes out and I feel the ice creep its way down my arms and settle into my hands.

I'm about to do it. I'm about to kill my father. I close my eyes for one more breath, and then open them, my finger barely pressing the trigger before a crunching noise, like shoes on top of hardened candy, startles me.

My father's eyes widen and his grin grows wicked.

I pause. Dread makes a home in my gut and I refuse to believe the thoughts coursing through my head.

Kevin can't be here. He can't. He's in the van, helping with surveillance.

I study my dad's face and realize his eyes aren't on me anymore. I have two choices. Take the shot, or see who he's looking at with the chance that he may be pulling my leg and waiting for me to get distracted. I glance quickly at one of the men behind my father and notice his eyes trained on something right above my shoulder.

Someone is behind me.

My breath quickens. I move to follow my dad's gaze.

"Stephanie, get down!"

Shots ring out and I fall to the cement at the same time I see two things: my dad crashing to the ground and firing off a shot, and that shot landing square in the middle of Kevin's chest. He falls against the ground, his eyes stunned. Behind me, men have already swarmed my father's body.

I'm up on my feet in one quick movement and running toward Kevin.

*No no no no no no no no no no…….*

"Kevin. Kevin. Ohmigod Kevin please…" I'm slapping his cheeks and pressing my hands into the wound on his chest growing red and this can't be happening. I can't lose Jude and Kevin in one day. I wrap my arms around him, the blood spilling onto my legs and arms and *ohmigod so much blood...*

I beg for him to come back but there's nothing I can do. I hear one of the men behind me say something about time of death and my feet slide out from under me.

My dad is dead.

I don't have time to process. The freedom I thought I'd feel disappears and is replaced with just an emptiness. I turn around and fall on the ground, my arms still around Kevin's body. I can feel him breathing, but he's not responding to me and I just need someone—anyone—to look at me. A man passes me and I grab at his ankle.

"Please. He needs help."

Medics come and have their turn with Kevin, placing him on a stretcher and reading his vitals. One of the emergency personnel shakes her head and whispers "shit" as she opens his shirt. I turn away, noticing the blood bubbling up and out of his wound.

"Who is this kid? Why doesn't he have on a vest?" She sounds pissed and she glances at me with an accusing stare.

"His name is Kevin. He was working with Jude." I whisper. I reach out and touch his fingers, now cold. "He was supposed to be in the surveillance van."

She moves to clean him off while they position to take him away. "That's what happens when you try and be a hero. Damn young people making foolish decisions. Getting themselves killed."

I squeeze his hand tighter and she slaps my hand away.

"Let him go."

I choke back a sob as they place him on the stretcher and carry him toward the door. His body is the third I see taken — but this time I'm the one calling after him.

"I told you not to promise…." I whisper, trying not to think of the medic's words—the way she said *getting themselves killed* and *let him go*. Because in this moment I know with absolute clarity: there's no way

I can let this boy go. I'm in—I'm all in—and I can't think about the fact that I may have realized this too late.

My hands are shaking and I'm covered in blood. I follow Kevin's stretcher. No one pays any attention to me running down the stairs after him. Why would they? The man they came for, my dad, is in a body bag. I focus on Kevin as the men in black swarm around me. When I get outside, the sun has painted everything with gold.

A medic passes by me and hands me a blanket.

"Are you hurt?"

I blink at him for a few moments before shaking my head.

"No. No I'm fine…is he…" I point toward Kevin being loaded in the ambulance and the medic interrupts me.

He points to a nearby car. "He needs you over there, miss."

Max is waiting, his face long and heavy. I walk over to him in a daze. He looks toward the ambulances and then runs his eyes up my exposed skin, checking for wounds.

"Are you okay?"

I swallow, hoping for words.

"I think that's a relative statement."

He nods, narrowing his eyes.

"Jessa sustained a few minor injuries, but for the most part she came away unscathed. She's at the hospital now."

I look away. Unscathed? Hardly. You don't walk away from Sam Tiller unscathed.

I bite my lip and fight back the tears threatening to spill. I just need to see Kevin. I need to know he's okay. Max watches me for a few seconds before pushing off the side of his car and walking over to the passenger's side door. He opens it.

"Do you want a ride to the hospital?"

I don't even respond. I just turn and wrap the blanket closer around me and fall into the seat as he shuts the door.

## CHAPTER TWENTY-ONE

We pull in to the hospital and I don't even wait for Max to park before I hop out of the car and run for the doors. I don't even really know where I'm going, but I aim for the first entrance I see and wince when I'm hit with the stale air of hospitals everywhere. The scent carries with it memories I'd rather forget.

I get to the front desk and ask them for Jude—or Kevin—or anyone really who knows what's going on with the two men just brought into the ER. The nurse taps a few sentences into her computer and looks up at me apologetically.

"I'm sorry, ma'am. They're not allowing visitors for either of those patients. Are you family?"

I open my mouth and then close it.

How do I answer that question?

"She's family."

I turn, my hands clutching at the front of my shirt.

"Emma." I crush her in a hug and she leans back to look me in the eyes, her gaze falling on my arms, still stained with blood. Her face whitens and I grimace and step away, my hands clasping together in front of me awkwardly.

"Is Jude…"

I can't finish the sentence. I don't even know what I want to say—okay? alive? the same? She rubs her forehead and leans her elbow on the counter.

"He's doing well…considering. He had on a vest, but the bullet was lodged in his shoulder. He lost a lot of blood."

I exhale, the image of him sliding down the wall making me wince. Emma lowers her chin and looks at me with her serious eyes and I can't help but stare back—she always knows how to make sure I'm paying attention and this is no different.

"He's okay, Stephanie. Jude's in surgery right now. Looks like he'll walk away from this with a nasty scar."

"How'd you get here so fast?"

She offers a weak smile. "We've been here." My eyebrows shoot up and she continues. "Once we realized Jude would be here for months at a time trying to close out the case, we came with him."

I look around her shoulder.

"Where's Benjamin? And Pacey?"

She jerks her thumb toward the door. "They're with my mom back at our apartment."

I scratch at my throat, suddenly nervous. "You really have been here for a while."

She studies me and then reaches out to touch my arm before taking her hands and wrapping them around her middle. She looks tired. Worn.

"I would have called you, Stephanie. I missed you—*we* missed you." She wipes at a stray tear on her cheek and then throws a furtive glance at the nurse before looking back at me.

"Listen. There's a coffee shop down the hall. I-I haven't heard anything about Kevin." I breathe in quick at the mention of his name and she pauses for just a moment, thinking.

She lifts her hand and runs it through her hair. "Do you need anything? Do you want to go sit? Are you hungry? We can get some coffee…"

"I think I'm still processing you being here…"

A small laugh escapes and she rolls her eyes. "Yeah well…you and me both, kid. You and me both." She frowns. "At least let me help you clean up a bit. I had a feeling you may be needing some fresh clothes so I went ahead and brought some extras." She stares at my skirt and looks back up at me.

"How long have you been wearing those clothes?"

"…over 24 hours."

She shakes her head and motions for me to follow her. "We're going to get you in some fresh clothes. Stat."

"Your husband gets shot and you bring *me* an extra pair of clothes?"

She shrugs. "Distractions. I need them." She fingers the bottom of her cardigan and shifts in her leather moccasins before turning to walk again. I know she probably threw on this outfit in a rush to get to the hospital, but she looks put together even now. I stop myself from reaching for another hug and opt instead to simply follow her, thankful for the familiarity in the midst of the chaos swirling inside.

We walk into the bathroom and she pulls out leggings and an oversized t-shirt. She hands them over to me and smiles apologetically.

"It's not the best, I know but…"

I breathe a sigh of relief when the clean clothes touch my fingers. Gingerly, I place them on a nearby counter to avoid staining them with blood. I shake my head and cut her off.

"…but nothing. These are perfect."

She grabs some lavender-scented wipes out of her purse and hands them over to me. I rub the wet cloth all over my face and neck and grab the grime off my arms before leaning over the sink and scrubbing away the blood. My hands are shaking and it's difficult to get them still enough to rub them up and down my arms. I see the water turn various shades of red and brown and I wonder if I'm washing Kevin away. If this, in all its morbidity, is the last I will see of him.

That's when I start to cry.

It's slow at first—just a few tears rolling down my cheeks. But then it's an avalanche—building strength and volume and energy. All of the anger, all of the fear, all of the anticipation and vigilance, it just diffuses into sobs wracking my body. I can barely stand. The weight of the past 24 hours finally takes its toll and I collapse. Emma wraps me in her arms and I bury my head in her neck.

"I was so scared. He wanted to kill me."

Emma's breath catches and she squeezes tighter.

"I know, Steph. I know. It's okay now. You're okay. You're safe—really. He's gone."

I'm crying so hard the pressure pushes against my temples and forehead. I keep moving my arm, still wet from washing, to wipe my nose. My eyes settle briefly on the way the stale-brown blood stains the porcelain around it and I remember everything.

The way my mom sounded as she took her last breath.

How Jude slid against the wall and caught my eyes before falling to the ground.

The thud of my dad's body on the concrete.

The shallow breathing of Kevin underneath my arms.

It's too much. I fall into another fit of tears and wonder when these images will leave me. I've been waiting for this moment—this freedom. I thought I would feel relief—maybe even excitement. But the only thing

I can think of is how much this hurts. And that's the really twisted part I will never tell another soul.

Because deep down in the crevices of what makes me, there is a little girl crying over the death of her father—monster and all. And how do you talk about that? How do you process the grief over losing someone you hate, when that same person ended up shooting the one you love?

.:::.

I'm not sure how long we're in the bathroom, but once the crying slows to a few renegade tears, I'm able to change. We find some seats in the lobby next to Max and I pull out Emma's hair brush and run it through my hair. Once I get the tangles out from the braid that got horribly twisted during the ordeal, I feel a little more human.

I breathe deep, quieting the nerves inside. We still haven't heard anything about Kevin. I'm feeling restless.

I need to talk to Jessa.

I realize that these past few hours are the first in a while that I haven't had her by my side and I've gotten used to her being here. I know she's okay, thanks to Max's update when I first walked out of the parking garage, but I have no idea where she is or if she's even *here*. I pull my phone out of my purse and shoot a text to Ren seeing if he's around. After a few minutes with no response, I turn to Max.

"Do you know if Jessa's here? At this hospital?"

He nods while looking at his phone. "She's here and already giving the doctors hell from what I can gather. She should be out soon, if nothing else because she's annoying."

I laugh and then cock my head.

"Wait. Where do you get all of this information?"

Max glances at me out of the corner of his eye. "I have my sources."

"Oooh. Mysterious cop is mysterious." I wink, knowing I'm toying with the line between appropriate behavior and offensive. I'm still not sure what this relationship is between Max and I. If anything it's been more like a sibling relationship than a police officer and his charge.

He rolls his eyes and looks out the window.

"You know, Stephanie. After this is over we're going to need to get a statement from you."

I pause mid-brush and look at him.

"I know."

"And we're going to need to talk about you stealing my gun."

"Oh that was yours? I was wondering…"

"It's not funny."

"I'm not laughing. But you may need to find an explanation yourself. It's not every day a police officer just leaves his gun unattended."

"If you would have shot your father with that gun…."

I hold up a finger. "It would have been self-defense and you know it."

He chews on the inside of his cheek and I glance toward the inside of his jacket. Just like I thought, his gun rested securely against his belt. I point toward it and look him in the eyes.

"And it wasn't stealing. It was simply borrowing."

He stares at me for a while longer and I smile, turning toward Emma flipping through a magazine. Her left foot is tapping a rhythm on the carpet and I know she's nervous. I nudge her shoulder with my own and we share a smile.

One of the doctors walks into the lobby and Emma stands. I turn and look at her as she walks over to the doctor. I press my feet into the floor, keeping myself from running over and interrupting their conversation. I watch their body language, twist my head slightly so I can listen for key words and just wait. After a few minutes Emma nods her head and reaches out to squeeze the doctor's arm.

"Thank you." She calls after him as he turns to walk back into the hallway.

Turning around, she catches me watching and smiles. I return the gesture, noticing the way relief has etched itself against her relaxed shoulders and easy steps.

"Jude's surgery went really well," she says as she sits down next to me, gathering her things. "He's waking up right now and the doctor mentioned I could go back and see him." She pauses and finds my gaze. "They will only let me go back there, though. At least for right now."

"Okay. That's fine. Did you ask about Kevin?"

Her eyes grow wide. "Oh no. I forgot. I'm sorry. I should have—I think they are in the same wing."

I hide my disappointment and puff my cheeks with air.

"Do you think he's okay?"

She blinks and grabs my hand, a small smile playing on her lips. "I think we would know if something happened. Jude always tells me no news is good news in these situations."

My head falls against the wall behind me.

"No news is good news," I repeat, placing my hand on my stomach where the butterflies of doubt and fear are flapping wildly against my rib cage. There are two choices I have right now: I can either dwell on the fact that we haven't heard any news from Kevin and I have no idea whether or not he's okay or I can just put it out of my mind. I'm horrible at the first choice—often freaking out about things that don't even really exist yet. The second option though? That's where I excel. It's how I've survived. Push it out of your mind and it doesn't exist.

Emma turns and glances toward the door behind us, the one she'll walk through to go see Jude. I sniff and squeeze my arms around me.

"Go see Jude," I offer, reaching up and wiping another renegade tear. Damn nerves. "I'll just stay here and wait."

She looks at me. "Really?" She searches my face. "Will you be okay?"

I nod. "I'm fine. Go see Jude," I repeat. "Tell him the bastard's dead."

That gets her moving.

She smiles and leans forward to kiss my forehead. I wrinkle my nose in protest but let her do it anyway.

"I have my phone if you need me," she says as she stands.

"I'm a big girl," I call after her. "Go kiss your husband."

She turns her head over her shoulder, meets my eyes and raises her eyebrows, grinning with secret intent. I roll my eyes and fake a gag.

And it's almost as if we're back in her house instead of in the waiting room of a hospital, the men we love wounded and on the other side of the doors. She pushes the red button on the wall leading into the hallway and the doors swing open, shortening the distance between her and Jude. I watch her take a step onto the linoleum floor, the doors swinging shut behind her. I sigh and stretch my arms above me, noticing every hitch in every muscle that prevents me from stretching fully. I twist my shoulders and tilt my head right and left before standing up. Max glances up from his phone.

"I'm going to grab some coffee. Do you want something?"

He shakes his head and I nod, turning toward the entrance to the shop across the lobby. I don't know who thought of a coffee shop in a hospital waiting room but it's basically genius. I offer a prayer to the gods of caffeine that it's not just drip coffee and that the beans won't be burnt and walk through the entrance. When I see the chalkboard art behind the register offering drinks with espresso, I sigh in relief. I order my drink—an iced Americano with a splash of cream, and turn around to walk back over to Max.

At first, I can't see him and I start freaking out a little. Outside of using the restroom, which is a high probability, I don't know why he would just disappear. But then I hear his voice, and notice a couple is standing in front of him. The woman places her hand across her chest and shakes her head. I can't hear what they're saying but they're visibly upset. I narrow my eyes. There's something familiar about them—I've seen them before and I can't place it.

Slowly, the woman turns and catches my gaze. Her eyes turn cold.

The recognition almost makes me drop my coffee. I grip it tighter and it rushes up the straw, spilling over the edge. I grab a napkin and dab at the drops of espresso on my hand and raise my chin, walking straight to the woman who is now avoiding my gaze. The last time I saw her, she was preparing Thanksgiving dinner at Kevin's house and doing her best to ignore me and convince her son not to leave the house. I remember that day. It was the last good day we had together, until she called Kevin and then un-invited me to Thanksgiving dinner, effectively cutting me out of Kevin's life.

I take a sip of my drink, as if it were my own form of liquid courage, and paste on a smile that spreads across my face.

I'm going to need it.

"Hi, Mrs. Matouse." I hold out my hand and leave it there until she's forced to shake it. "We've met before under difference circumstances. My name is Stephanie. I'm glad you're here." I swallow and take a seat next to Max, lifting my leg and placing it underneath me. I lean over on the arm of the chair and glance between the three, hoping for some sort of clue.

"How's Kevin? Do we know?"

## CHAPTER TWENTY-TWO

Kevin's mom looks at me, her nose wrinkling. "Why are you here?" She spits out.

I frown. "You didn't answer my question."

"I don't typically answer to whores." She looks away from me as she says it and I feel my fingers squeezing into the plastic.

So much for my iced Americano. It's in a puddle on the floor.

*Fuck.*

Max purses his lips together and glances quickly at Kevin's dad before going to grab some napkins. Once he's out of eye-range he turns and looks at me, pushing the palm of his hand down as if to say, *easy girl. Don't bite.*

I raise an eyebrow.

"I'm sorry. What did you say?"

"I *said*..."

"You don't have to repeat yourself. I actually heard you the first time; it's why I dropped my coffee. I just wanted to give you the opportunity to not be a total bitch."

Her face blanches.

"I am not a whore. And you can make up for your bitchiness by replacing my coffee."

Kevin's dad sighs and throws up his hand, looking at his wife in frustration. I just sit there, waiting. He twists his lips and sets his hands in his pockets.

"I think my wife was just startled to see you here. We were under the impression that Kevin was here at USC. We didn't…we didn't know he was still with you."

I stare at them.

"You didn't know he was with me."

Mrs. Matouse shakes her head quickly and looks me up and down. I wait for them both to look at me again before continuing.

"We…we haven't been together since Thanksgiving."

Their turn to act surprised. She throws the question back in my face with more venom.

"So why are you here?"

"Well. What part do you want to know?" I start counting off my fingers. "Do you want to know about my psycho-dad stalking me after I left town? Do you want to know about the threats I received? Or maybe my closest friend being kidnapped right underneath my nose. The story about being held at gun-point is pretty not-fun. Or oh! This is a good one. Your son following his *whore* even after I asked him not to may explain a lot."

I leave out the fact that he was working with Jude and Max throws me a surreptitious thumbs up sign. His involvement in the case is not my story to tell, and as far as I know, there are far more implications in outing him than just connecting the dots for his family.

She shakes her head. "You manipulated him."

I point at myself. I can't help the shocked expression painting its way across my face.

"Me? I mani—" I jerk my head back. "Oh no. No. You don't get to say that." I swing my leg out from under me and stand before she stumbles back and her husband steps between us.

He looks at me and smiles.

"It's obvious we're all a little *emotional* right now." The emphasis on *emotional* has me rolling my eyes before I can stop myself. I feel Max's hand wrap around my wrist and pull me back down toward the seat.

"Easy," he whispers out of the corner of his mouth.

I scoff and flick my wrist toward Kevin's mom, as if her presence explains everything. Because it does. I curl my lip in disgust and Max sends me a look of warning.

Kevin's dad turns his back to us and starts talking in hushed tones with his wife. I see her arms jut out and her hands wave around, at one point focusing in my direction. I stiffen and Max places his hand on my arm again.

I growl.

He leans over.

"Seriously. Stephanie. Calm down. If you want to see Kevin at all…"

That stops me. I turn and face him.

"I can see him? He's okay?" The hope within my chest blows wide like a balloon and I'm soaring before Max can even respond.

He nods hesitantly.

"He's…stable." He glances at me and crosses his ankle over his knee. "He's going to have a long recovery but he'll make it. The bullet missed his heart but punctured one of his lungs."

"Oh shit," I whisper.

"Right. But, he's not critical anymore and his parents mentioned he'd be able to see visitors in a few hours." He looks at me meaningfully. "So you know, maybe you should tame the crazed girlfriend approach?"

I push my tongue against the top of my teeth and force myself to keep the words at bay. Instead, I just throw him my best serious eyes.

"I am neither crazed or his girlfriend."

He shrugs.

"Whatever. I know commitment when I see it though, and you have a sense of protection about you when it comes to him. No one can talk about you guys except for you. That's commitment, albeit an immature form."

I frown.

"Since when did I give you permission to psychoanalyze me?"

He picks up the plastic cup sitting next to him on a table and raises it to his mouth. Setting it down, he looks at me.

"Since you stole—I'm sorry—since we *shared* a gun."

I cross my arms over my chest.

"Have I ever told you how much I dislike cops?"

He leans back in the chair. "I've gathered."

I study my hands and look back at him. "But Kevin's okay. Right?" I need to hear Max say it again; I need to hear it repeated until I can see him for myself.

He offers me a smile. "Kevin's okay, Stephanie."

"He's okay." I whisper under my breath, more for my benefit than anyone in this room. I watch his parents whisper in the corner, far removed from where we've taken residence in the waiting area and feel my eyes grow heavier and heavier until they close.

"Stupid bitch making me drop my coffee…" I mutter before eyeing the floor in front of me. I scoot off the chair and position my purse and the bag Emma left behind as a sufficient enough pillow. I can't remember the last time I really slept and so it comes quick and painless, my brain going fuzzy as the world around me disappears.

.::.

I wake up to someone shaking my shoulder.

"Hey. Steph. Steph. Wake up."

I moan and push the mysterious voice away. I reach for a blanket that isn't there and pry open an eye out of confusion. Ren is standing above me, his eyes full of laughter.

And he's holding an extra cup of coffee.

"Good morning, Sunshine."

I rub my eyes and blink a few times before propping up on my elbows.

"Do you need some coffee?" He holds out the cup and I make a gimme motion with my hands.

"You're my favorite, Ren. Don't ever let anyone tell you any different."

I bring the cup up to my lips and breathe in the sweet scent of a spiced mocha. I can tell even before taking the first sip that it's loaded with espresso shots.

He sits in one of the chairs nearby.

"Sorry I didn't reply to your text last night. I was here with Jessa last night until her dad showed." He shakes his head. "You should have seen his face, Steph."

"Was he angry?"

He brushes his lips with the back of his hand and raises an eyebrow. "No. That's just it. He wasn't angry at all. We haven't ever really been on the best of terms but he walked in and grabbed me in this massive hug. And then he went and sat with Jessa and they just started crying. Both of them."

"Wow."

"Yeah. So, it was awkward and I was exhausted so I decided to leave knowing she was in good hands. I went home and crashed."

"What time is it?" I ask him. A quick glance around the waiting room and I see Max crouched over in a nearby chair sleeping. Kevin's parents are missing.

He twists his hand to look at his watch.

"9:30 in the morning."

I stop mid-yawn. I think back to when Max was talking with me about Kevin and how he'd be able to see visitors in a few hours.

Ren smiles. "Relax. I already figured out a plan on how to get you back there."

I blink.

"What?"

He points toward the doors. "To see Kevin. I know how we can get you to his room even though technically it's still family only." He does the air quotes and rolls his eyes. "What's with his mom anyways?"

I widen my eyes. "Where do you want me to start? She's crazy, unstable, and called me a whore to my face." I twist and grab my purse from behind me and then hop up on my feet in one quick motion.

"Damn." Ren says.

I nod. "Yep. Not worth it, figuring her out. But seeing Kevin is so…" I look at him expectantly, my fingers twitching with anticipation.

He tips his head back. "Ah. Yes. Kevin." Standing up, he motions me to follow him to the doors and pushes the red button.

"What are you doing? I thought it's only fam…"

He places his finger over my mouth and I push it away with a puff of air from my lips. He smiles.

"Kevin's family has requested no visitors. But Jessa, on the other hand, needs as many visitors as possible before she's goes insane."

I bounce on my feet.

"We're going to see Jessa?!"

The double doors swing open and he grabs my wrist and pulls me with him. "We're going to see Jessa, and then we're breaking her out of her prison and going to find Kevin."

I give him an approving stare.

"You are high on my list today, Renfro."

He smiles and wraps his arm around my shoulders. "You too, Mystery-Girl. You too.

## CHAPTER TWENTY-THREE

"Shoo-fly. Stop bothering me."

Ren and I look at each other and stifle our laughter. It's obvious from the exasperated nurse walking out of Jessa's room and nearly bumping into us that she is not the highlight of their day. The nurse sighs.

"Oh. Sorry."

Ren raises his hands.

"No apologies needed. I get it. She is not her best when she is confined."

She smiles and walks away, and he reaches for my arm, whispering.

"When she was in the hospital last time her nursing team was relegated to this big burly guy and a few fierce women. No softies. They can't handle her. She gets too feisty when she feels trapped."

I think of her comment to my dad about stabbing him with her stiletto and a smile creeps across my face.

"I can imagine," I whisper back.

We walk in and she's flipping through the channels on the television above her.

"No. No. No. ….FUCK no…" She throws the remote down by her feet and falls against the pillows behind her before she notices us walk around the corner.

Her face lights up. "Ohmigod! You guys!" She reaches out for hugs and then winces, falling back against the pillow. Ren rushes over and helps her situate herself to where she's more comfortable.

I frown. "Are you okay?"

She nods and flicks her wrist toward her chest. "It's these damn broken ribs." She wipes at something on the corner of her mouth and levels me with a stare.

"Your dad has a mean kick on him, you know that?"

I grimace.

"Shit, Jessa. I'm sorry."

She waves her hand as if it's nothing and turns to smile at Ren.

"And he had a mean kick."

She looks at me.

"What?"

I step forward and sit on the edge of her bed. "He *had* a mean kick. He's dead. Kevin shot him."

She watches me for a few beats.

"Are you serious?" A smile starts to form on her face and she wipes it away.

"You can be relieved, Jessa. It's okay."

Ren takes to rubbing her back with his hand and she reaches for my own. She closes her eyes for a second before opening them again and finding my own.

"I'm sorry. Did you just say *Kevin* shot him?"

I nod.

She waits.

"Is he..."

"He shot my dad in the neck, right in the jugular. He came up behind me; I didn't even see him. I had the gun, and I was going to shoot my dad because he took a shot at Jude and hit him in the shoulder and I was pissed and Kevin came up behind me and shot him first." The image of my dad falling and bouncing on the cement flashes across my memory and I flinch.

"My dad didn't have a chance, but he took one shot on his way down and punctured Kevin's lung."

Her hands fly to cover her mouth. "Ohmigod. Stephanie."

"Kevin's okay. Just...I haven't seen him but they say he's okay."

"And Jude?"

"Jude is okay too. He had surgery early this morning to remove the bullet lodged in his shoulder." I grab her hand.

"I'm really, really sorry you got to meet my father."

She smiles but it doesn't reach her eyes. I recognize the haunted look and squeeze her fingers.

"Did he do anything to you?"

She shakes her head fast and wipes some stray tears on her cheeks. I see Ren's jawline tense and his hand pauses on her back.

"He made a lot of threats. Said a lot of words I'd rather forget. But other than kicking me and pushing me around, he did nothing."

"Did you really stab him with your stiletto?"

A laugh breaks out from the midst of her crying and she nods.

"I did. I wish you were there. It was amazing." She wrinkles her nose. "Although that's why he kicked me. Because I stabbed him."

I make a face and she shrugs. "He stayed away from me after that, though. Tied me up on that piece of cement and had your mom take pictures. Creeper."

She looks at me.

"Are you okay?'

I nod.

She narrows her eyes.

"Promise?"

"Check yes," I whisper and she smiles, satisfied. Shifting her head to look at Ren, she bats her eyelashes.

"Did you come to bust me out, my knight in shining armor?"

Ren rolls his eyes. "I am not your knight in shining anything, remember? I practically led Stephanie's dad right to you."

She places her hand on his face and brings him close, kissing him lightly.

"That, my love, was not your fault." She looks him in the eyes long enough for secret messages to pass between them and I look away, clearing my throat. She drops her hands against the blanket.

"Now that we got that settled, Renfro, be a good Moondoggie and bust me out of this hell hole?"

He blinks and she places her finger on her bottom lip.

"Yeah that didn't sound the way I thought it would in my head."

He smiles and pushes the wheelchair over to her bed.

"Come on, Gidget. Let's go for a ride." He finds my eyes and motions with his head to the door as he lifts her off the bed. She only grimaces slightly as he gingerly places her on the chair. I walk over and open the door so they can roll past me with ease.

"Where are we going?" Jessa asks.

"Well, my dear. We're going to go check on Kevin the Misguided Hero. It seems his family doesn't want any visitors with names that rhyme with Epiphany, but we're taking matters into our own hands, as we do."

She nods with finality and reaches for my hand. I let her grab it and walk beside her chair as we weave in and out of families waiting outside of rooms and nurses dodging us as soon as they see Jessa.

"Do we know why Kevin's parents don't want an epiphany that looks like Stephanie?"

I laugh and study the linoleum. "It's a long story."

"Well," Jessa says, waving her other free hand. "It's a good thing we have the time and the most boring hospital staff around, now isn't it?" She winks at me. "I want the full story when we get back to my room."

I'm about to tell her of course, because at this point I can't imagine ever going without telling Jessa anything, when Ren stops the wheelchair. I look at him over Jessa and he motions to the room next to us.

"Room 502. That's you." And he smiles at me before pushing Jessa further down the hall, much to her dismay.

"Renfro, roll me back this instant, I want to see the epiphany!"

"Relax. We'll come back. I figured they would want some privacy."

"*You* want privacy," she shoots back, and Ren throws his head back and laughs.

"You got me, Jess. It's true. I want us to find some privacy with those broken ribs of yours." He pauses the rolling long enough to get the attention of a nurse walking down the hall. Obviously she doesn't know about Jessa because she stops.

"Excuse me, do you know of an empty room where we can get some privacy?" Ren winks at the nurse and she frowns and shakes her head and keeps on walking, passing me by and muttering about the *stupid youths overtaking the hospital with their stupid decisions.*

Ren catches my eye and I wave and he motions me closer to the door. I find a spot on the wall opposite the door and lean against it and try to remember how to breathe. I stare at the numbers until they start to swim in my vision and I shake my head.

What am I even going to say?

*Hey Kev, remember that time you took a bullet for me? Well…funny story…I realized I love you but also I kind of hate you because why the fuck did you not let me kill my own father?*

Lame.

My head falls into my hands and I sigh.

I have no idea how the hell I'm going to find the courage to walk through that door.

.:::.

Ultimately, it's my need to eavesdrop that gets one foot in front of the other.

Just as I am about to lose my shit because I can't just do the thing and open Kevin's door, I hear Jude's voice coming from his hospital room. I look around.

I know I shouldn't listen.

My feet propel me forward and I lean my ear against the wood paneling.

*Should* and *do* are two very different words in the English language.

Jude's voice breaks the silence again and I hold my breath.

"Welcome back, tiger."

Kevin mumbles something unintelligible and Jude chuckles.

"Yeah it's good to see you too, kid." He pauses and I can almost see him studying his hands. "So now that you're awake…do you know how badly I want to punch you right now?"

Kevin coughs.

"W-what?" His voice is soft and strained. I wrinkle my nose.

"You were supposed to stay in the van."

"I heard shots."

"Kevin. It's a raid. There was going to be shots. Someone was going to get hit—you know this. You *knew* this. I don't understand why you bailed on your station. How'd you even get the gun?"

"It's complicated."

"Shit, Kevin. There's nothing complicated about stupidity. *What's complicated* is that you could have missed Sam and hit Stephanie. *What's complicated* is that because of your absolute insistence that you come out of this a hero, you almost got yourself killed."

The hospital room grows silent and I step back for a moment to make sure no one is walking toward the door. Glancing around the hallway again I lean my shoulder against the wall and continue to listen.

"Kevin." Jude's voice has quieted down to a low pitch, one he reserves for Benjamin, his son. "Sometimes, being a hero is more about walking away and trusting that what you love will still be there when you return."

"He was going to kill Stephanie."

"Our men had him, Kevin. We had him and you came into the middle of a firestorm when I explicitly said you needed to stay behind. I said it for a reason."

Kevin coughs again and I hear the rustling of sheets and the pouring of water. The conversation pauses as Kevin drinks and then Jude continues.

"Remember what I told you in the hospital? How you are the person Stephanie needs to shine the beauty in her shattered pieces?"

"…Yeah. I remember."

"You haven't found that piece yet. You haven't seen how strong she is—how she is so much more than a shattered thing. Once you see that, you'll be content with just being her mirror. You'll see just how capable she is of standing on her own and you'll want nothing more than to show her every single day what she can do by herself."

Kevin begins to speak but is interrupted by the door suddenly opening and me stumbling into the room. I send a dazed look toward Emma, watching me with an amused expression, and turn toward Jude and Kevin.

I wave. Awkwardly.

"Hi."

Jude rests his hand on the hospital bed and glances between Kevin and me. I see Emma out of the corner of my eye motion for Jude to follow her and he pats Kevin on the knee before standing up and wincing with the pressure it places on his shoulder.

Emma wraps her arm around his middle and squeezes his side with her fingers.

"Let's go get you some drugs, huh honey?"

Jude grunts in response.

"Uhh. Nap."

He turns and points at Kevin. "Remember what I said, kid. Oh and, this is your official resignation. I'm signing it for you."

Kevin shakes his head.

"I've been off the team for a while, Jude."

Him and Emma laugh on their way out the door.

"Yeah, Kevin. You've been off the team. Tell that to the guy who's gun you stole." He levels him with a stare.

"And tell that to Stephanie's dad."

I raise an eyebrow and twist my lips together, fighting a grin.

I kind of like seeing Kevin squirm under Jude's gaze. I watch him roll his eyes and shoo Emma and Jude out of the hospital room with his hand.

And then those baby blue eyes are on me.

"Hi," he says.

I smile.

"Hi."

"How much of that conversation did you hear?"

I avoided his gaze.

"Enough."

"You know he's not right, you know."

I blink and look at him.

"Jude?" I laugh. "What's not right about him labeling you a wanna-be hero?" I feel myself getting angry all over again and I try to breathe.

"Kevin, I had him. I had my dad. I had the gun raised and pointed and I was pulling the trigger and I could have done it…I could have—"

He interrupts me. "I know."

I sit down on the chair next to his bed.

"Well then why did you have to shoot him? Why couldn't you have just let me take the shot?"

My eyes are watering now, and just like I had no idea how much it would affect me to see my father killed, I'm not expecting this emotion either: the fact that killing him was taken from me. It's one thing to choose to take someone's life. It's something completely different when they're taken from you.

Kevin reaches for my hand and takes a moment before responding.

"I knew you could do it, Steph." He looks at me. "I always knew you could do it. I just didn't want you to have to be the one to pull the trigger."

## CHAPTER TWENTY-FOUR

I open my mouth but no sound comes out. Finally, after a few moments, I shake my head in confusion.

"You...what?"

Kevin grimaces and turns to face me.

"I always knew you could do it—ever since the moment you mentioned back at home how you wanted to kill him. I knew you had it in you. But I didn't want you to have to be the one who killed your father." He grabs my hand. "You've been through so much because of him, why add killing him to the mix?"

I frown.

"I think I have my reasons."

"Absolutely. All of them valid." His thumb rubs the top of my hand and I glance down. "Look at me, Stephanie."

I look away and then sigh and then turn to look him in the eye.

"What."

"Are you mad? At me?"

My breath catches.

"No," I mumble.

"Then what's going on here?" He brushes my hair back with his finger and I close my eyes against his touch.

"I almost lost you," I whisper.

"But I'm here."

I pull my hand away and wipe at my tears.

"But you almost *weren't*. Do you know what it was like turning around and seeing your body on the ground like that? Do you know how it felt to try and stop the blood from gushing out of that wound?" I point to his bandage wrapping around the left side of his chest and then my hands press up against my own lungs as if to remind them to move. It's not working very well. "You said we had forever and then suddenly we didn't. How was I supposed to handle that?"

He just looks at me.

"But I'm okay. Right now I'm okay. We're okay." He smiles. "We still have that forever."

"Stop that," I mutter.

"Stop what? Stephanie, I won't ever leave you. I've told you this. From the moment I saw you in that coffee shop—"

I hit the bed. "God, Kevin. Stop. You have to stop! You don't fucking know." I look at him in the eyes. "Seriously. I need you to stop promising me things you don't know if you can deliver."

His lips turn downward.

"Why wouldn't I keep that promise? Why would I ever leave you, Stephanie? When have I ever showed you otherwise?"

My head falls against his arm laying on the edge of the bed.

"Kevin, this is what Jude was talking about…this right here."

He sighs.

"What are you saying, Stephanie."

"I'm saying, I need to know you to love me for *me* — not because I'm some helpless girl you can save. I need you to know that loving me is risky because it doesn't guarantee anything." I find his eyes.

"Since I've left I have these mood swings, Kev. One minute I'm okay and the next all I hear is my dad's voice in my head and I just go batshit, you know? It's scary as hell. And I can't figure out a way to stop it. Are you going to be okay with that? I need to know that all my shit is not going to make you lose your own."

"I won't lose my shit, Stephanie."

"I will run, Kevin. At any given moment I will run and I will not want you to find me because everything I've ever known is coming to haunt me. I'm trying not to—I'm trying this crazy thing called *staying*. But sometimes, sometimes I get overwhelmed. And I run."

"I'll run with you, if you let me."

I smile.

"Stephanie, for as long as we've known each other, you've tried your hardest to get away from me." He grabs my hand and kisses my fingers. "But you can't. You have me."

"I have you?"

"You have me." He moves his lips to my wrist and my forearm and I catch my breath, leaning in closer until I'm not sitting on the chair anymore but leaning both of my arms against the good side of his chest. For the first time since I walked in the hospital room, I relax. He stares at me with those iridescent blues and I'm struck, my pulse turning electric all over again. He pulls my hand down and presses it into his own.

"When my mom and dad were in their good days, before everything went to hell, my dad would always talk about this mantra they had—them against the world." He looks at me. "I can't tell you how many times he'd start talking about how he knew my mom was the one because she was the only person he'd fight the world for—how she was the only one he'd be willing to stand next to and find the next adventure holding her hand instead of trying to run up ahead and beat her."

He laughs.

"And when I got old enough to know how to play the system and would ask one parent because I know they would say yes over the other my dad would just look at me and shake his head and remind me, 'it's us against the world son; don't think for a moment you are not included in that world.'"

"He has it tattooed on his ring finger, you know. *UATW*—the letters wrap around his finger." He rubs his finger around my ring finger, showing me where the letters stain his father's skin.

I look at him, barely breathing.

He squeezes my hand.

"You are the only one I'd fight the world for, Stephanie. The only one I want to find adventures with—whether it be runaway trains or abandoned buildings or tattoos." He runs his finger against my new tattoo, leaving goosebumps in his wake. I hear his voice fading and I look up in time to see his head drop off to the side. I glance at the whiteboard signaling his automatic dosage and note that he should have been given pain medication a little while ago. I push myself up and position myself carefully next to him on the bed, weaving my way through the wires and sheets until I'm pressed up next to him. I wrap my arms around his waist, careful to avoid the wound.

"You're the only one I'd stay for, Kev," I whisper against his hospital gown, the scent of sandalwood coming up to greet me. I close my eyes and inhale, and rest my head against his shoulder, and am just falling asleep when the door to his hospital room opens.

Jessa's head peeks around the door first, her eyes bright when she sees me on the bed. She points at me and breaks into a huge smile and throws a thumbs-up sign my way. I roll my eyes and place a finger over my mouth.

"He just fell asleep."

Ren nods and takes care at pushing Jessa in with as little noise as possible. They end up rolling back toward the door, in case a quick getaway is needed. Jessa leans forward and places her hands gingerly on her knees and then motions with her index finger toward the cloth draped against the wall.

"You just give me the word and we'll roll this curtain closed." She winks.

"Jessa."

Her eyes widen and then a slow smile creases across her face.

"You look happy."

"I'm...content." I push down the blanket on his leg and look back at her. "We still have a ways to go but we're getting there."

Jessa fingers a loose thread on her gown and then glances up at Ren. A look passes between them before she looks back at me. I sit up.

"What."

They both laugh nervously and Jessa lifts one of her hands, waving me off.

"It's nothing. Just that we ran into Jude in the hallway and started talking with him." She leans forward again.

"Listen, Stephanie. I've talked to my dad. There's some programs available for you to receive therapy if you were open to it."

I jerk my head back.

"You think I need a shrink?"

She leans her head on her hands, her arms resting on the side of her wheelchair.

"I think everyone deserves the chance to sit in a room and talk about themselves for an hour."

My mind goes to the money I have stashed in the bank. I know it's not enough to cover everything. I give her an apologetic look. "Maybe when I save up more money? Right now I only have enough for my first year at USC."

Her eyebrow lifts almost imperceptibly.

"What if I told you that these programs could offer you *free* therapy and tuition? They're meant to help you get what you need to succeed."

I wrinkle my nose. "Would your dad being my therapist be…I don't know…weird?"

"Absolutely. Which is why we've connected with a colleague of his we both trust. She's the leading therapist on the West Coast with specialized training in severe trauma and EMDR techniques for those with PTSD."

"Sounds severe."

Jessa laughs. "Trust me. Therapy isn't for the weak—but it's what saved me."

Ren squeezes Jessa's shoulder and then looks at me and shrugs. "And it's *free.*"

I shift uncomfortably and try to avoid the wires draped over my arms. I look at Kevin, crashed out next to me.

"I don't know. Talking about myself seems redundant."

"In the best way," Jessa adds. "Just think about it, Steph. You definitely don't have to make any decisions right now."

Jessa reaches her hand up to grab Ren's.

"Stephanie, it's obvious to everyone you meet that you are, in my dad's words, *a highly functioning human with a whole lot of human shit for a past.* It's what makes you so strong. But it's gotta crack somewhere." In a quieter voice she adds, "remember? You can't run forever."

I nod.

"Storm-wood" I answer back.

"Storm-wood." Jessa responds, smiling.

I know nothing about counseling, really. Only what I've heard from Jessa and other friends back home. All I know is that you talk about yourself with some older and wiser person who takes notes and nods and *mmmms*, while you go through all of the shit you've been dealt in your life. And apparently you cry. A lot.

Sounds like a party.

I sigh.

"I'll think about it. Promise."

"Excellent." Ren fist pumps and I throw a pillow at him. Jessa ducks to avoid getting hit by the shrapnel of cloth and then yelps in pain from the movement.

"Sorry, Jessa!" I throw out, purposefully ignoring Ren's groans in the background.

"Hey!" He gives me the stink eye from behind the edge of the pillow and then hugs it close to his chest, pouting. "I don't get a sorry? That could have taken my eye out!"

I grimace. "Really? You're complaining about a pillow?"

"First thing on the agenda for you in free-counseling? Anger. You have entirely too much anger in that body of yours."

"I find it sexy." Kevin's voice, scratchy from sleep, causes us all to pause mid-motion.

I widen my eyes in surprise and turn my head to where it's resting on his shoulder. I didn't even notice him shifting in and out of sleep.

"When did you wake up?"

"Right in time to see you throw the pillow." He fumbles for the switch for more medicine and glances at Ren. "You're lucky she wasn't standing next to you." He winks at me. "She throws a mean punch."

Ren laughs. "I don't doubt it."

I slide against the railings of the bed and turn toward Kevin.

"I just remembered a question I meant to ask you earlier."

Kevin's eyes shift toward Ren and Jessa and then back at me.

"Yeah?"

"Where's your mom and dad? I saw them earlier in the lobby."

Kevin weaves his hands through his hair and sighs, holding tight the strands of on top. I can tell he hasn't washed it in a while. When he lets his hands fall into his lap the hair he just pulled sticks up straight against the rest of his hair.

"Um. They left after my surgery."

I tilt my head in confusion. "Wait—to go back home?"

He nods slowly.

"They uh…they just needed to know I was alive. And since I was, my mom didn't want to hang around and give me the impression that she approved of any of my choices lately." He catches my eyes.

"My dad just followed her home, as he always does."

"Just like that? They left? But didn't they just get here?" I look at him confused.

"We may have had a fight. I can't remember it all because of these damn-beautiful drugs, but I remember my mom yelling and me just telling her to leave." He pushes himself up gingerly with one hand and winces. "She didn't argue."

I balance on my knees and help him position himself with the pillows surrounding him and fall back against the railing. I look down at the sheet, toying with the threads sticking out.

"So what about you? Are you're going to stay here? In LA?"

*With me?* I add silently.

At first, he doesn't respond and I start to freak a little.

"Shit," he mutters. His face darkens and he rubs the front of his cheeks. He holds his hands there for a moment and whispers so only I can here him.

"I'm really hurting. I think—I think this bandage may need changed, too."

I snap into action, the question forgotten.

"Right. Let me go get a nurse."

He drops one hand and hits the ON CALL button and throws me a half-smile.

"I can do that—I just wanted to let you know I already pressed the morphine button and it'll put me to sleep in approximately five minutes." He shudders. "And I promise you don't want to see them change out this bandage." He looks down at the gauze wrapped around his shoulder and torso and I briefly lean over to touch it, his eyes on me the entire time. Before I can even react, he learns forward enough to kiss me on the side of my temple and I close my eyes, opening them to his dopey-eyed smile.

"See you soon?" He asks, slipping a piece of paper in my hand.

I look down at the folded white edges. "What's this?" I ask.

"Read it later," he whispers, wincing at the pain.

I slip it into the side pocket of my purse and then squeeze his arm.

"I'll see you soon."

Sliding off the bed I grab my purse and motion for Ren and Jessa to start heading out into the hallway. I clasp my hands in front of me awkwardly.

He crinkles his eyes, the only response I need, and I turn to leave.

"Hey Steph." His voice is so quiet now I can barely hear him. When I turn around his face is white and I know he's in pain. I try to avoid staring at the red mark slowly growing on his bandage.

"Yeah?"

Nurses and doctors start pouring into the room then, each intent on separate jobs. One nurse looks at me out of the corner of her eye and shakes her head, pointing to the door.

"This isn't visiting hour, honey. Why are you here?"

I look at her apologetically and glance through the crack in the door at Ren and Jessa waiting outside.

"I'm sorry. I'm just leaving."

And as I turn to walk out the door, I hear his voice call out to me above the murmur of nurses and beeping monitors. What he says sears me to the bone.

"You're the only one I'd stay for too, Stephanie."

I walk out the door and meet Jessa and Ren, not even thinking about the fact that he never answered my question about whether or not he would stay. There's no way for me to know I won't be able to say good-bye. When we come back to his room later that day, his bed is made and there's a solitary note left behind.

"I'm sorry" it says, in his hurried scrawl.

I freak at first, hollering at nurses and begging for them to put out a search party.

"He left! He left and he's still hurt…"

One of the nurses walking in to clean the room reaches for my hands and gives me a sympathetic smile.

"Honey he's fine. He requested a transfer."

I sniff and look around wildly for a pen. "What hospital? Where did he go?"

She twists her lips and shakes her head, glancing at her notes.

"He asked we not share that information with the public."

"With the…with the…public?" I'm hyperventilating. I can't catch my breath. Jessa motions for Ren to push her toward me.

There's nothing for me to do. I fall apart there in the hospital room.

## CHAPTER TWENTY-FIVE

The next few months are a blur as I settle into a routine of simultaneous numbness and grief.

It's a lot of meetings with Max, giving statements to local authorities and federal agents. If I'm not at the station with Jude, I'm over at their apartment, hanging out with Emma and Pacey and Benjamin. It provides a bit of home in the midst of swings of grief. Emma is more of a mother to me than my own ever showed. I finally see that now—finally see what me leaving did to her. Our relationship is slow but instinctual.

As for Pacey? He's flourishing. After the case closes, I get to attend the adoption hearing and speak on Emma and Jude's behalf.

"Are these people fit for parenting?" The judge asks me.

I laugh and then break into tears and then glance at the judge apologetically.

"You have no idea how fit these two are as parents." I whisper. "They've saved my life multiple times, and that's not a metaphor."

At the end of the hearing, the judge pronounced Pacey a Stevens and the entire place erupted. I kept looking for Kevin, thinking he may show, but he never did.

I think I've stopped looking.

And then there's the therapy.

I started the week after Kevin disappeared. My therapist's name is Katie Cohl, but I affectionately call her *The Boss*. I thought she was hypnotizing me at first when we started EMDR treatments, her waving her fingers back and forth in front of my face. It never worked for me. She had to start tapping her finger on my knee, a slow rhythm of questions and silence.

It's helping.

One week, she asks a question and I flinch. She recognizes the movement and sits back in her chair, gently twirling her pen back and forth between her fingers.

"What's going on in there, Stephanie? Where are you right now?"

"I just don't understand why he left."

She nods in understanding and then lets the silence build before speaking.

"What would happen if you stopped thinking about the why and started thinking about you?"

I frown. "What do you mean?"

She leans her elbows on her knees.

"You've been through trauma together. You guys are irrevocably linked." She opens up her palms in front of her. "But how are you without him? Are you better dealing with things now or do you need him to process?"

I go quiet, thinking.

"Don't hide from the answer, Stephanie," she says softly.

"No."

"No what? No you're not better? Or no you don't need him?"

"…I think no to both."

Her eyebrows shoot up and down quickly and I know I've hit something. I see her write something down on her notepad and look back at me, her eyes gentle.

"Go on."

I fidget in my seat and pick at the tissue in my hands.

"I don't think I'm better without him. I think about him all the time and I would have hoped our promises meant something."

"But you've said yourself that promises aren't meant for keeping."

I close my eyes.

"I hoped this one was."

"You're expecting perfection from an imperfect human, Stephanie."

I frown. These are the truths I don't like to hear.

"But I don't need him. At least, I don't think I do. I was able to shoot my dad. He just took that away from me. I'm not sure we can work through that."

Her eyes narrow and she crosses her legs.

"You've said that he told you he didn't want you to have to kill your father."

"Yes."

"Is it possible for you to think of this as noble? Maybe even a sign of his love for you?"

I sneer and she jumps in quick.

"Stephanie, if you would have had to pull that trigger—you wouldn't have come away unaffected. There would be muscle memory. Scents would be ingrained into your triggers and just the slightest aroma similar to what you experienced that day would send you reeling. You may have experienced regression with the severe PTSD you already possess because of your father. Our brains aren't meant to handle too much at once. We're placed in an emotionally hijacked state for a time. You know this." She tilts her head. "You've experienced it."

"You make it seem like I'm walking through some existential crisis."

She laughs.

"You are! Your whole life has been a series of decisions of whether or not you could or should live through a certain moment. Of course you're experiencing some angst where safety and love is concerned."

I blink and look out the window in front of me, watching the way the ocean moves and bends. It quiets me for a moment and she takes a few deep breaths, writing more in her notebook. Finally I look back toward her and find her watching me, a small smile playing on her lips.

"What?"

"From everything you've told me of him—your adventures, the way he made you laugh, how he protected you—there's nothing in me that makes me wonder if he truly loved you."

"Really?"

"Think about this, Stephanie. You guys are what, 18? 19?"

I nod.

"You're out of sync. Your brain hasn't even fully developed yet and you're dealing with situations most adults wouldn't even dream of facing." She sets her notebook on the table beside her and then places her hands on her knees.

"I want you to think about something."

I bite the corner of my lip.

"Um. Okay."

"I want you to think about the fact that Kevin did not come away from this unscathed. I want you to consider his own lack—the parents who don't understand, the trauma of false allegations, the severity of taking another person's life—all of it, everything he's experienced."

My breath starts to quicken and I swallow. I reach for another tissue.

"Okay."

"What if his leaving was out of self-preservation? What if, in his own finite understanding of love, he thought he was doing you a favor by allowing you the space to live and breathe and figure out who you are separate from any trauma?"

The tears start to fall.

"What if," she whispers now, her eyes searching my own, "the promise still rings true in a way you never anticipated?"

I stare at my hands for the remainder of the session, her quiet breathing in rhythm with my own, the tears falling softly on the carpet below.

.:̇:.

I'm thinking about this conversation one morning as Jessa and I pound our feet into the pavement toward Santa Monica pier. It's become a ritual of sorts, this running. We do it early, at the first break of dawn before there's really anyone around and everything is quiet.

The Boss suggested I take up running, and when she did, I laughed at her. But it's working. When I'm running, there's nothing for me to think about except for the way my feet hit the ground and the way the wind pulls at the tendrils of my hair and how I'm able to breathe—in and out, in and out.

A rhythm of peace I haven't known until now.

We stop at the corner of the pier, taking our shoes off so we can run toward the shore. As our feet kick up sand around us and the sun starts to break the horizon, I can't help but smile.

There she is—right there and so close I can almost reach out and touch her.

Hope.

Nestled between water and sky, as constant as the sunrise.

I sit there and stare while trying to catch my breath. Jessa collapses on the sand next to me and grabs at her ribcage.

"I think I broke another rib."

I kick her foot. "Pansy."

She scowls and then sits up, resting her hands behind her. "So you haven't heard anything. Anything at all."

I breathe in. Out. Close my eyes and then open them.

"You know I would tell you."

She throws some sand in frustration.

"I just don't understand. I don't get why he would just up and leave." She points at me. "And don't start giving me words from The Boss. I know. I know he loves you and didn't know what he was doing and blah-blah-blah." She grows quiet. "It doesn't make it suck any less."

A laugh escapes me and I bend down next to her, kicking the sand around me to form a softer seat.

"Yeah. Tell me about it."

She looks at me.

"He really said nothing. Left nothing other than that ass-hat note."

*Note.*

I straighten, my body rigid.

"He left me a note," I whisper.

"Yeah. I know, Sherlock. We all saw it."

I scramble to my feet. "No. *Another* note. Before you guys walked out of the hospital room. He slipped me a note and told me to read it later but in between everything that happened I completely forgot."

She stares at me for a few seconds before leaning forward and slapping my legs.

"STEPHANIE TILLER WHAT THE FUCK YOU HAD A NOTE THIS WHOLE TIME?!"

I laugh. "Ohmigod." I grab my shoes and socks and start running for the street. "Jessa, I gotta get my purse! I have to read it. Now."

She chases after me, yelling obscenities so loud that nearby surfers are distracted enough from their preparation to stop and stare. I laugh even harder, the realization of a note from Kevin heavy on my breath.

*He wrote me. He wrote me. He knew. He was trying to tell me something this whole time and I missed it.*

With one quick look toward the sunrise, I make a quiet plea that maybe, hope is here to stay.

⋮

We're out of breath when we get back to her place. I rush for my purse and zip open the side pocket, pulling out the creased page and waving it in front of Jessa's face before collapsing on the couch and opening it.

She leans over my shoulder.

"Is it a poem?"

I stare at the page in disbelief.

"Yeah…it's…it's my poem. It's one I wrote when I first moved here."

She wrinkles her nose.

"How'd he get it?"

I look at the added scrawl on the bottom, the *Soon — xoxo, Kevin,* and I sink lower into the cushions.

"He must have pulled it from the trashcan after I threw it away."

"That's weird."

I smile.

"Not for Kevin."

I stare at the page again.

"I remember when I wrote this," I whisper, running my finger along the lines. "It was right after I got here, on New Years Eve—I was so drunk on this champagne I stole from a couple down the hallway and really, really missing him."

*They say that wounds*
*need air to breathe -*
*that the reliance of bandages and*
*gauze only weaken the skin.*
*They say to rip it off —*
*one quick painful second and then*
*healing is on its way.*
*But what of the bandaid?*
*What of the adhesive that*
*held the wound in tact?*
*Where does it go to heal?*
*Where does it go to find*
*that sometimes*
*open air and separation*
*can cleanse*
*almost anything?*

Jessa leans her head on my shoulder and I swallow.

"It was the only poem I wrote that even remotely suggested that we may have a future—that this separation and me leaving was only temporary. These words? They're me admitting that we're meant to be together; we just need some air to breathe."

Jessa lets out a big sigh.

"So you're saying…."

I fold the paper and then place it in my hands, close to my chest.

"I'm saying this is him letting me know he'll be back. That him leaving is only temporary."

"The promise still rings true," she breathes, just loud enough for me to hear. I smile hearing The Boss' words in her mouth.

"The promise still rings true," I repeat, hope blossoming into a ripening flower and taking my breath away.

## CHAPTER TWENTY-SIX

He shows up a week later, right in the middle of my shift at work. It's a slow day, a rainy one—rare in Southern California. Apparently, on days like this, most stay inside to protect their glistening tans from humidity and rain.

I'm sitting a table in the corner reading *East of Eden* when I see his shadow pass in front of me. I glance up and nearly spill my coffee.

*There are no words for this. Shit. What do I say? What do I do with my hands?*

Jessa walks out of the kitchen then, gasping and catching my eye before turning back into the kitchen, the double doors swinging behind her. I silently thank her for the privacy.

I swallow and keep staring and he smiles, pointing to the book.

"That's easily one of my top five pieces of literature. Do you love it? What do you think of Cathy?"

My breath catches at the familiar line and I blink.

"I hate Cathy. She's the only character in literature I'm legitimately scared of…"

He laughs. "Seriously. She's batshit crazy. And that takes a lot for me to say that—I've known some crazy-ass people in my life."

I crack a smile and he leans his hands on the table. "Can I sit?"

"You left me," I whisper.

He nods and scrapes at something invisible. "I did."

"You promised."

He looks at me then, his eyes narrowed.

"I can't explain why, Steph. I just…it made sense at the time. In my own way, I had to make sure this promise could stick."

I raise an eyebrow.

"Like a test?"

His head shoots up and his eyes go wide.

"Oh God no. Not that. I just…I freaked. I bolted. I thought…I thought you really did need space."

"Bandaids," I say and he smiles, understanding.

"Yes. Bandaids."

He looks at me then—really looks at me—and I see the way his eyes are haunted now in a way they weren't before. I motion for him to sit in a chair next to me and he falls into it.

"How many of my poems did you save?" I ask.

He scratches at something near his ear.

"Just that one. It seemed…the most hopeful."

"It's the one where I allowed myself to picture us together again."

"And now?"

I watch him and lean back in my chair.

"I think it's possible."

He rests his chin in his hand and stares at the window.

"I think possible is good. Possible can turn into a promise."

I cross my arms against my chest and tilt my head.

"Will you leave again?"

He levels me with a stare.

"Will you?"

I run my fingers through my hair and he watches me. I place my hands on the table between us, palms down, and I stare at the way my fingers reach for him. I want to reach over and kiss those lips. I want to kick his shins. I want to grab his hands and take off for somewhere completely *other* — a place where we can just be. One of my fingers curls under and I chance a glance at him.

"Where do we go from here, Kevin?"

My thumb has taken to tapping the table beneath it and he reaches over and places his hand above my own, quieting the movement.

"Kevin…"

His other hand comes up and he rests his fingers on my lips and I resist the urge to lick his skin.

"I've missed you," he whispers.

I close my eyes.

"You didn't answer my question."

And then he's kissing me, his lips overtaking my own and his tongue searching me and I have to grab the sleeves of his sweater to keep from climbing on top of him.

We pull away from each other, panting, and he rests his forehead against my own.

"I think here is a good place to start."

# ACKNOWLEDGEMENTS

In March of 2014, I sat in my living room with KP talking about writing. She looked at me and asked, "and are *you* writing? Or are you just, you know…helping other people." I couldn't answer her. She shrugged and said, "you know what you're supposed to do, Elora. So do it."

We all have those moments where a question someone asks unlocks something inside and pushes us to the next level of our purpose. KP, something unlocked when you reminded me of my purpose, and it lit a fire under my ass to write this book. Thank you.

My conversation with KP was just the beginning. There were so many people who helped me during the crazy few months of penning the continuation of Stephanie's story. These are just a handful of those who made it happen.

Russ, there really are no words for the support and belief you give me. Thank you for putting up with the countless hours of me writing or talking about what I'm writing or lamenting about what I'm writing or wondering about what I *can* write. It's not easy being married to an author, and you shine. I love you.

Blanche, I hope you know how many stories I stole from your life. I love you, sister. Christina had *Every Shattered Thing,* and you got book two. Thanks for telling me the crazy-ass abandoned hotel story (I'm still mad at you). And tell Aarika thanks for telling me the catching the sunrise story at your bachelorette party. Your life is print-worthy, girl.

Teresa, you told me to *just write the damn thing* and I did. Thanks for wearing the white hat and reminding me to get the poison out, even when I didn't think I had any more words.

Sarah, you held my hand and got serious when you knew I needed it. You are my person. So much of Stephanie's relationship with Jessa reminds me of us. Now we just need a trip to the ocean. Thank you for taking the risk on me.

Ritz, thank you for saving my wrists and shoulders and back from certain peril. But more than that, thank you for seeing the intricacies of Stephanie and Kevin's relationship and helping me flesh them out. From the very beginning—even before I started writing this story—we spent hours discussing the issues they would face as they tried to work out the past. Thank you for being a sounding board of realism. This story is better for it.

Rachel, thank you for reminding me to write dark chocolate.

Lisa, thank you for helping me untangle all of the crazy-ass messes this manuscript was in the beginning. You saved me from about a thousand reader eye-rolls. I'm certain. Also, I think it's kind of perfect that you were sitting in the chair watching me as I finished this book. I'm grateful for you, friend.

Shelby, thank you for believing in Stephanie and seeing her strength. You two are fellow-warrior spirits.

Lindsay, your attention to detail saved my ass. Thankful for your edits that won't be noticeable because they're so damn good.

Stacey, thank you for believing in these words of mine. Thank you for reading Stephanie's story and seeing the possibility between these pages. You're a kick ass agent and I'm thankful to be in your care.

Finally, to the ladies of the Storytellers: this book is for you. Thank you for the nights spent sprinting and the laughter involved with Teaser Tuesdays. You guys breathed life into this novel.

# ABOUT THE AUTHOR

Elora Ramirez has been telling stories her whole life.

It started when she was four, when she taught herself how to read and write as a way to entertain herself while her grandmother kicked and danced in aerobics class. She cut her teeth on books from Dr. Seuss and writing anywhere she could find the space -- including her Fischer Price kitchenette, the pages of picture books, and Highlights Magazines.

She's matured a bit since then, now choosing to write in the margins of her books and on the mirrors of her apartment ideas and thoughts surrounding story and what makes us human.

Founder of Awake the Bones, she's not content to stop at writing her own books and loves sharing with others the alchemy of becoming a #novelistwild. She's coached over 300 women in finding language to tell their own story well and facilitates an online writing community that's more sisterhood than anything else.

Intuition and hustle get her through the day, as well as her dog-toddler viszla who barks at squirrels outside her Tree House and her chef-husband Russell who always greets her with a kiss.

Follow her on twitter (@eloranicole) and her blog, eloranicole.com

Made in the USA
Middletown, DE
02 May 2021